Praise for THE ARTIST'S WIFE

"Phillips has gotten inside Alma's head and made her sing. ṣ..
is selfish, witty, and mean. Her fictional memoir, told from the
other side of the grave, is, like Nabokov's 'Speak, Memory,' a
kind of sad and insolent poetry."

New York Times Book Review

"[A] gorgeous second novel.... a perfumed voice, laced with the
bitter, sexy scent of truth. It is a voice that instantly seduces, car-
rying you through her life and passions in a daze of aesthetic
pleasure. And there's your warning. Opening this book is an
invitation to possession – I could almost hear Alma whispering
to me, haunting me, when I wasn't reading.... Beneath this
book's rich English prose is a whisper of Austrian German – as if
you were suddenly fluent beyond your wildest dreams, watching
a foreign language recompose itself before your eyes into English sentences more beautiful than any you could ever have imagined yourself.... For all its careful craft and stunning prose, the
novel itself charges past. It manages to be that delightfully rare
thing: both beautifully wrought and a rip-roaring page-turner."

New York Newsday

"Highly entertaining."

Kirkus Reviews

"Artful, intelligent and quietly powerful... evokes the life of the maenad-muse Alma Mahler Gropius Werfel, who was born Alma Schindler near Vienna in 1879, died in New York City in 1964, and in between the ages of 16 and 50 made just about every heterosexual male who came within sniffing distance of her go wild with a combination of diffuse longing and specific lust. Coming of age in the hothouse of fin de siècle Vienna; ingenue temptress of Max Burckhard and Gustav Klimt; piano pupil and foreplay-partner of Alexander von Zemlinsky; skeptical caryatid on the monument of Gustav Mahler; lover of love-mad Oskar Kokoschka; bored war-bride of Walter Gropius; surrogate mother of lazy-boy Franz Werfel; serial adulterer; merry deflowerer, in middle age, of a Roman Catholic priest; refugee from the Nazis... Alma would be a powerful seductress, from beyond the grave, of any red-blooded novelist, male or female.... Phillips deftly culls a few telling incidents from a long life and a voluminous record.... Psychologically acute."

The Bookpress (Ithaca, N.Y.)

"Max Phillips has conjured from his reinvention of Alma Mahler one of the most compellingly passionate voices of either our century or hers. And beneath its beautifully articulated surfaces, The Artist's Wife is rich with deeper meanings."

Madison Smartt Bell

"The crucial test of a successful historical novel is whether the past is brought to vivid and viable light. Phillips' second novel passes with flying colors."

Bookpage

"Alma Mahler was the femme fatale of intellectual and artistic Vienna during the first half of the last century... a heroine one uneasily yet ineluctably identifies with."

Boston Globe

"Alma Mahler emerges as a fascinating character whose life intersected with many early-20th-century luminaries."

Philadelphia Inquirer

"Phillips has created a colorful, complicated figure, and this book may spark more interest in Alma and the men she inspired."

Washington Post

"A fantastic book for lovers of art, sex, and the social milieu of Central European 20th century history. Me, in other words."

Alison Goldfrapp, Jane

"Alma Schindler cut a romantic swath through early 20th Century Eastern European culture the way Attila the Hun swallowed principalities and kingdoms in the same geography.... Phillips creates a compelling voice for Alma through her observations from beyond the grave... Linguistically elegant and inventive... It's amazing that Phillips is able, in a fairly compact novel, to render convincing depictions of a number of the 20th Century's most important figures."

Memphis Commercial Appeal

"Alma's forthright narration succeeds in conveying the personality of a complex, indomitable woman who... lived life exactly as she wished, bravely and without hypocrisy."

Publishers Weekly

"Max Phillips' new fictionalized portrait of Alma's life, *The Artist's Wife*, is gossip of the highest order, outweighing anything in *People* or *The National Inquirer*.... And what a voice! A siren's voice... at once sensuous and world-weary, most delightful in flirtation with her famous lovers, but irresistible in solitude as well."

www.bookpage.com

"Insightful and entertaining."

Tampa Tribune & Times

Also by Max Phillips
Snakebite Sonnet

THE ARTIST'S WIFE

Max Phillips

THE ARTIST'S WIFE

A NOVEL

WELCOME RAIN PUBLISHERS

New York

THE ARTIST'S WIFE
by Max Phillips
All rights reserved.

Copyright © 2001 by Max Phillips

First published in the U.S. by
Henry Holt and Company, LLC
New York, New York

Direct any inquries to Welcome Rain Publishers LLC.

Library of Congress CIP data available from the Publisher.

ISBN 1-56649-273-4
First Welcome Rain edition: January 2003
Designed by Max Phillips

1 3 5 7 9 10 8 6 4 2

For my father and mother

Ultimately one loves one's desires and not that which is desired.
FRIEDRICH NIETZSCHE

THE ARTIST'S WIFE

I

DEATH, ALSO, I FIND to be a disappointment. There are no arches of cloud or tunnels of fire. Instead, there's knowledge. Your own little cupful is emptied out into the general ocean, you vanish as a drop of blood vanishes in the cool sea, and after that, you swim through all the moments that ever were, the way water swims through water. Your second husband addresses his egg with a butter knife and thinks, *Whore*, the wind lifts the corner of your page and you smooth it back with a child's fat hand, the fingers shine in places with dried pear juice and you draw your thousandth-to-last breath. Your shoes pinch. Well, at eighty-four years old, all shoes are tight and, besides, you're not wearing any shoes. You think, *I shall never marry.* You walk to the road on legs swollen with pregnancy, close one eye, and hold up a thumb to blot your house of orange clay from the hilltop, but you've never lived in a house of orange clay – you see, one swims not only through one's own moments, but through everybody's, everyone who ever lived. And so, yes, the dead know everything. Your cat's-eye sapphire earring with the loose clasp has slipped through a hole in your pocket. It sits in the lining of your gray lambskin coat. Your car keys you knocked across the sill above your kitchen sink and into the window box outside. There they are on the chalky blue bottom, which is set like an abandoned chessboard with the husks of flies.

In fact, there's no end to the questions – the living won't leave us alone. Tapping, humming, burning incense, muttering endearments, the mystics, the mourners, the professionally morbid, asking, Have you heard from my Aunt Betty? Will I find love, or money? And: You? Oh, I've heard of you. Tell me, how did you live?

How greedy you are, how interested. I was awfully interested in myself when I was alive. But now my old self, my old husbands, old enemies, old children all seem a bit transparent, like ghosts, or abstract, like facts and figures. And so *noisy* – what a fuss we were always making. I will say this, we could be amusing to watch.

Maybe that's all you want, to be amused.

Anyway, I don't mind telling the story. None of us here mind anything anymore.

THE PROPER PLACE to start, of course, is with my father. As it happens, he was killed by a prince. This was his old friend Prince Regent Luitpold of Bavaria, who was a great lover of jokes. In the summer of 1892, while his guests were all eating dinner on the terrace of his castle, His Excellency cranked open a secret valve so that a great rush of water flew out and knocked everybody across the stone floor. The prince staggered back and forth, cackling. Water rolled down his fierce little monkey's head. He clapped for servants to run forward with towels and schnapps, but Papi lay still in a puddle. A great pain moved up through my father's body then, as clear as a sentence in plain German, though afterward he couldn't recall what it had been about.

At home in Plankenberg, the doctor told us this was exhaustion of the nerves. He polished his pince-nez and talked enthusiastically about sea air. By 1892 our family was finally out of debt, so we could have our first trip for pleasure, and we decided to go to Sylt in the North Sea and rent a small house near the beach and take healthful walks. But in Sylt my father just lay in his room with a blanket pulled up to his chest and his finger between the pages of a volume of Schiller. He listened to the waves and to his daughters' voices. In his intestines, he had his own secret valve, closing, a blockage from which he'd soon die. When he felt a little stronger, he opened up his book and read: *Peaks thunder, the frail narrow footbridge sways. | No fear feels the archer up dizzy ways.*

Me, I wasn't so crazy about Sylt. Papi was sick, and there was nobody to talk to. Just Mami and Gretl and my father's student Carl Moll, a big round pale-bearded giant who went with his teacher everywhere and saw to the running of his household. The only thing I really liked were our trunks, because some of them were quite enormous and I was proud that we owned such large things.

One morning I woke up especially petulant and bored. It was bright out, but not too hot yet. I rested my feet on the cool wall and lay there with my book, which was about a big Russian fish that wore a crown and bestowed treasures. I was almost thirteen, and my body was fussing me. If I looked down the collar of my nightdress, I saw two puffy little hills in a sort of cambric twilight, and on the horizon a little twilit wood. I put out my belly to be fat, and then twisted around to be thin, and then I buttoned my collar over my nose and walked around like that with no face, making ferocious eyes. Then I got dressed and went down the hall to have a look at Papi. He was lying all neat and small in his own bed, with his own book. His cheeks were yellow and gray, like a new-plucked chicken. When he saw me in the crack of the door, he made himself look sly, as if he were pretending to be ill just to be lazy, and said, "You must be very quiet, Tigress. Because I'm asleep."

I said, "But you're talking to me."

"Perhaps," he said, "I'm only dreaming of you."

"I'm not a *dream*," I said, very offended, and went downstairs and out the door.

There were two ways down to the sea. One was a cobbled road, which was boring, and the other was a steep path that began in a little saddle of honey-colored clay. I sat myself down in this and looked out across the clean dark waves. They looked very new in the morning sun, but they smelt old. I kept thinking about Papi's chicken-skin cheeks, and it made me gather my skirts squeamishly away from the weeds. Down on the beach, my sister was examining the tide pools. I could see her long toes, plucking at the rocks. There she was, not giving me a thought. I shouted, "Grete! Grete!" like two stones rapped together – what a loud child I was – and waited until she was watching me before I began to climb down.

Grete was a year younger than me. We lived way out in the country and had no friends except each other. I was a big blond girl, but she was dark and sleek and could move fast when she wanted. If you'd asked me, I'd have told you I loved her, and been happy to tell you just why. My whole life, I was very fond of talking about love. Gretl was holding a wet brown ribbon-thing on the end of a bit of reed. "I found it in the pools," she told me. "I was going to go down to the ocean and see if it swims."

"It's just a bit of kelp," I said.

"Oh. I thought maybe it was an eel?"

"No. Just seaweed."

She dropped it in the sand and wiped her fingers on her leg.

"Do you want to wade?" she said.

"No."

She kicked her feet in the sand, to dry them. "Do you want to play Prisoner?"

For Prisoner, you got an old trunk or scratched a square into the dirt. Gretl would be prisoner inside this and I would pinch her all over until she confessed. Then I'd execute her, but before she died she could make a speech. If she was good, I let her come back as an angel, and she'd walk around doing angel things while I pretended I couldn't see, crying out, "What was that? Who goes there?" Sometimes I'd be the prisoner, but Gretl was afraid to pinch me too hard, and I'd keep my face calm until she started crying with frustration, and then I'd escape. So we both saw it was best if she was the prisoner.

"No," I said.

"Do you know a game?" she said.

"No."

"Please?"

"All right," I said. "Dig a hole."

"A hole?"

"As deep as your elbow," I said. "Three sides should be straight down and the other should be sloping."

One sloping side seemed like a good thing for a hole to have. She went to work at once. When she was finished with the hole, I'd figure out what you might do with it. She dug quickly, with her hands like paws. We felt better now.

"We've hardly seen Papi at all," she complained.

"He has to rest," I said.

"We wouldn't tire him."

"He has to *rest.*"

"We could put a divan on the beach," she said, panting, "with an umbrella to keep him cool. And a screen all around. Moll could help us. We could sit with him and be quiet." She waved out her dirty hands to make everything quiet. "We could all be together. It would be nice for him. There could be music."

She was full of her own ideas now.

"Impossible," I said. "He may have a wasting illness, you know."

I'd read about wasting illnesses and they sounded very fine. Princesses got them.

"A bellyache only?" she whispered. Mami had said bellyache.

"No, it's different. He told me. He's told me many things, as the eldest."

"Things?" she whispered.

"Serious things. He wouldn't want you to worry, as you're young. His condition is serious." The hole was already pretty deep and soon I'd have to think of something.

"He may die," I said, and I saw myself addressing a grieving Empire. There were flags everywhere, and I explained to everyone what had to be done.

Gretl was standing there, all muddy, with tears in her eyes.

"You're lying?" she said. "No?" Then she just stood in her hole and wept.

It wasn't enjoyable anymore.

"We must love him very much," I said, "and then he'll get better."

"Yes!" she said. "Let's go to him now!"

"No. It's best for his condition if he rests. You leave this to me. He'll be fine. Never mind the hole," I said kindly. "It's all right. Come here. What a mess, your face is all snot." I cleaned her face with my handkerchief and made her blow. She leaned into me and smelt sweet and helpless. I always loved Grete best after I'd made her cry, and I put my arms around her and kissed her and smelt her sweet hair until I was calm myself. "It's no good getting upset," I said. "Besides, I know what we can do."

I'd passed through town the previous day with Mami and noticed a woman in a café, by the window, unpinning her beautiful hat. Gretl's hair reminded me.

We went to Mami and Moll and announced that we wanted to go across the island to town and have lunch, all by ourselves, and that we wanted money.

MY WORLD WAS as full as a garden in which weeds and strange blooms hide the paths, as full as an old map in which the unknown places are decorated with monsters, but it contained only two cities: Plankenberg, where we lived, and Vienna.

Vienna was ruled by the Emperor Franz Josef, whose face was on all our money. He was an old man and very tall. When he died, they'd pickle his heart and put it with the other Habsburg hearts in Saint Augustin's. I'd seen him once on Corpus Christi Day, leading the holy procession with a candle in his hand. I thought he nodded to my father in respect, but my father couldn't nod in return, because I was sitting on his shoulders so I could see.

Plankenberg, of course, was ruled by my father. His name was Emil Jakob Schindler, and he was the most celebrated landscape painter in the Empire and a very impressive fellow. His uncle was a member of Parliament who helped abolish the lash, and his mother's portrait still hangs in the Gallery of Beauties. He was good friends with Franz Josef's court painter, Makart. The two of them used to give big Renaissance balls, with Liszt playing the piano and garlands of roses swinging drunkenly from the ceiling. He sang Schumann lieder in a fine tenor voice, and was once Lenardo in a private production of *Lenardo und Blandine.* Blandine was a brewer's daughter named Anna Bergen who'd been sent to Vienna to make her début at the Ringtheater under Mottl, but she got pregnant and married my father instead.

I was always convinced that marriage brought a narrowness into my father's life. He had luxurious tastes and was always in debt, which he and I both thought was only fitting for a genius, but Mami didn't agree. I used to sleep in a drawer of my parents' wardrobe until Makart made me a crib. That's the sort of thing she always wanted to talk about, that and the bills, but Papi just turned his back and napped. But when I was nearly five he had a success with a couple of collectors and we leased a castle near the flower-town of Tulln. Plankenberg Manor was four hundred years old and had a little onion-shaped dome that rang the hour. Inside, it was all polished leather and venetian glass, everything tufted, swagged, tasseled, and fringed. Papi used to go around patting and straightening. The artist's eye! Myself, I'd go down to the pantry and inspect the silver. They kept it in a varnished cedar box, which smelt warm and spicy. It had an oval lid, and when you closed it, the box was very solid and satisfactory.

Papi used to tell me how the Plankenberg ghost went around looking for golden-haired girls, taking strides as long as a coal barge on its great double-jointed legs. He put a painted wooden Madonna in a niche halfway up the stairs and heaped up flowers all around it. Its smile was very frightening, very still, shaped with three dabs of a tiny red brush, two dabs for the top lip and one for the bottom, and Gretl and I used to run past it at night, when its eyes got enormous in the shadows and you couldn't tell what it was thinking. Papi used to frighten the wits out of us. I was crazy about him. He kept his studio upstairs, so our bedrooms all smelt of linseed oil. He'd furnished the place very fashionably, like Makart's studio, with ferns and Turkish rugs and a mandolin in a corner that nobody knew how to play. The chairs all had legs like lion's paws, and while Papi worked I'd kneel on one and ride, as if it were a flying beast I'd tamed myself, and dream that I'd built a great Italian garden full of white studios, like caves, where princes lived for their art and the air was full of Schumann lieder.

Once Papi painted me as I stood in the kitchen garden. He used a hinged palette, which folded for traveling. Whenever he stopped for a minute to consider, he'd roll the brush slowly between thumb and forefinger, his fingers very certain, his mouth solemn and kind, and I'd think All right. Now we're getting somewhere. Now I'm going to learn all the secrets. He took a flexible little knife and mixed up mauve, grass green, apricot, and vermilion. These were all very splendid but I didn't see how they pertained.

"Wait, Tigress," he said.

Scrfff, scrfff went the brush.

"Are you tired, Tigress?"

"No," I said.

"You're being very good," he said. "You're being very good and still. There are grown-up ladies who couldn't stand so still. That's why I'd rather paint a poplar, a larch. No witless chatter. Better posture, too."

"I might be tired in a little," I said.

"We'll rest," he said. "Have a look."

I stood before the canvas as he wiped his fingers one by one with a rag, and then he laid his hands on my shoulders and rubbed them. A great feeling of ease moved down through my body, and I wanted to be picked up and carried, but this wasn't grown-up and so I didn't mention it. Papi's skies were always very dense, like an endless thickness of lead crystal. By the time the light squeezed through a sky like that, it was pure, and made everything glisten a bit. There I was, glistening, there between the leaves. I held my face near the little hills and valleys of the paint and tried to see how the strokes of mauve, grass green, apricot, and vermilion wove together to make the cheeks of an excellent little girl. He said, "Are you looking at it, dumpling, or eating it?"

"But I like the smell," I said.

"You'll get paint on your nose. You'll get your nose on your nose."

"It's *me*."

"I hope so."

"What will you do when it's done?"

"Put it on the wall."

"Why?" I asked. Up-on-the-wall meant old things, treasures, from journeys Papi must have made back in mythic times, back when he went around with the other great old mythic fellows.

"So people can look at it," he said.

"Everyone will look at it?"

"Yes."

"You made the flowers so big," I said, a little frightened.

"They are big."

"The big flowers are all looking at me."

"Sunflowers," he said, "always turn to look at the sun."

When I was eight, he read to us from *Faust*. The devil came to Faust as a black poodle. This was exciting, because I wanted a dog. But soon the story went wandering, like the singing of an evil kettle, all complicated bargains and a stumbling girl, and at last Grete and I were weeping with the strangeness. Then he gave it to us, saying, "This is the most beautiful book in the world."

Well, Gretl didn't see much of that book. I kept it for myself. I'd stare at it, sniff it, even taste it. I'd ruffle the pages against my cheek, then open the book wide, so the binding made a noise like a comb biting into snarled hair, and look down the little woven tunnel in the spine at this and that in my room. Faust spoke of two souls in his breast. This sounded very uncomfortable. He sang of Gretchen's beauty. He climbed up into the sky, which was where the angels sang to you, apparently, and made you wise. I wanted to carry the book everywhere.

"What is that," Mami cried.

"It's beautiful," I shouted. But she took it away.

My parents were always quarreling, and I always took Papi's side. In fact, I couldn't really see the need for my mother. She knew no good stories. She wasn't handsome. She'd never made her début under Mottl. Instead, she went around trilling under her breath and let her daughters be *prime donne* in her place. I had no respect for anyone who sacrificed for others, and Mami went out of her way to be nice to us. We weren't sent off to convent schools like most girls of our sort, or to any school at all, and we did what we liked, so that we soon taught our governess fear. We also wore what we liked, and I got used to running around my whole life without underdrawers, which I also couldn't see the need for. But I was quite an ungrateful child. When I got measles, it was Mami who slept in a chair pulled close to my bed, but all I remembered was that Papi came and scattered flowers across my counterpane as if I were a toy Madonna.

"Papi," I told him, "you are putting things on my *bed.*"

"Flowers, Tigress."

"Mami won't like the mess. Papi, there's a noise."

"Your Mami is snoring."

"You sound very far away...."

He rubbed his thumb and forefinger quickly together beside my left ear, then my right ear. "Can you hear that?"

I didn't answer.

He touched my ear, looking very sorrowful.

"Is it late?" I asked.

"It's very late."

"Am I better?"

"You're much better."

"You don't know *that,*" I said, accusing him, and he laid his palm on my forehead. His hand was big and cool. It seemed to curve around my head the way clouds curve around the earth. My head seemed hollow. I felt I was growing large, very unpleasantly. My legs were endless beneath the comforter. I was a mountain at the edge of the world, and Papi was a neighbor mountain, and Mami was a distant mountain in the horrid quiet. "See?" he said, "you're *much* better."

"No," I said, "you mustn't take your hand away now. Because it's cool. Gretchen went up to heaven, I was just thinking, or else I was asleep? And Faust said he was sorry, and they all sang to her."

"Ah, but you're a luckier little girl than Gretchen, for we'll sing to you right here on earth. I'll sing about a little house with wings, in which you can travel all over the world."

"Yes."

"And the roof will be of crystal, so you can look up from your bed and see all the stars as you fly along. And the stars will be cool, like peach ices. And the peach-ice stars will sing with us, and their song will make you cooooool. And sweet."

"Your hand is getting warm." He took it away. "I don't want to go up to heaven...."

"But what a foolish Tigress! Didn't I say we'll sing to you right here?"

I thought he sang better than the angels anyway.

Soon after I recovered, my father was commissioned by Franz Josef's son Rudolf to make ink drawings of all the towns of the Adriatic coast for the Crown Prince's book *Die österreichische-ungarische Monarchie in Wort und Bild*. We got the use of a steamship, which waited in each port until Papi was done, and we took Moll to be our nanny. At the end we rented a small stone villa on a hill in Corfu, so Papi could rest and paint his own pictures. We had a pianino sent up from town, and for me this was the whole point of the trip. I was crazy about that pianino. It was just the right size. If you closed the lid over the keys, it was solid and satisfactory, like the silver chest. If you lifted the top and sang in, the wires inside sang back. The measles had damaged my ears, and for the rest of my life I never heard properly again, but if I struck a key, the note was clear and meaningful. So that's when I first began to make music: when I'd just freshly gone half deaf.

I liked to play with my arms spread wide, which made the music more dramatic. I'd twiddle with the right hand and growl with the left, and rock stubbornly back and forth on my little bottom, and wear a lofty look, as if I wasn't much interested. But I was in paradise. Because I saw how, in that row of keys, you could find everything: the gold of the onion dome, the dark striding trees, my parents' shouting, the devil's whistling, the sad comfort of velvet on my cheek when I was bored. There were other things, too, that had never been heard of and that only you knew about, and only while you were playing them. I thought, Papi's doing his work in the corner room, and I'm down here in the parlor doing mine. I'm his apprentice now, not Moll. He's going to teach me everything.

The day we came to Sylt, he walked along the beach with me and said, "*Play, play to allure the gods.*"

And he bowed, carefully, because of the little valve inside, that was already closing.

MY CAFÉ TURNED OUT to be quite nice. The glass cabinets were filled with good things, and an elderly waiter unfolded our napkins ceremoniously, *flick snap* for Gretl, *flick snap* for Alma, heavy white napkins embroidered with blind white suns. We ordered sherbet, and when we were done we ordered some more. Gretl ate slowly, in little dabs with the spoon or fork, each little dab important as any other. But at last the dishes were empty and the nice napkins were marked with our sticky mouths and lying in a heap on the table. Outside, there were flat gray clouds, sliding in quickly. It was that terrible moment, when you've gobbled all the sweetness in the world and there's nothing left but queasiness and regret.

We left without speaking and started walking back across the dunes. The rest of my life, I always remembered that walk. There was a path through the sand made of heavy boards. The fence on each side was staves of wood fastened edge to edge with twisted wire. The wind put a cold palm on my face and pushed me back. There was thunder, and I had a taste in my mouth.

"I don't feel well," Gretl said. "I don't feel well at all."

I said, "Let's run."

When we got to the cottage, we found the front door hanging open. There was no one in the front hall, no one in the parlor. We flew upstairs. Through the wall came a noise. We turned and all at once a doctor was there, thrusting us furiously aside. He ran into Papi's room and we had a glimpse, just a glimpse, of a swollen red thing in the bed, eyeless, like a newborn puppy, and dressed in my father's pajamas. It seemed to have been born from the warm wrinkles of our parents' bedclothes. It rolled under Moll's hands, its red jaws clamped. And then Moll ran at us, huge, and cried, *"Girls! Your father is – busy!"*

He swept us back from the doorway and bustled us to our room. Through the wall came Mami's pleading. I was ashamed of the taste in my mouth. Moll stood at the door like a jailer, his big eyes stuck upon us.

"What," I whispered, "what did you – where is he. Where is he going."

Moll's big lips moved.

"I can't *hear* you," I said, and I began to weep.

II

In the Stadtpark in Vienna they've got statues of Mozart, Schubert, and Johann Strauss. When I was fourteen years old, they made one of my Papi. It was fashioned so that the rocks of Papi's beloved earth seemed to rise up and make him a sort of armchair, with his folding palette tucked into a convenient cleft, and they set it between some shrubbery by the pond. He lay back as if he'd eaten too much, my poor father that died of bellyache. But Moll was pleased with the design, and organized a grand ceremony to unveil it.

Moll had become a dealer in other men's art. He'd taken charge of my father's work, which he auctioned off with great success, and of my father's widow, whom he was engaged to marry in the fall. He moved us from our castle into town. Josef Hoffman built our house and Moll was very proud of it. He painted himself there in his study, very thoughtful with the light on his forehead, very large behind his small desk. It was stupid to be so large and I did not believe his grief.

They unveiled my father's monument on a harsh bright day. The waves in the pond, the busy ducks, everything made a single dull stupid noise – my hearing wasn't any better. The orators hummed and mumbled. I couldn't tell if they were saying the right things about my father. I was quite grouchy, and believed that I was **bored and that** I must not be grieving properly. If it wasn't that there was a little breeze, I wouldn't even have known my cheeks were wet. I felt ashamed to have no Papi. I felt everyone must be looking at me, since I was so tall. "Can you be brave?" Moll said. "You're being very brave."

"I'm all right," I said.

"We should never have subjected you to this," Mami said. "Shall I take you home?"

"Please," I said, nearly sobbing, "*please* don't trouble."

Up came Privy Councilor Burckhard, one of Papi's old café friends. "We lost a fine man," he told my mother. "And now, Fräulein Alma, I've also lost the little girl I used to know. For you've become quite the young lady."

"I'm sorry," I muttered. "Become...?"

At one time it had amused him when my governess used to lead me out to say good night to the guests, all brushed and shining in my nightgown and lifting my chin in order to be elegant. Perhaps Burckhard wasn't used to seeing my face so high up, because somehow or other his eyes kept wandering lower.

"A young lady," he repeated, without mercy.

OUR NEW NEIGHBORHOOD WAS CALLED the Hohe Warte, the High Watch. It sat on top of the highest hill in Vienna. Our house was enclosed in that little loop where the Number 37 tram turns around and goes back. Across the street were some broad flat steps, and these went twisting down past Saint Michael's toward the Grinzingerstrasse, where Mozart used to live. Here I lived a life that I considered – as the young do, as the living do – unique, poignant, and full of drama.

I had a gang of girlfriends there that I called my *colleagues*. We all ran around with our hair loose, like holy women. When we had masques, I always took the leading male role. We gave Gretl the small parts. I loved to eat, and as I got older I became a bit of a drinker, even for a Viennese. I was pretty good at drawing.

Hoffman built me a music room that I was very proud of, and I had my piano lessons there.

But the main thing about me back then – and even then I knew it – is that I was very good-looking. By the time I was seventeen, I was almost a hundred and seventy centimeters tall. My eyes were long and blue-violet. The whites were also a little blue, like skimmed milk. My hair was dark blond and my nose was long and smooth. Beneath it there was a dimple in my lip that I liked to fit my pinky-tip into. I had what they called the *mollige Figur*, plump and big-bosomed, but with a narrow waist. In fact, my waist was thick, but this I didn't know, because I was careful never to notice myself unless I was well corseted.

It didn't take long for the gentlemen to start coming round. It began with my father's old friends. Their words used to float high above my head, like cigar smoke or instructive ceiling murals, but now they were addressed to me. "It's a delight to discuss my researches with you, Fräulein Schindler," one might say. "You possess such a ready understanding – if I shut my eyes, I could quite forget you're a young lady! But what man in your presence could bear to shut his eyes?" Or maybe: "Fräulein Schindler, I believe you're your esteemed father's greatest work." Or: "I can see why they call you the most beautiful girl in Vienna."

Well, I was Papi's daughter, and charm always came easily to me. I knew how to move my shoulders. To show pleasure, I closed my lips as if tasting something superb. If displeased, I did not pout – a girl of seventy kilos must not pout. Instead, I leaned back and looked expectant, for surely this man would now do something fine, to erase this bad impression he'd made on me. To understand my suitors' words I was obliged to remain quite still, with my eyes upon their moving lips. The result was that even the most tiresome man was convinced that he fascinated me. But if they noticed my boredom, I crinkled up my eyes, because I'd learnt that this made me look kind.

For a joke once, I took everyone's rings and put them on my fingers. "You give yourself to all comers," Mami said.

I said, "I don't give myself to anyone." And I waggled the rings at her.

I had a lot of admirers and I gave them all hopes. I often had hopes myself. I was always meeting some marvelous man, bold and handsome and with such a way about him. All right, I'd think. Now I've found a man of higher instincts. Now we're getting somewhere. But then the next day I'd notice that his neck was fat, and that he didn't dare address me by name, and soon I was right back where I started again. My nature was a stream running over shining pebbles. If I lifted one out to admire him, he turned into a dull dry lump. Then I'd go to my piano and improvise for hours, and imagine myself wed to some lieutenant, some hydraulic engineer, the way you might stand above a ravine and entertain yourself with thoughts of falling.

Before Papi died, I'd been bossy and carefree, but now I was full of doubts. I was quite popular and so forth, and considered myself superior to everyone I met, but inside I couldn't see what was so great about me, either. I adored parties and I was always chattering away, but afterward I'd feel I'd been cheap. People used to insist that I play the piano for their guests. At home I'd take out my diary and write, *I played like a pig.* I drank five seidels of punch once and woke up in the night with vomit on my bodice, and wrote, *I'm utterly vulgar, superficial, sybaritic, domineering, and egoistic!* I felt I had no one to ask about things anymore, that there was no one anywhere who'd understand what I was feeling. I felt like a loose tooth, that might fall out if you wiggled it. Sometimes I dreamt of doing away with myself, because I thought death would be restful, which shows you how much I knew about it.

My great consolation was music, by which, since I was a Viennese, I meant Wagner, and my favorite place was the Hofoper, the

Court Opera House. This was a splendid building on the Ringstrasse with a big auditorium in which twenty-five hundred people could sit and admire each other. It employed fifty stagehands and a dozen mechanics to work the enormous cogs and pistons of the stage machinery, and the boxes rose up in tier upon tier, weighted down with red velvet and gilt plaster garlands, so that as a child I knew God must sit in the highest one, marking time with a forefinger upon His knee. When Papi gave me *Faust*, I assumed Faust's heaven was a sort of Hofoper made of clouds. I pictured his whole story on the big stage. I put me and Papi up there too. Off we went through the deep blue light, in this realm of mountaintops and ancient forests and the prows of ships, where one dealt only with great struggles, betrayals, and renunciations. I felt Papi and I had a sort of invisible life that gathered above our everyday lives like the flame above a candle, and that this invisible life was all that mattered.

I screeched all the Wagner roles until I ruined a good mezzo-soprano voice, and then I stopped singing and just played the music, attentively: the *Meistersinger*, the opening of the *Rheingold* – the endless water, bright and blurry, with that Eb rippling up from the double basses – and Isolde's Liebestod, which I couldn't get enough of. When the light was gone I'd improvise for hours in the dark, trying to make a little of that fine feeling for myself. Pretty soon I saw I didn't have the technique, so I began to learn composition. I studied figured basses once a week with Robert Gound and counterpoint with the blind organist Josef Labor. He told me, "Compose or socialize. Right now you're better at socializing." I was too deaf to hear the click of a watch, but I wasn't too deaf to hear that, and in four years I wrote over a hundred lieder. It was a matter of constant scribbling and scratching out, until your eyes stung and your fingers were numb and your sit-upon ached from the piano bench. But sometimes when I played one through, I felt I was climbing a winding stair up to some angels' choir loft, seeing the light getting stronger up ahead, watching the figure in the carpet grow clearer beneath my feet.

OF ALL PAPI'S FRIENDS who came round to see me, Max Burckhard was the most persevering. For Christmas when I was seventeen, he sent me two enormous linen hampers full of books. He stuffed everything in there, from Plato to Nietzsche. That was his declaration. After that, the siege was on. One afternoon he came in while I was playing *Tristan*. "What are you doing there?" he said. "Apologizing to Wagner? I'd think you *would* apologize, if that's how you tickle away at him." He plonked himself down beside me so that the piano bench squealed, and his hands blundered around on the keys. His elbow flung back and forth by my nose. It was dressed in thick dark worsted and smelt respectably of tobacco smoke. "See?" he said. "Without fear."

"Without...?"

"Fear," he said loudly.

"You're not playing very well," I murmured.

"*Very* badly," he said. "But add technique to that – *that's* Wagner."

The Burgtheater was where Austria came to learn manners and style, but its former director was careful to be a ruffian. Burckhard was an athlete, a critic, and a scholar. He was a confidant of the Burgtheater comedienne Schratt, who was a favorite of Franz Josef's, and she told Burckhard to offer His Excellency fresh-baked poppy-seed crescents, and that's how he came to run the Burgtheater and introduce Vienna to Ibsen and Hauptmann and make the Court very unhappy. He was a pagan and hated Christianity. He loved to sail alone in great purple storms. He'd climb to his hunting lodge high in the Alps and stay for weeks without changing his shirt, and pay guides to bring him tinned food and candles so his reading wouldn't be interrupted. They said that because of him, two marriages were on the rocks. They said Krastel's daughter was expecting his child. *He takes what he can get*, I wrote in my diary. *Just what I'd do! Use your elbows!* I told him I'd been reading his books and complained that *Zarathustra* was unclear.

"He's clear enough," Burckhard said tenderly. "It's you that's unclear."

He took hold of my waist as if it were his waist. "D'you know," he said, "I believe you hear me well enough."

I knocked his hands away.

I was breathing deeply and easily. I'd greatly enjoyed him taking hold of my waist, and I'd quite enjoyed knocking his hands aside. I hoped he'd take hold of me again so I could knock him away again. He understood this. In fact, we understood each other. He shook his hands, surprised, because I'd struck them quite hard. We were standing chin to chin.

"You're a sensible height for a girl," he said.

We started spending a lot of time together. He brought me a dozen cognac pastilles and a book by Darwin. We went to the champagne pavilions in the Kaisergarten and swilled the stuff down like students. We had a high tea of melon cut in cubes and thrown into a paper sack. We ate this with bare fingers. It was piggery, lovely piggery. We cycled to Hallstatt, and he mixed up a punchbowl full of peaches, wine, and two bottles of Heidsieck Metropole. What a ride back to town we had! When you've had a drop or two, nothing's better than a cycle ride. He gripped my hand as I seated myself in his sailboat and I found myself staring at his straddled loins. It had never occurred to me before to notice this portion of a man.

Still, I thought, all that stuff can wait. At that point, I'd never even kissed anyone. You understand, what I loved in Wagner was purity. Besides, my friend Louise had recently horrified me by explaining that people go about their proceedings just as dogs do. My God, I thought, the whole business? The daft faces, the dreadful pivoting motions of the male? After that, whenever a man introduced himself, I imagined him rocking up and down on top of me and could scarcely bring myself to shake his hand.

One day Burckhard and I started bickering at the shooting gallery in the Prater. That was a very fine place. There were glass balls floating on jets of water so you could burst them, and a drummer boy who beat his drum if you shot him in the heart. "You enjoy tormenting that little soldier," Burckhard said.

"He's only doing what he was made for," I said.

"You're a good shot."

"Yes. You oughtn't ever to challenge me to a duel."

"Why should I want to?"

"You're always so vexed with me. See, I got the eagle then, and made him flap his wings. So it's not always the little soldier."

"I'm only vexed with you when you play the coquette with little soldiers."

I said, "You make too much of the poor Herr Lieutenant."

"And you make too little of him. And of the engineer, Martz. And that fat fellow with the earlobes, haven't you noticed his ears? Like a Buddha's. A sad thing, to be a Buddha without wisdom. In any case, one duels with enemies, not with young misses who make themselves trivial over lieutenants."

"But mightn't I become an enemy? If I go on making myself trivial? What a shame, I've no more bullets."

He took the gun from me. "I prefer enemies to friends, in any case. Enemies mind their manners."

We became friends anyhow.

"Come now," he'd always say. "What are you reading?"

No one else talked to me that way. I'd been running from man to man since Papi died, and from notion to notion, and I was starving for a little certainty. Well, Burckhard had that. He understood that I dreamt of doing large things, and he was actually a good listener. In the end, he had a great effect on what I suppose you could call my ideas.

He was a real Nietzschean. His motto was: Who needs help doesn't deserve it. One's only duty was to reach heights. Morality was a Jewish stratagem. "If you're lacking in the animal virtues," he used to say, "you devise laws to cripple the fellow who's fully equipped. If you're spiritually sterile, you devise criticism to cut the artists down to size." He explained that Jews were bitter, dark, and priestly, and that they got influence unfairly by means of slyness. Of course, I was an anti-Semite too, like everybody else, but Burckhard was way ahead of me. He also had opinions about women. He'd quote: *"That in woman which inspires respect and fundamentally fear is her nature, which is more natural than that of the man, her genuine, cunning, beast-of-prey suppleness, the tiger's claws beneath the glove, the naïveté of her egoism, her ineducability and inner savagery, and how incomprehensible, capacious, and prowling her desires are."*

Well, I rather liked the sound of that. It was gratifying to think I was not a selfish little flirt but instead was following the promptings of a great and restless soul. I'd smile at Max – I called him Max now – in a capacious, prowling way and go on doodling ensembles I might like to own in the margins of my diary. I was always doing a real fan dance with this diary. I took it everywhere and made a show of not letting anybody look in it. I always used purple ink, which fades, and would one day inconvenience my biographers.

I once told him, "Sometimes I feel nothing really moves me. That I'm only half a person. Don't smile, it's hell being fickle. You always think, All right, *this* time I'm *sure.* Like one of those nightmares in which you think you've finally woken? Only you look around, and the room's not quite right, because you're only in a dream of waking, and then another, and then another.... I'd like to do something really remarkable. Compose a really *good* opera, something no woman's ever done. But I'm – oh, maybe half good enough? Just now I'm dismembering Mozart's first sonata in F major, like a chicken. I want to see how he does it."

"Let me tell you a secret," he said. "Heuberger wants me to do the libretto for an operetta. But I'm simply too lazy. Would you like to compose the music? It would encourage me to work."

Well, my God!

Of course, nothing came of it.

At a certain point I'd always start declaring that I would never marry. Then I'd say, "Do you suppose I'll ever marry?" And then I'd start talking about my future husband, whom as it happened I knew all about. I gave Max a whole list of qualifications. He'd be fixed and certain in his beliefs, this husband of mine, and he'd also have an open and questing mind, and he'd devote every moment to his work, and he'd know how to enjoy life, and he'd raise me up on a pedestal, and from this pedestal I'd gaze up at him in the heavens. Above all else, he'd be an artist. And above that, he'd be pure. And he'd be brave. "Cowardice is the most dreadful quality in a man," I said. "All these pallid fellows who put saccharin in their coffee! A man must rule."

"I begin to feel sorry for this gentleman," Burckhard said.

"He'd know I was his, and possess me with utter naturalness. He'd have no fear, and so there'd be no possibility of regret. Oh, stop huffing out your chest, Max. You'd never do for me. You're a sort of – eunuch." Burckhard laughed, but oh, he didn't like that. "That's what it amounts to, all these women – it's like no women. I'm not going to be one of your little females."

"D'you know what your problem is?" he said. "You can't decide whether you want to be the tenor who slays the dragon or the soprano he dreams of while he's doing it. And you're trotting round looking for some wise baritone to advise you. And my voice might be deep enough, but you're pouting because my soul's not pure – no purer than yours, in fact. Ah, I like to see you blush. We do understand each other."

"And that would never do for a love affair," I said at last. "It'd be a scandal."

"All right, then," he said. "Let's not have a scandal."

I remember it was the most gorgeous evening. Above us in the sky, great pink figures stirred lazily, as if after love. I was quite happy. We were both big, healthy, and good-looking, and strolling at our ease along the Ringstrasse. To either side, the buildings looked like temples. The roofs were crowded with gilt gods, observing us with interest. Some of the passersby probably knew our names, because we were both people who got talked about, and in a minute we'd pick out a nice place for a snack. As we walked in, we'd see ourselves up on the wall in one of those old mirrors that hung everywhere, golden with tobacco smoke. We'd look as if we'd been framed and varnished. I loved Vienna. It's like a vast and ancient cabinet with a hundred thousand mirrored compartments, and in each compartment is some curious or charming thing, and one of them is you, and inside of you your talent unfolds, in secrecy. The chief thing about the Viennese isn't that some of us have done splendid things. It's that every one of us is always about to do something splendid. She can feel it.

I told Burckhard, "Yes – let's not. You enjoy your little females, and I'll wait for my man. If he exists. Ah, the only thing for it is to write my opera. I can do it if I want. I was born on a Sunday."

NOW, ALL THIS TIME, the Empire was falling apart, and it's not like we didn't all know it. You had Austrians, Hungarians, Germans, Czechs, Jews, Gypsies, Croats, Serbs, Slavs, Slovaks, Slovenes, Romanians, Ruthenians, Italians, Poles – we didn't even share a language to disagree in. But it had been falling apart for a hundred years, and we were certain it would go on falling apart forever, and meanwhile we could do what a Viennese loves best, which is to sit comfortably over coffee and discuss all the problems. I recall how everyone's favorite was syphilis. We preferred to call it *Krankheit*. Disease. Krankheit gave an agreeably scientific tone to a sermon, and for poets it was as useful as the moon. There was a waxworks devoted to it in the Prater. The newspaper artists showed it as a comely young woman of the latest mode. They drew her with such enthusiasm that sometimes I'd stand in my shift and beckon mockingly to my mirror, squinting to make my eyes hollow, but I was too pink and the effect was never satisfactory. Every block had a specialist, who'd make you drink a solution of ground glass or rub your body with mercury until your teeth fell out. Nietzsche died of it. Makart died of it. After I died – of old age, by the way – I learnt poor sleek Gretl was a paretic. Her true father was a syphilitic painter named Berger. When she got older, she had to be put in an asylum, and at last the Nazis destroyed her with the rest of the incurables. So she got here before me.

So everything was going to the devil, but on the other hand, in a minute we were going to have a new century. And this, everybody agreed, was going to fix all our problems. If you went into any café, you'd find a bunch of ambitious young fellows discussing spirit travel, phonetic alphabets, and free love, and generally working out the details. You always saw Schnitzler and von Hofmannsthal at the Griensteidl. They used to call it Café Megalomania. At the Louvre, Herzl would be inventing the Jewish State, and at the Café Central, Trotsky would be beating Stalin at chess – Stalin, in that candy box! – and Karl Kraus would be guarding his plate with his elbows. Kraus had just founded a journal called Die Fackel, The Torch. It had fearless red covers. He flew about Vienna with his pencil and everywhere saw injustice and bad grammar. At last he dismissed all his writers, saying, "I was jealous. They drove away readers I wanted to drive away myself."

In art, the big idea was the Gesamtkunstwerk, the total work of art. It was Wagner's word. Wagner wanted his operas to be total works of art, so that music and painting and theater and design and dance were all combined to raise up the spirit. Since the Künstlerhaus wasn't interested in this, all the best men resigned and started the Vienna Secession, and of course, Moll begged them to have their meetings in his beautiful house. They'd sit with their coffee in our parlor and plan it all out. They were going to have a journal called *Ver Sacrum*, and a Wiener Werkstätte to sell properly designed goods, and a Temple of Art crowned with a sphere of gilt-iron laurel leaves. When they built it, everybody called it the Golden Cabbage. I always saw the painter Gustav Klimt at these meetings. He had a brown face and a smooth thick neck like a mastiff. He spoke little and unwillingly, with a warm strong Viennese accent, but the others all wanted him to be their president, and sometimes he'd peer over at me, as if he hoped I'd save him, because I was pretty, and tall.

Klimt was quite a notorious fellow. He always wore sandals and a monk's robe. They said he kept models ready at hand like tubes of paint, that there was always a flock of nude women in his studio, lounging, stretching, waiting to catch the master's eye. In fact, he'd choose one and make the others wait in the hall. He was a gold engraver's son, and these were girls of his class, poor girls who meant to be dancers or milliners. They didn't torment him with thick legs or educated speech. They didn't object to what he called *relaxation*. Each summer he took his mother and sisters to the Salzkammergut. He'd row out into the Attersee with a canvas a meter square and an ivory tablet with a small square hole, and look for compositions along the shore. When he got back, sometimes his sister gave him a letter from a model named Zimmerman, who was living with two of his children in a stinking little room in the Eighth District. Klimt would put in twenty gulden when he replied, and explain that to send more made the envelope thick, so that people would open it and steal the money, and complain that he'd been embarrassed. He'd write, *The postman arrives and blows a little trumpet, and everyone in the house runs to meet him, so the whole world knows from where a letter comes and where it is going.*

Klimt's biggest scandal was the university murals. The city university had hired him to paint Philosophy, Jurisprudence, and Medicine for the ceiling of their Great Hall. Klimt took the female gender of "*die*" *Medizin* quite literally, and when they saw the oil sketch, the Ministry of Education complained about the indecency. He'd painted Suffering Mankind flying up into the clouds. Like me, she wore no drawers, and so you looked up into her armpit and her female apparatus. Across this Klimt painted a bit of colored gauze for the sake of good manners, but when he heard the complaints he got angry and scraped the gauze away. The painting was put on view and everybody went to see it. I thought it was ugly and exciting. Klimt's ladies were beautiful but very thin, with fidgeting long hands and knees like knuckles, and Suffering Mankind's belly shone like a shield. She seemed to rule the world from up there, but she was so malnourished that it made me cross. I wondered, Hadn't he ever painted a fine strong girl with a healthy bust? I supposed he'd made some poor woman climb up on a ladder and stand there quite nude.

Anyway, I decided to go and see him.

I brought Gretl along to be my chaperone, and we took a fiacre to his studio, which was surrounded by flower beds. I knocked on the front door and found it unlocked. Inside, I saw Chinese paintings on the walls and an African sculpture that stood on the floor like a coat tree. There was a black-and-red Japanese cupboard, and two young women in cheap clothes who stopped talking when they saw me, and two skeletons on hooks with their mouths open. There was a door. I said that I had business with Herr Klimt and that my sister would wait here for me, and then I went quickly through the door and into his workroom. One wall there was all windows. Through the white curtains, I saw a ghost of the wild flower beds. The model stand was covered in striped cloth, and on it was a naked woman, and seated on a stool before her was Klimt, turning around in a fury at this interruption and holding his pencil like a sword, but when he saw me he was still. All about me was the smell of linseed oil and tobacco. It was a familiar odor – a Papi-smell. I announced, "I've come to see the great man in his studio."

Klimt painted a woman in the stars, in some heaven of complicated gold, but down in the world she'd sit on a dirty chair with dirty feet, on a coarse cloth, wrinkled, so that when she got up there were red marks across her posterior as if she'd been whipped. The model wrapped herself in a kimono that smelt of sweat and went to fix tea on a gas ring. She offered me a cup in a servant's tone. A tired woman, a coarse type, even a bit heavy in the middle. I was disappointed. All over the floor were drawings and cats. I said, "The cats are walking on your sketches. And what if they do their business there?"

"It's the best fixative there is," he said, "the small business. And if they do the other, well, a cat is also entitled to her opinion. If you had told me, Fräulein Alma, that you were coming, I... would be prepared for visitors." His little eyes were unhappy.

I sank down with my arm around my knees and my seat upon my heels. It was an improper posture for a young lady of nearly nineteen, but I believed that I remained graceful, and I picked up a sketch. From my drawing lessons I knew that the first important thing was the distribution of weight. I felt that Klimt was studying the distribution of my weight.

He said, "Perhaps you won't like them. They represent ideas of some sort."

They were drawn in pencil on Japanese rice paper, which shimmered like the skin of a boiled egg. The women were almost invisible except for the central tuft. Just a few lines, scarcely touching the paper – zoop! and you have an arm; zoop! a leg – but then in the middle, his pencil would get very busy and interested and this one place got scribbled very dark. And here was a young couple lying down together. His back was very broad. She had a drowning woman's mouth, and gripped him with her legs as if she was trying to drag him under. It was nothing like dogs. It was like some cataclysm. It was an outrage and besides, it seemed like very hard work.

"You work on a painting and get all sorts of ideas," he said. "Not every idea is useful, but there you are."

"She does not," I said, "look very comfortable."

Klimt laughed. "Oh, I think Willi made her comfortable enough!"

There I was, down among his drawings with the cats, so now he felt easier. A pretty woman taking a pose in his studio, with these he had experience.

My legs were getting tired and I stood.

"Well," I said, and stepped onto the stand, "at any rate, I shan't want any company."

I shook the dust from a flowered cloth with a snap that stirred the drawings and made the cats run. Then I swung it around myself. I drew up my skirts a bit to reveal my calves, which I had decided were fine. I looked up into the heaven that had so upset the Arts Commission of the Ministry of Education, and stood before the whole world, shining and shameless, with my calves exposed, and at last Klimt shrugged and sat down on his little stool.

Before him was a bit of furniture like a child's desk. To this he clipped a new sheet of paper. He took up his pencil again in that peculiar way. His eyes grew empty and strict, and for a while he kept his pencil down by his knee. Then his heavy arm moved out like the leg of a ballerina, fine and searching, and the end of the pencil wandered and at last flicked, flicked. I lifted my face still further. I would teach him to paint life instead of death. The air across my legs felt truthful. To remain motionless was more difficult than I'd imagined, and soon one ankle hurt from the distribution of weight. The model leaned in the corner with folded arms. Her kimono was coming undone so you could see her brown scribble. She was pregnant – that was why her belly was thick.

When I saw this, I shook away the cloth and marched over to Klimt. On his paper a podgy young girl lifted her chin in order to be elegant, and thrust out her stomach.

I snatched her up and ripped her in two. Outside, Grete was still patiently waiting between the skeletons. Behind me I heard the rising laughter of a woman and a man. I told Grete not to ask questions and we went home.

I'D NEVER BEEN LAUGHED AT before. It was a new experience.

Klimt became my new marvelous man.

I began to see him everywhere. We danced a quadrille at the Camera Club. There was a big dinner at the Zierers' and he asked for my place card. He tucked it into his pocket. I went home and embraced a pillow with my golden arms and examined the effect. I flung myself belly-down on the bed and started dreaming at a great rate. I went prowling barefoot amongst the cats and drawings, which were now all of Klimt and myself. He was working away there on his little stool which made him look so large and bristly and satisfactory. I wore the old kimono. I washed it and then it was clean. I washed his brushes. We warmed ourselves with tea, and the gas ring lit me from below, becomingly. I advised him: You should paint a seraph, a messenger; she has come with the message, in golden mailed gauntlets, she should otherwise be nude and for the sake of modesty she should hold a sword, *here*, but the handle of the sword should be a serpent and the blade should be a river of fire and by means of this blade she should fly. And at her left is a great dragon that has been tamed by her beauty and at her right is a fish with a crown. And she should point the way, and she should not be flimsy but strong and well-born. I held out my pointing arm to show him. He admitted that it looked very fine to paint. He said, To think, when I first met you... Oh! I cried, don't remind me! Then we laughed together, and he rested his face on my belly and said, The child will justify everything.

That spring my family made a tour of Italy. I spent the whole trip in a highly agitated condition. Mami was pregnant with Moll's first child, whom I'd decided was going to run me and Gretl out of the house, and the sun shone down everywhere so you couldn't think. I'd brought manuscript paper along and wrote cradle songs and fantasias. I went around having realizations about life. At last Klimt telegraphed and asked if he could join us at the station in Florence.

He didn't show up at the appointed time, and Moll was obliged to buy a platform ticket and go looking. He found Klimt on a bench with his case pressed between his knees. Klimt was fidgeting at the catches with his big thumbs and wanting to take the next train back to Vienna, because he was far away from his sister's cooking and he couldn't make himself understood.

Moll brought him back to the hotel and we gave him lunch. Over the soup, Klimt told me that five women were completely dependent on him. I thought, Poor devil! He pulled open his pocket, and there was my place card, still. The next day, he came by after my nap, when my hair was all anyhow, and asked if he could take out my hairpins. He did so, gently, one by one, until my hair fell over my shoulders like a cloak.

Now, here was a difficulty. Moll was Klimt's friend, and so he knew all about Klimt's relaxations, about which he was always eager to hear. But now Klimt wanted to show Moll's step-daughter around Italy. Moll couldn't object to this unless he considered me as a possible source of relaxation, like some milliner's apprentice with black feet and a goose-pimpled der-rière. In the end he agreed, very unhappily, and Klimt showed me around Florence and then Venice, very unconcerned, because he was a great innocent and besides, he knew quite well when to remain so.

What did concern Klimt was that someone might speak to him in Italian. "Let's not go over there," he would say. "It looks complicated." I spoke no more Italian than he did, but I'd take him where he wanted to go and make the Italians speak what German they knew, and afterward Klimt would say, "I suppose they're laughing at me." Then we'd find a place where he could sit and drink beer, which he knew how to do, and this comforted him. He was all right as long as Italy was paintings and beer. He didn't mind bridges, and he was at ease in small boats. He didn't notice the smell of trapped water that was everywhere. He nourished himself with beer and Giotto, and there were many later, lesser artists that made him quite cheerful. He led me away from some Tiepolos, saying, "My God, what an awful painter. No construction. He just piled it all up there, like storing old furniture in the attic. But I'll give him this, he could paint a nice soft piece of cloth. And the arses on those *putti*, like spun sugar, like beefsteak! A hungry man could live off one of them for a month."

"Herr Klimt," I said, "you must not speak to me as if I were one of your females."

"Females? Have I *females*?" he said.

"It's very rude," I said fiercely, because perhaps it was all silly rumors and the poor man had no females. "You must learn to speak correctly to a young lady."

"You'll teach me," he said. "I thought I was a well-mannered fellow."

I shouted, "I came to your studio in good faith and you insulted me!"

"You ran away. For no reason. Because you didn't like my drawing, for heaven's sake. I'd've made you another. We could have gotten some work done."

"Work?"

"Yes. You're a god-awful model but a celestial subject. It's criminal no one's been painting you. What the devil has old Moll been thinking?"

Tiepolo had made him brave.

We were crossing the Piazza San Marco. It was spring, and the famous pigeons walked stupidly in circles. Down by the steps, the boats were nodding their masts, and the Venetian men swung their hips like prostitutes, although somehow this was not unmasculine, and I was much noticed. I took Klimt's arm. There are all sorts of ways to take a man's arm. On the far side of the piazza were some iron chairs painted green, and I knew Klimt wanted to go there and see if there might be beer. I made my voice small and drowsy and said, "And now you're speaking rudely of my stepfather. You must learn not to be so wicked, Herr Klimt. It's because you've no woman in your life."

"No woman? I thought I had a hundred women. I thought I had females."

"You haven't the right sort of woman."

He stopped walking then, and I swung round and halted myself with a hand on his breast. He had a strange odor, like fresh-dug earth, but warm. The taste of his mouth had been darkened by cigars. Against my stomach I felt the engine of his nature. His arms were powerful but his hands were delicate, and I felt his thumb lightly behind one ear and his forefinger behind the other. I had no air and I wanted him to carry me somewhere because my legs were all at once so sleepy.

"I'll take you away," he muttered. "I'll come and take you away."

"To where?" I asked.

"I'll take you away. I'll *kidnap* you," he said.

"Yes," I said. "All right."

That night I wrote in my diary that Vienna's foremost artist had kissed me amongst the pigeons and that I had to decide what I was going to do.

Soon after this my mother read my diary, as she often did, and she and Moll forbade Klimt ever to speak to me or to enter our house again.

On 19 May 1899, Klimt wrote a letter of apology. He never in his life wrote anything so long, before or after. The envelope was thick as your hand, but somehow no one tore it open looking for money, and he addressed it to my stepfather. *Lieber Moll!* he scrawled across the whole first page, so that the exclamation point ran off the edge. His pen leapt wildly beneath, with blots and big gaps where he couldn't bring himself to write a word. *You are seeing things much more grimly than they are, as a result of your paternal cares.* He wrote, *I am a poor fool.* He wrote, *then came your telegram – I followed you – not knowing what I did. I noticed your wife's perfectly comprehensible and natural efforts to keep me and Fräulein Alma apart. One thing was quite clear – It could not be allowed to happen – . –*

Then that evening in Venice came. I am an embittered man, he wrote. *I had been drinking rather more quickly than was wise.*

When I turn these things over in my mind, I fear for myself what I have feared for a long time/my father died from a brain disease/my   was in an asylum/my elder sister went mad a few years ago/perhaps there are the first signs in me – then, dear Moll, I am probably one of   /the madness that will kill me will not be a happy one. He wrote, *I'll do whatever you say – because you are cleverer than I.*

Dear Moll, forgive me if I have caused you trouble.

And he wrote: *as for Fräulein Alma/I think she won't find it difficult to forget.*

WHEN KLIMT CAME to the house, my parents wouldn't let him past the front hall. "Are you angry with me?" he asked them. "Don't hold it against me, I beg you, don't hold it against me!" I stood at the top of the stairs and listened to the whole sorry business.

I marked my diary with a big dark cross and wept. I felt this was all the most awful humiliation. I'd had things all planned out, you see: I was going to sacrifice my purity to his genius and thereby become some sort of holy whore. But now I saw that I was only meant to be relaxation – a girl that forgets – and that all he cared about was fat Moll. And now I'd gone and kissed a man, and my purity was lost, and I couldn't ever marry. And I could practically still taste his goddamned cigars.

It was generally an awful time, because the next thing you know, Moll told me Gretl was engaged to a painter named Legler. Well, my God, Gretl, that runt? whose mind was so crushingly practical, who had no temperament and no rhythm, so that when we played duets I was always in a fury? This Gretl was going to be married first? "What?" I screamed. "And never said a word to me?" At the wedding, Mami's eyes gleamed lustfully, or so I thought. That night, I dreamt Gretl had married Klimt. Then Mami's baby came, and they obliged me to hold it, which I found highly embarrassing, and they asked me to give up my music room to make a nursery. I decided I'd run away. But charming Papi had left no papers. Everything had gone to Mami. I saw it all: I'd given Klimt everything and now I had nothing.

I won't bore you, I went on like this for quite a while. Then in the fall I began studying composition with Schönberg's teacher, Alexander von Zemlinsky. A tiny man, chinless and frog-eyed and no one with whom anyone need fall in love. So one afternoon I slid into his arms as we played *Götterdämmerung* four-handed. I'd been missing a lot of notes and didn't want to continue and needed kisses from a brilliant man.

I lived a long life and I was unkind to many men, but I was never again so wholly unkind as I was to Alex. I led him, as the English say, a merry dance. I obliged him to admit that he wasn't a virgin, and then I obliged him to explain whom he'd been not-a-virgin with, and then I scolded him for naming these women, like a fellow with no sense of chivalry. I told him I wanted his child. He declared that this would be his greatest happiness. I said that I'd want his child if the idea were sensible, but that it wasn't. He decided children were not essential. I told him I would never marry. Fine, he'd never marry either. I made him read Nietzsche and corrected his spelling of the name. He mumbled, "Men like me may deserve such happiness, but we never get it." To such a gentleman it's almost necessary to be cruel. And so in the mirror each morning I found a cruel young woman, lewd and false and quite pale enough now to make a satisfactory Krankheit.

After lessons, when the other students left Alex's flat, we'd remain behind and relieve our bitterness.

"Did you *hear* his *adagio*?" I'd say.

"Did you *see* the way she looked at him?" he'd cry.

"Dullard," I sang.

"Cow," he crooned.

"No better than she should be," I agreed. I was breathless, like a girl that crushes an insect with her heel. "One of these spoilt little misses that fancies herself a musician."

"A sorry little weakling," he drawled. "Eaten up with spite." We were both breathless. He lowered his voice. "They say in the evenings, after he locks up that so-called export business of his..." And his voice grew softer and softer, lower and lower.

I wanted to be with a man as awful as myself. I didn't want there to be any purity anywhere. I thought it was an advantage that Alex was Jewish. I figured that meant he was just as bad as I was. We kissed so hard our teeth ached. I loosened my clothes and let him explore and was excited by my sacrifice. With weeping eyes I wrote: *The touch of his hand deep inside me – and such a blissful glow swept through me – one little nuance more and I would have* been a god. His male element would grow prominent, and sometimes I'd pet it through his trousers. Then he'd shake and cry out, and afterward seem ashamed and wet, and I was glad I never let him unbutton.

Now, I said to myself miserably, *now you're being sensible.*

As it happened, Zemlinsky was never able to provide the final nuance. But I learnt that by closing my legs around one of his and heaving my *os pubis* against his hip I could conclude matters for myself and not be obliged to suffer dissatisfaction.

III

THE SOPRANO ANNA VON MILDENBURG, who would soon become my enemy, used to talk about meeting the great man as follows. She'd been rehearsing Brünnhilde in Hamburg when the door popped open. There stood a little fellow in a gray summer suit with a dark felt hat in one hand. His face was burnt black by the sun and his bright eyes were full of aversion. Her accompanist pressed his lips together to make an M: Mahler. Mahler flung his hat onto the piano, shooed away the *répétiteur*, and made von Mildenburg sing *hojotoho* until she laid her head upon her arms and wept.

He stood over her, biting his lip, then gave a shout of laughter and began to rush around with his hands in his pockets, saying, "Go on then, cry! Blub blub blub! until you sink into the mire of mediocrity!"

And soon he was writing his Annerl each time he left Hamburg, complaining about his sisters' poverty and instructing her to disguise her handwriting when she replied, for like previous of Mahler's sopranos, she'd become a labor of love.

Gustav Mahler was a fidgety little man with a fine head. He was thin and clean-shaven, like a youth, and hopped about in nickel-rimmed spectacles. When he got enraged, a sea-green vein appeared at each temple. In a restaurant he'd cry, "Waiter, what's that gentleman eating over there?" As a birthday gift to himself he climbed the Amthorspitze. He couldn't pronounce his r's. Like Klimt, he was the eldest son of a poor Bohemian family, and paid their bills, so that he was always in debt. There were thirteen brothers and sisters, but eight died in childhood and another shot himself at twenty-one. He was from Iglau, a garrison town, where he taught himself the concertina before he was three years old. He'd run after the military band in his little shirt, oomping. He'd been Kapellmeister in Prague, Leipzig, Pest, and Hamburg, and now he was Artistic Director of the Viennese Court Opera, and from this post you could be promoted only to heaven. He was a Jew. Even Wagner's widow had to admit he was Wagner's greatest interpreter, but she still started such an outcry that Mahler had to be baptized a Catholic before he assumed his duties. He saw to it before he left Munich, then prowled through the Hofoper, gripping his lapels and declaring, "Tradition is Schlamperei." Slovenliness.

In those days singers hired *claqueurs* to sit in the audience and shout out for curtain calls, but Mahler forbade this and put detectives in the gallery to keep an eye on things. He sent latecomers to a latecomers' box. He revised the instrumentation of Beethoven's Ninth and distributed a pamphlet explaining his corrections. His own First Symphony was very unpopular. I went to the première and found it awfully loud. The newspaper artists drew him conducting an orchestra of squalling elephants, hooting Red Indians, and screaming sewing machines, and the *Reichspost* complained about his *Jew-boy antics at the podium*. For all his energy, his health was uncertain, and his sister painted his throat daily to prevent abscesses. His hemorrhoids had been operated upon three times by Franz Josef's own surgeon, Hochenegg. I was in the audience watching when he nearly died from a burst aneurysm of the intestine while conducting *The Magic Flute.* But he wouldn't stop and spoil the music, and with his jagged white face and twisted eyes and his Jew-boy's arm snap-ping up and down, he looked like a dying Lucifer and I told my friends, "No man can go on like that. It's impossible."

He made me nervous, but I was quite mad for him as an artist. He was known as a tyrant. He feared nobody. Prince Mon-tenuovo once instructed him to engage the soprano Forster, whose voice was extinct. She'd been Franz Josef's mistress, and the Emperor was going to pay her fees. Mahler said, "Very well. But each time her name appears on the program it will be fol-lowed by the words: *By superior order of His Majesty.*" Forster didn't get her engagement, and I went around crying, "That's the way to treat them!" I was just as big an anti-Semite as ever, but like most Viennese I had my own little list of Jews I knew were all right. Besides, I knew something Burckhard didn't know, and this is that dark, bitter, priestly men could be awfully intriguing.

One day on the Ringstrasse I met Berta Zuckerkandl, the anatomist's wife. Her father managed the *Wiener Tagblatt* and she'd become an art critic. Each Sunday she held a salon, which she freely admitted was the most brilliant in Vienna. She had a square jaw, weary eyes, and a wide, weary lizard's mouth. "Come and meet Mahler," she said.

I said, "I've been trying for the last six months to keep from meeting him."

She told me he lived with his sister. "Justi keeps an eye on him for the family, so he doesn't overdo it with work or women. Country dolts. The man's a hermit. We've got to coax him out of there somehow." And she looked me up and down. Like any *salonnière*, she had the eye of a procuress.

I said, "No, thank you."

"You're looking well," she said coldly. "You've grown quite plump."

But it would be a coup to drag Mahler from Justi's table to

hers. So Zuckerkandl gave a dinner for her own sister, Sophie. Sophie had married a mining engineer named Clemenceau and become sister-in-law to the famous statesman, and Mahler had once met the Clemenceaus and liked them. Zuckerkandl promised Mahler that if he came, there'd be Clemenceaus and no strangers and the sort of food he liked. To me she just said, "Don't be a dolt. He's Vienna's biggest man."

The whole mob was there, Mami, Moll, Burckhard, even Klimt, whom we'd forgiven – it had been two years. She seated me between these men. That's the way she did things. Across the table was an empty chair: Mahler was late. The air was simmering with the odor of candied potatoes. Finally, in came a small dark man of forty-two years, frowning intelligently. His clothes were of good quality and he wore them badly. Like any concertgoer, I was already familiar with how he moved – herky-jerky but very certain. At this time, Mahler ate only whole-meal bread and rennet apples, because Wagner, the Master, had declared that vegetarianism was the last hope for degenerate humanity, so there was a nice bowl of shiny apples in front of him. He picked one up and sniffed it. Zuckerkandl said, "Herr Operndirektor, may I present Fräulein Moll?" and I loudly said, "Fräulein *Schindler*," and he gave my hand a little jerk, since I was not Sophie Clemenceau and he did not wish to meet any young women who were not Sophie Clemenceau.

That's a relief, I thought. He's not interested in me.

Mahler was not interested. In *me*.

Because of my deafness, I often chose to be silent and stately and let people admire my long neck, but that night the words spun on my tongue, and my glances were rich and flashing. Burckhard got suspicious and Klimt squeezed his little eyes shut and mumbled, "That's good! That's good!" Soon Mahler envied us our merriment. He cried, "Share the joke with the rest of us, can't you?" His voice was deep for such a little man. I looked up, as if I hadn't quite heard him, and then away, as if I hadn't quite seen him.

After a while, the talk turned to Beauty.

"Ah, but what is beautiful?" I said, and stretched out my young neck and waited.

"The head of Socrates," Mahler said absently. "One sees the solidity of his thought." He was examining my throat the way a silk peddler examines a bolt of silk.

His answer pleased me, so I frowned and put away my neck. "I think Zemlinsky is beautiful."

Mahler shrugged. "His face is like his music. Both lack a chin."

Meanwhile I was doing what I always did with any new man. I was imagining that were were wed. I told myself that most great men were rather small. I told myself that a fair woman looks very well with a dark man. Part of my excitement is that I was sitting next to Klimt, which unsettled me and made my lips feel strange, but it's also true Mahler was quite attractive in his way, and besides, he was Wagner's greatest interpreter. I seemed to see his hard dark fingers unfastening my manuscript case. I saw him stooping over my lieder, nodding. Then we composed the first husband-and-wife symphony and the critics declared: It's astonishing! One cannot detect where the Meister's ideas end and where those of the young Meisterin begin! *The King and Queen of Music* was vulgar, I decided. We should be known everywhere simply as *The Mahlers*. And all this time I kept drinking and saying whatever came into my head, to show him I wasn't afraid of him, so that by the time we got our coffee in the next room we were at it like husband and wife. I very nearly screamed at him that he'd been ignoring the manuscript of Zemlinsky's *The Golden Heart.* "You have no right to keep such a man waiting for a year!"

He twirled back and forth, he stamped like Rumpelstiltskin. "How can you stand up for such rubbish? Didn't you say you'd studied with Labor?"

"I have been schooled in music. And also in common courtesy!"

Mahler held his mouth open for a time, as if to cool his brains.

Then when he spoke he was so calm and pleasant that I felt like a child. "You're quite correct. The work's a muddle, but he's a serious man and deserves a serious answer. I'll write tomorrow and ask him to come see me."

I'd made a fool of myself. I left early.

Afterward, Mahler went around saying, "She was quite rude to me, that young woman!" He was like me: He wasn't used to back talk.

He was in raptures.

The next evening Mami and I had tickets to see Gluck's *Orfeo* at the Hofoper, with Bruno Walter conducting. The performance that night was skillful but rather rushing. I wouldn't have minded a bit more clarity. I looked up toward the Director's box, the location of which was known to every educated Viennese, and there was Mahler, flirting away at me like a *fille de joie* and pointing with his chin that Mami and I should meet him in the foyer at the interval.

When the interval came, I rose through the applause like a swimmer and we walked toward the doors to the foyer. My gown was pale salmon with a sour-ivory fichu. The floor sloped up-ward like a beach, and I could feel the muscles of my legs as they carried me forward. Mahler took us to his office for tea. The rooms were luxuriously appointed, and in the far wall a vent opened into the auditorium so that he could hear the music in secrecy. He went to his desk and poked at a button. "Did you sleep well last night, Fräulein?" he asked.

"Quite well. Why shouldn't I?"

"I didn't sleep a wink. Not all night!" he said proudly.

"No? That is unfortunate." He was making me nervous again. I put on my music-room face – chin up – and began to shuffle through the scores on his piano.

"The pressure of your duties…" said Mami, the old soprano.

She was thinking, To have sung for Mahler!

"To execute my duties is actually effortless. It is the execution of the duties of others that remains a martyrdom. Herr Walter is a young man of particular promise, but tonight's performance was spoilt by his kindness. One cannot approach musicians longing for friendship, since with every orchestra one must ruthlessly correct the same bad habits. They won't observe the markings and have no respect for the rules of dynamics."

A fat woman is at the mercy of any skinny man. Mami offered up her words like spoonfuls of soup. "It's very important."

"It is the hidden innermost pulse of a work. But if they see a crescendo they at once play forte and rush until the notes pile one upon the other. My God, do they think they're paid by the note? One's tempo is correct only if it allows every note its value."

It was my own opinion exactly, and I ruffled more furiously at his sheet music. Mami watched us, her nose red and white with satisfaction. She told Mahler our house was a nice place for a busy man to come and take it easy awhile, and begged him to visit.

"Visit? Of course I'll come and visit! Now, when can I visit?" He snatched from a drawer an immense green datebook, into which he'd folded notes on dozens of slips of paper. These went flying.

"Herr Direktor, you're losing all your little papers!"

"Yes, they're going all over," he said complacently.

"Almschili, Herr Operndirektor is coming to visit!"

"Is he?" I said. "Now, here's a piece I should like to conduct myself."

"I should be delighted to hand over my baton," he said. "I am convinced you would be entirely brilliant."

"That doesn't sound like an objective judgment, I'm afraid."

"There is no such thing," Mahler said, ablaze with happiness, "as an objective judgment."

MOLL SHOUTED at my mother, "You took an innocent young girl into the private rooms of that filthy roué?"

Later he tried to speak kindly to me. "He's not young. He's not strong. You couldn't call him a beauty. To my certain knowledge he's in debt. Composes, too, and they say it's no go."

Burckhard said, "It would be a crime to squander yourself on a degenerate, rachitic old Jew."

"Don't go getting a swelled head," said Mami, "but I believe Herr Mahler likes you."

The snow was falling when Mahler trotted into my music room, rubbing his hands and smelling of cold. I was tending the fire, gracefully down on one knee like an angel in an Annunciation, so that he should see I was lissome, but domestic, and yet not negligible, because I held an iron poker in my hand. I was pretty jumpy. I'd just had the walls redone in white and pale green, and my books were still piled on the rug. He crouched here and there, twisting sideways to read the titles. "Nietzsche? You're reading Nietzsche?" he said merrily. "You ought to throw this rubbish on the fire."

Mahler had never had an affair with any woman who was not a soprano under his direction.

I took hold of the book, my throat lively with nerves. "With pleasure," I said, and held it up as if I was about to throw it. "Once you explain why I ought to."

"Once...?"

Mahler looked up at the book. He seemed astounded to see it so high in the air.

"You would surely agree," said I, "that it would be better for me to be properly convinced of Nietzsche's worthlessness here and now than to burn him on your instructions and forever long to read him afterward."

The fire lit us. I felt the book's weight down my arm. I felt my pulse there. His words had been a danger, but I'd been brave and quick, and Mahler was affronted again. For him this was a voluptuous feeling.

"Well, then," he said, "why don't *you* convince *me*? Is it really that good?" He took it from me and began turning the pages. He flung himself into one of my chairs and slumped there with my book, like an adolescent, his mouth a bit open.

And there we were. Mahler reading, me staring at him.

"So, Herr Direktor," I said.

My voice was trivial.

"So, Herr Mahler," I said loudly. He nodded and kept turning pages.

I asked him where his people were from – Iglau, wasn't it?

"How nicely you say *Iglau*," he said. "No, Kalischt – not even Kalischt, but nearby, in such a miserable little hut, we didn't even have glass in the windows."

"You grew up in the country, then?"

He shrugged. "There was a pond in front. One muddy fish that went round and round. I threw rocks at it. That's a fine instrument you have there, a Bleuthner. You don't find the movement a little stiff?"

"It shouldn't be too easy to play a note. You ought to have to commit yourself."

"Yes," he said, pleased. "I like a Bleuthner."

"Did you find that, living in the country, you were presented with a palette of sort of ready-made motifs? So that the works of Nature seemed more pertinent than the works of Man? I wish you'd put down that book."

"You seem full of ideas," Mahler said.

"Don't you like ideas, Herr Mahler?"

"Well," he said, very jolly, "I like *mine!*"

"There's something I feel I ought to tell you. I didn't care for your First."

"Why not?"

"I'm afraid I thought it willfully naïve."

"Ah."

"That giddy stuff with the piccolos. Bits of *Frère Jacques*. A *czárdás*. My Sweetheart's Two Blue Eyes. These – snippets. You're not so simple as all that."

"I wrote it at your age," he said mildly.

"Then, bang, bang, the world ending." I couldn't seem to stop myself.

"Well, maybe you'll feel differently later."

How it thrilled me, that *later*!

"I thought perhaps you'd be angry," I said.

"But no one else liked it, either."

"And that doesn't discourage you?"

"I knew what sort of symphony I wanted. I didn't imagine I knew what sort everybody else wanted."

"Don't you like praise?"

"I love praise."

"And it doesn't bother you when you're not understood?"

"No, it's very bothersome. It makes everyone twice as difficult the next time round."

"But you don't, actually, *care* what your critics think. Or what I think. Either."

"Oh, no, I listen to everybody. You never know."

"That's not much of a compliment to me."

"Don't you get enough compliments, Fräulein? I'd think you would."

"You seem so sure of everything, so armored, so – self-contained."

"You make me sound like a mollusk."

"As if you had everything you needed."

He hesitated. "Not everything," he said.

I've got him, I thought. The biggest man in music, and I've got him.

My Nietzsche was spread out on his chest now. He looked like a man with the blankets pulled up to his chin. I took the book from him – for an instant, I felt his warm breastbone against my knuckles – and flipped through the pages, saying, "Shall I read you something I've always liked? Ah. Here. *I teach* *you the friend in whom the world stands complete, a vessel of the good – the creative friend, who always has a complete world to bestow."*

He snapped himself forward and was on his feet again, hands in his pockets. He paced round the room again. He gave the andiron a little kick and turned to me.

"That doesn't sound so bad," he said.

Seeing me blush, he blushed, but it didn't occur to him to drop his eyes.

Mami poked in the tip of her nose to say, "For dinner, Herr Mahler, we're having Paprikahendl. And we hope for Burckhard."

"I don't like either!" he said gaily.

"Ah," she cried, "then you're not dining with us?"

"Of course I am dining. Nothing could induce me not to dine. But I must phone Justi and tell her I shan't be in to dinner. Just like that, with no warning! She won't know what to think!"

"Surely she must be used to it, a busy man like yourself."

"No. This *never* happens. Since we've been in Vienna, this is the *first* time!"

There was a telephone at the post office in Döbling and I offered to bring him there.

Mami and a servant got Mahler into his coat and hat and muffler, and he supervised this procedure, and even helped, and then patted himself here and there to see that everything was in order, so that his muffler came undone again, but at last we set off down the hill. A love-struck violinist once wrote that Mahler had the gait of a prancing horse. In fact, any horse that walked as Mahler did would be shot and rendered into glue. He'd canter

ahead so that I couldn't keep up, and then stop to tie his shoelace
so that I nearly knocked him down, and each time we had to find a
good place to put up his foot so that he could tie the lace properly.
The snow squeaked under our soles. I couldn't think of anything
to say. I brought him to the post office and he took up the apparatus. "This is Mahler," he said.

I stamped my cold boots.

"Is there someone there, please," he said, "who knows my
'phone number at home?"

And when I stared, he remarked, "It's not so simple, to marry
a man like me."

SO IT SEEMED I was engaged.

"A quiet little ceremony," he said. "Perhaps only Justi and
your lovely parents? Engagement rings are tasteless and absurd
and I'm sure you don't want one any more than I do."

No ring!

It was quite a courtship. For one thing, the technical aspect
wasn't so good. Mahler kept himself very clean, but his body had
an odd, sharp smell and, besides, his embraces were clumsy.
Back then, love affairs weren't so common among young bour-
geois men. You got your learning in brothels, and poor Gustl was
too squeamish for that. He'd unbutton his sopranos and twiddle
them and send them home.

So he had no experience, the famous roué. "*If only,*" he murmured, "*if only you were a widow!*" He grew blacker and blacker with
our kisses, the veins clutching his temples like claws, and then
went home all swollen. The doctor prescribed hip baths full of ice.
I was afraid that our incomplete love might endanger his health.

I met his sister. She seemed changeable and imperious. In my
diary I wrote: *Justi watches me Argus-eyed and immediately passes on
her anxieties to him. What if it should strike her that I am lacking in warm*

feeling, that within me there is nothing but calculation, cold, clear calcula-
tion? But then I wrote: *His health, his race, his age, his debts, even his*
music, all these make his position terribly precarious. So where then is the
calculation?

He sent me all his songs. They struck me as mannered. He
was a genius, all right, but I just didn't like them. I'd think of
how Alex and I would work together, kiss awhile, work, kiss, and
how when I played a nice bit, he'd stroke my back and murmur,
Well done. I hadn't told Alex anything yet, and I still couldn't
decide if I ought to. Because the big question was, Would Mahler
believe in my music like Alex did?

One day while Mahler was in Dresden I wrote him a very short
letter, explaining that I had an appointment with Gound and
that, after all, I couldn't go on neglecting my work.

Two days later, he replied.

When I'd read this reply several times, I wandered into the
parlor. "I've had a letter from Gustav, Mami," I said, almost
sleepily.

"Ah, but he writes you twice a day!" my mother said. Then she
said, "My heavens! How many pages have you there?"

"Twenty," I said. "I have disturbed the Herr Direktor. He asks
me how it is that I claim to be possessed of a *personality.* He begs
me to explain what I mean when I say that my ideas do not always
agree with his; he reminds me that I have none of my own, and
would not think I had, but for the flattery of *highly confused com-*
panions besotted with my looks. He asks – ah, here – *I must now*
ask myself again what this obsession is that has fixed itself in that little
head I love so indescribably dearly, that you must be and remain yourself.
He is horrified that I wish to go on with my work. This I must
renounce entirely if we are to be married. He writes, *You have only*
one profession from now on: to make me happy! He is kind enough to
offer that I may regard his work as mine."

"May I see that?" my mother said. She took the letter, and after some time she said, "This is monstrous. You must break off with him at once." She was trembling.

"You haven't read all of it, have you?" I said.

Again my mother bowed her head. As she read, she munched with her lips. I have to admit, I was kind of enjoying her horror. Out the window, the dusk swam around the garden like blue honey. I felt like I was swimming through great warm honey-blooms of anger, stroking lazily with my legs. I said, from memory, "*What you could become to me, Alma, the most sublime object of my life, my courageous companion, my stronghold, my peace, my heaven, in a word, my wife, in whom I constantly find and renew myself...* He'll send his man round tomorrow for my answer. He doesn't want us to marry unless we understand each other. I've upset him, Mami, I really have. He thought it was agreed that I'd give him what he wanted."

Mami had finished. "This is monstrous. You must break off with him at once."

"It requires courage to write a letter so monstrous. Not many men would have such courage. *You must give yourself to me uncondi- tionally, shape your future life, in every detail, entirely in accordance with my needs and desire nothing in return but my* LOVE ! Now, what could be more forthright? How can any girl be disappointed if she takes up such an offer as that?"

"No gentleman –"

"He's not a gentleman. He always says, *I'm not like you! You can trip lightly through life, but I've got mud on my boots.* And you gave up your music, Mami."

"I don't care what he has on his boots. Even the son of a tavern keeper – He's a Jew after all, then. A common little Jew, for all his talent."

"I wonder if that's what it is," I said dreamily. I thought, What a grand renunciation it would be. I'd give up my own music

for the sake of his greater gifts. I felt warm all over, and decided
I'd stop endangering Gustav's health.

SO I WENT with Mahler to his rooms and prepared to be
deflowered. I unpinned my hair, the way he liked it. I removed
my corset and loosened my shift, and presented myself to be
swooped down upon.

"You're so beautiful," he said, holding his trousers by the
cuffs. "No man could ever deserve you."

Well, I agreed with him, but wasn't he supposed to take me
anyway? My legs were cold and I got into the bed.

Mahler was very tidy about removing his clothing. I was startled at the size and hairiness of his parts. One of his testes hung a
bit lower than the other. He later assured me the arrangement
was common. He got into bed and hitched along on his elbows
until our faces were near.

"Now it's just you and me," he murmured.

"What?" I said, and then quickly, "Oh, yes." But I still hadn't
heard.

He kissed me and then climbed on top of me. He weighed sixty-
three kilos, less than I did. I remember his grinding teeth and hard
thin struggling limbs, like the legs of a beetle turned over upon its
back. It was obvious what he was trying to do, but the condition of
his anatomy was too inconstant. I couldn't understand this,
because Alex would have a constant condition for hours. I took
hold of it. It was clean, warm, and unpleasantly dark. I tried to
encourage it with my hand but it shrank back like a cat that doesn't
want you to pet it. "I *said* I didn't deserve you," he cried.

Oh, it was miserable. I had such a sense of being all wrong
that my joints felt rickety, as if I had the flu. I kept smoothing
down the sheets around him, as if that might make things a bit
better. I wanted to comfort him, but wound up crying myself,
with shame and disappointment. After all, I'd given up my music

in order to be enslaved by a dark genius and I did feel I was owed simple physical competence.

Once I was crying, we got along much better. I laid my wet cheek against his breast. His heart frightened me. It creaked, like a gate swinging open and shut.

"Things will go better next time," he said.

Next time? I thought. The man's mad.

But three days later we had success. Ouch, what a business. But Mahler's happiness was very great, and so I wrote just three words in my diary: *Bliss upon bliss.*

The following night Mahler and Justi had a dinner party to present me to Mahler's friends. My mood was maybe a little complex. I recalled myself all nude and golden in Mahler's dark arms, and felt sore from my trial and full of mystery. But I was also afraid I was pregnant – in fact, I was – and imagined that I already felt sick. I wanted to sit quietly and gravely with him, my cheek on his chest, and be solitary queen of the flat again, but although he kissed me quite worshipfully at the door, he at once returned to Justi and the details of hospitality. I took out my diary and wrote, *A.Z. is a genius, and I share his feelings for his art. But Mahler is so poor, so frightfully poor, I'll have to lie my entire life, and with Justi, that female! peering and prying all the time – but I must be free, utterly free!* And then in came the guests.

First came Siegfried Lipiner, who considered himself a poet and was Librarian of the Austrian Parliament. Of him Brahms said, *That deceitful Polish dog interests me.* Then his wife Clementine, and his former wife Nanna, and Nanna's new husband, Albert Spiegler, who was a scientist and Mahler's childhood friend and in addition was Clementine's brother. Then Mami and Moll, and the archaeologist Fritz Loehr and his wife Uda, and the young conductor Bruno Walter, whom Mahler had accused of kindness, and Justi's fiancé Rosé the famous cross-eyed violinist, and Anna von Mildenburg, who in Hamburg had been Mahler's

Annerl and by now was Vienna's foremost dramatic soprano and old Lipiner's mistress.

They had nothing to do with me, these old Lipiners and Spieglers. Mahler, I felt, had dragged them around since his youth like leg-irons. They treated his box as their own, but they'd still only known about his engagement when the *Neue Freie Presse* spied it out, since Mahler was so secretive. Mahler fell into a rage when he was congratulated, as if he were ashamed, and his friends saw me as young and unsuitable and scheming. Old Lipiner called me *Mädchen*, and von Mildenburg held out her arms and devoured me with a wet smile. She and I were pretty much the same type, powerful and well-fleshed – *That coarse fat thing*, I thought – and she had big fanatical eyes crowding up against a strong nose that perhaps looked best beneath a winged helmet. Back in Hamburg, she used to chase Mahler through the back lanes after a performance. She'd throw herself at his feet, burst into tears, and parade though his rooms nude, so that he was disgusted. To lure him back she pretended to be ill, and when he rushed to her side he found her with a Dominican friar to marry them. She was still determined to have him, and now she leaned close, with her gobbling smile, and told me I was pretty, and that she wanted to know everything about me.

The meal was served, and I ate and said very little. The hoarse odor of the red wine, the thick sweetness of duck stewed in apricots and rice steamed with raisins and cumin, the rush of considering and self-important words, all these spilled over me like a drunkenness. Justi had polished the crystal cruets, and now evil gleams swam inside them, like sprites or spermatozoa. The weave of the tablecloth was horrible against my wrist. I had wind. Mahler's friends were happy to ignore me, and I felt like a pregnant strumpet, too clumsy to give pleasure, who still wanted to be lady of the house, and my fiancé was avid to please them, and I suspected I was after all as fat as von Mildenburg. I thought

I might be sick, or maybe sing. At last, in response to one of her questions I announced: "I know very little of Gustav's music, and what little I know I don't like."

There was blessed quiet.

Mahler beamed and laughed his hard gasping laugh. He brought me next door to his room to sit together and kiss, saying, "Wasn't it frightful in there? Here we'll be comfier." The dinner was a shambles. Through the wall we heard chairs scraping back and then people leaving. All the Spieglers and Lipiners were furious.

What I thought was: Good. He needed to choose. He's chosen.

THE MOST DIFFICULT THING was to tell Alex. I came at the regular time for my lesson. He rose slowly to his feet, but he wasn't quite perpendicular and he steadied himself with spread fingers against the edge of the piano. I'd seen such a face just once before, when Mahler conducted *The Magic Flute*. Then out came a grinding together of bones. "Such a man... deserves," he said, "such a great... happiness. I wish you both, the two of you... I wish..." He said, "Great happiness."

WE WED in secret in the sacristy of the old Karlskirche. Moll and Rosé were our witnesses. Justi and Mami were the only guests. I was ill with the baby, and Mahler held a soft felt hat spotted with rain. His galoshes made him stumble when he knelt. Then we got on a train for St. Petersburg, where he had contracts for three concerts. This was our honeymoon. It was a rule for Mahler to get a migraine each time he traveled, and at each station he leapt out and rushed up and down the platform to soothe his skull, with no coat or hat, astounding the Russians wrapped in furs. "Let them stare," he said calmly. "The chief thing is my head." In Petersburg we rented an open sledge with three horses harnessed abreast and drove round through the falling snow. When we passed the black Kazan Cathedral, our driver stopped and threw himself down in the snow and prayed until he was all covered up. Yes, I thought, this is married life. A new world. The Neva was frozen thicker than a man is tall, and tram lines were laid down across it. Near evening the fashionable came out to skate on it, circling and nodding as couples do upon the Ring. It was strange to see their calm faces moving through the dusk at such speed. We both got colds, which shut off the Petersburg smell of wood smoke and leather. Gustav's work went very well. For weeks the orchestra had thirsted for Gustav Mahler and his bold new *tempi* and they didn't care if his French was poor, and he found them excellent and obedient. He conducted Beethoven's *Eroica* in the huge Assembly of the Nobles. His arms worked powerfully and his mouth gaped blackly open in the lectern light. And when the ovation came, it was my face Mahler searched for, and I knew he was my purpose and my meaning.

JUSTI SAID, "I had Gustav when he was young. You can have him now he's old."

IV

WHEN I WROTE my memoirs, I called the next chapter Splendid Isolation 1903. This was a favorite phrase of Mahler's. He wanted us to live together, he said, in splendid isolation.

The chapters after that I called Splendid Isolation 1904, Splendid Isolation 1905, and Splendid Isolation 1906.

AFTER WE GOT BACK from Petersburg, I moved into Justi's old room and began to get acquainted with my husband.

The first thing I found out was that he took a cold shower each day at seven. Seven! I wasn't the most disciplined little miss, and this just horrified me. Half asleep, I'd hear him ringing, with the water trickling from his ears, for his breakfast to be put on the worktable so he could eat as he revised. He always wanted a freshly ground café au lait, milk, butter, two slices of coarse diet bread, and a dish of fruit jam, a different sort of fruit jam each day. He smoked one cigarette and was at the Hofoper by nine. When he returned at lunch, he'd ring the bell on the street as he came in so that his soup would be waiting on the table when he arrived at the fourth floor. All the doors had to be standing open so that his time wouldn't be wasted. I had to eat the way he did, plain, flavorless food, cooked until it was dead to spare his digestion. It was enough to ruin mine. If there was bad news I had to keep quiet about it so as not to trouble his chewing. Otherwise

I got a look of black rage. Then he and I took a walk, nearly a run, round the Ring or Belvedere Park. I was pregnant and couldn't keep his mad pace, and to encourage me he'd call back I love you! without turning his head. I'd be waddling along behind him with my teeth clenched, thinking, Love, eh?

Each summer Mahler went to the Salzkammergut to work on his own compositions. This year, since I was his wife, I went with him. He'd built a house in Maiernigg at the edge of the Wörther-see, and it wasn't my idea of a nice place at all. The furniture was raw wood joined with iron nails and covered with cheap cre-tonne. There was a single leather sofa, which we dragged from room to room according to need. Behind the house there was a path that twisted back and forth between the firs to a one-room brick hut, seventy meters up, which I wasn't supposed to enter. Mahler called this his Häuschen. Each morning at six he rang the cook's bell and climbed to his Häuschen. The cook had to climb there by a separate path with his breakfast tray and put milk on the spirit stove and matches beside it and be gone before Mahler came so that his solitude wouldn't be spoilt. The Häuschen had a piano, a big table with a straightedge for ruling out the mea-sures, and a shelf full of Goethe and Kant. Mahler ate at a table outside if it was fine and then settled himself down to write, and meanwhile I had Justi's old job: making the whole village silent. I rushed out and paid organ grinders to stop in the middle of a note. I bribed children with sweets not to splash in the lake. I gave the neighbors Hofoper tickets so they'd lock up their dogs and farm animals, and if they had a particularly loud animal I'd buy it and have it slaughtered. Of course I couldn't play any music myself while he was working, and later on he'd be resting, so the only time I could play was when he felt like a duet after dinner, and then he'd keep stopping to correct my technique. At midday he had a swim by our boathouse and floated with his bony toes sticking up. He whistled for me, and I sat and waited

on the boathouse steps, all wrapped up against the sun and fret-
ting about my skin. As we walked back he whistled

to let the servants know he expected to find another invalid's
meal on the table.

He had me pack his trunk and copy out his rough scores. He
asked me to do something about his debts. He'd sent great sums
to his brothers and sisters, but if I mentioned this, Justi cried,
"Oh, what does it matter? If the worst came to the worst, I'd go
begging with him from door to door!" I made a budget, as Mami
had done for Papi, and Mahler gave me his salary. I didn't notice
that now I was the one to bring a narrowness into a great man's
life, but Mahler noticed, and not silently.

My final duty I executed half in dreams, because Mahler never
came to me until I was asleep. Then he'd snatch and dig in my
nightclothes like a thief. His fingers were rough and his organ
was disproportionate, and I never had my little nuance anymore,
because I felt it wouldn't do to work one's *os pubis* against the
Artistic Director of the Viennese Court Opera.

None of this was my idea of married life at all, and I was
awfully bitter about things. I'd expected to be Mahler's muse,
and instead it seemed I'd become his housekeeper. He scarcely
spoke to me except to give instructions, and then he'd send more
advice in little notes. *It seems that my example has not taught you very
much. You get lost over and over in irrelevancies. Do me a favor, therefore,
and think how you can improve yourself.* We never went out, because
he thought gay society was rubbish, and I was quite shabby,
because he thought fine clothes were rubbish too, so I'd sit
home, fat and pregnant, my ankles puffed up like an old lady's,
thinking how my baby would be a bastard. I might call myself a
Nietzschean, but oh, this bothered me. It was around this first

summer that I really started drinking double-time. I'd pour rum in my morning cocoa, have a schnapps with my morning pâté and wine with lunch, and sip Bénédictine until bedtime. Drinking made me calmer and a little deafer – it seemed to swaddle me – and I'd roll my head round in a circle on my neck and listen to the little crackling of ligaments inside. In bed, I'd lie awake revising old lieder in my mind and complaining to myself. I rather respected Mahler for being more self-absorbed than me – he was like Papi in that way – and I told myself that I'd expected marriage to be a great trial, like when Siegfried had to forge Nothung, and I had to be worthy, and maybe this is what Jewish marriages were like, very stern and Old Testament, and that Mahler did have all those Jewish brains, and maybe this marriage was just too intelligent for me. And then I'd think, *Why, I could knock this little fellow down!*

In the fall we went back to Vienna.

I said, "It'll be Christmas soon."

This was an accusation. Mahler gazed at his book.

"Nothing's the way I thought it would be," I said. "I thought we would…"

"Yes?"

"I've nothing to do," I mumbled.

"But you're mistress of the house!" he cried in perplexity.

"I cannot be expected…" I said, very calmly and clearly.

He waited.

"I can't – the drawing-room rug is a disgrace. It shames us every time we have a guest. If we ever had any guests."

"But Almi, buy a good rug, then! Buy ten good rugs, only don't be so unhappy!" He laid a comforting hand upon the arm of his chair, since he was too far away to lay it upon my arm. "That is," he added slyly, "if you think your *budget* will allow it.…"

"It'll be Christmas soon."

"Again," he sighed.

"And we won't take any proper notice again."

"How does a Christian get attached to such pagan foolery?"

"It makes the year nice to pay a little attention. Otherwise it's just cold."

"I haven't the patience."

"I had a dream the other night. A green lizard came – crept up. Inside."

"My God, is the child all right?"

"The maid heard me shouting and dragged it out by the tail. But it held my insides in its jaws, and I was left broken and empty, like a wrecked ship."

"Come here," he said. I smelt his sharp smell. He set his lips to my forehead. "Cool," he said.

"When I was a girl, we'd put lamps on the floor to make a stage and have a Christmas masque. And afterward we'd eat bishop's bread with apricot sauce. And on New Year's we always had a lead casting."

"I've heard of those."

"You pour a bit of melted lead into cold water. Papi poured for me until I was twelve. Then I poured for myself. It makes a shape, and you look it up in a little book, and it tells you how the year will be."

"We haven't an apparatus for melting lead."

"There isn't any *apparatus*, Gustav. You use the stove."

"Really?" he said. "As if one were scrambling an egg? I'd no idea the melting point was so low."

So now it was a scientific matter and we had a lead casting.

We hung lanterns of lacquered orange paper in the windows of the flat. I made a careful toilette. I closed my eyes as the Friseurin braided my hair over and under with her strong fingers. I'd sweetened my mouth with New Year's punch against the usual taste of vomit. I was heavily pregnant and wore a loose straight gown in the Reform style from Schwestern Flöge, with broad beige and teal stripes. Mahler thought this looked like mattress ticking but was pleased to have a wife who understood such advanced clothes. He himself wore a black vest, green with age, and fetched out from somewhere an awful bowl of dark Rotwelsches glass, and set it on the sideboard and began to polish it. It was scribed in silver with a view of some palace and the year 1818.

"What happened in 1818?" I asked.

"I don't know," he said, polishing the sideboard and then the floor before it. "But doesn't it look fine?" And he fell into a little frenzy of polishing until the servants made him stop.

It was just going midnight when we got the lead properly melted. The cook stood with fat folded arms. We were in her kitchen, making a smell.

"First," Gustav said, "we must cast for the child." And he wound a rag around the handle of the iron saucepan and – plip! – poured a tiny drop into the bucket. It made a little coughing noise and sent up a blossom of steam. "We'll let it cool a bit."

"Gustl, it doesn't take that long," I said. "Give me the spoon. Well, you didn't use much, did you? It's just a little round... pebble. You've made our child a pebble."

"It's fat like the world," Mahler said, "because our child is the entire world. And it shines. I didn't expect it would shine. And now you must cast yours."

"All right."

"Carefully! You've got a good grip now?"

"I was always a bit afraid I'd splash!"

"You're doing excellently. Bloop! *What* a commotion. And now the spoon. Permit me? Ah."

"It's awful," I said.

"It's excellent. It's a bird."

"A toad, maybe."

"What talk. It's a beautiful soaring dove. Now, what does your book say about doves?"

"Where are its wings? It's a pretty poor dove that hasn't any wings. Here. TOAD or FROG. *Orators & Combatants. Contemplation of Leaps. A Year of Contention.* That sounds about right. Gustav, what are you *doing?*"

He was poking at the blob of lead with a fork. "I'm making a little hole here, while it's soft, so I can wear my soaring dove on a string around my neck."

"You're murdering my dove!"

"Not a frog now? Yes, I do seem to be making a mess."

"You've spoilt it." I began to cry.

"Well, I think that's enough. You'll clean this up for us?" he said to the cook. "Let's go back and sit down and be comfortable."

"You've spoilt it."

"Here, next to me." He patted the divan. "Let's be friends a little. Oh, now, Almschili, you're not weeping about a bit of lead? I don't believe," he said judiciously, "you love me enough. You should have thought of it before we married."

"Gustav," I said, weeping, "it's bad luck – we never cast your future."

"What does an old man want with a future?"

"Everybody wants a future," I cried.

It wasn't too long before, fat as I was, I went back to having little flirtations. I got very chummy with Gabrilowitsch the pianist, whom Mahler had befriended at Essen. He was a Russian Jew, and as ill-formed a little man as one might make oneself without practice. "A *potent* musicality," I assured him, and crinkled my eyes. Then there was Charpentier, with his black cape and bitten nails. Mahler was doing his *Louise.* Charpentier stepped on my foot, squeezed my knee, and tried to convert me to socialism. These men were all musicians, of course, and I didn't go to bed with any of them. It wouldn't have been pure. Pfitzner I met when we were in Krefeld for the première of Mahler's Third. One afternoon the maid brought in a card. The room they'd given us had an enormous double bed in a black-curtained alcove, and when Mahler read the card he asked me to hide in this marital grotto.

"You don't mind, Almschili?" he said. "It's a man who's written a bad opera, and he insists on seeing me. Well, it's poor manners on his part, but he still shouldn't have to suffer his refusal under the eyes of a woman."

Mahler shut the velvet curtains and I lay there stifling in the dark. There'd been a lot of wine at lunch. It was nice to hide my hot face. The curtains, my drunkenness, my deafness, all made me feel as if I were submerging my head in the sea. There was silence, pressure, a great volume of some preventing element. The visitor had a high, piping voice. *Only*, he said, and *chance*, and *understand*. Mahler replied, "Fine feelings are all very well. But Herr Pfitzner, there are no potatoes in your stew – only a kind of pleasant sauce. It won't do."

I thought, *Won't do!*

I was so tender-spirited from hugging the pillow that I flew through the curtains and clasped the man's hand. Behind his spectacles, his little eyes were startled, like sparks. "Don't be sad, Herr Pfitzner," I cried, "it's just my husband's way. Gustav, I know you're not an unfeeling man. I know you haven't forgotten your youth."

The both of them gaped at this scolding angel who rushed from secret beds. Mahler was too astonished to be angry.

"Alma," he said musingly, "this is Hans Pfitzner. Herr Pfitzner, this is my wife, who flies about."

Pfitzner had cringing shoulders and a floppy mustache. Back in Vienna, he came to our parlor when Mahler was out working, begged to hear my lieder, and said, Ah, if only he could work with me to develop such gifts! He embraced my hips and cried, "I am in your hands!" I patted his neck. I left his score open on Mahler's piano each day, and because it was my husband's habit to play whatever he found there, at last he got used to *Die Rose vom Liebesgarten* and agreed to produce it. But he wrote: *My opinion of P. remains unaltered. Great emotional appeal and very interesting in color. Frog-spawn and slime with a continual urge towards life, but creation stops short at the molluscoid level.* "Flowers, nothing but flowers."

All right, I thought. I'm stuck.

MY MAMI TOLD ME, "Nothing can prepare you for the pain of childbirth."

"Well, you've prepared me now," I snapped.

She hadn't, of course. It was a cross birth, and the labor was endless. It was as if my twenty-three years had been a brief dream, and now I'd woken into the true world, a red place, where creatures ripped at swollen creatures with curved steel tongs. Mahler stamped around the flat crying, "How can a man visit upon his dearest such torment," and so on. But when they told him how the infant had appeared wrong end foremost, he gave out his great tearing laugh and said, "That's my child! First thing, she shows the world her bottom! That's what she thinks of us!"

All I thought was, Thank God I'm not in labor anymore. And then I remembered: My God, now I've got a child to see to, and just when I'm so exhausted!

The baby lay as if stillborn, blue and sticky. We named her Maria, for Gustav's mother, and called her Putzi. Her head was like a curd of milk with a few shabby hairs. I hoped she wouldn't require anything complicated or unpleasant. In my diary I wrote, *I haven't found the right love yet to give my baby.*

But Mahler was devoted. When Putzi was ill, he took her in his arms and walked around for hours, singing to her. He was sure this was the only thing that could make her well. When he conducted before foreign orchestras, he wrote every day to ask after her. *How is Putzerl getting on?* he'd write. *What advances are being made in the two opposed regions of her being, beneath and above, back and front?* When she was older, she'd go into his study each morning and they'd talk for hours of matters that concerned them, and he told her the tale of Gockel, Hinkel, and Gackeleia. For these talks he brought her to his Häuschen, where I was forbidden to go, and she'd return hand in hand with him, smeared all over with jam, her black hair in a state, her blue eyes dark and defiant. It scandalized Miss Turner, the English nanny.

Mahler found a level spot near the lake, had the gardener fence it in to be a playground, and put down ten florins' worth of fine sand.

"Beside the water – are you mad?" I said jealously. "She'll be murdered by snakes."

"Poisonous snakes," he said, "are only found in particularly warm and dry spots – ask any doctor." He fussed over the sand, raking it and picking out little bits, and walked around wiggling the fence posts. And when Putzi played here, he got down on his knees and elbows and they'd each peer at the other as a man studies a billiards table before making his shot.

We took Putzi to the ballet and afterward she walked everywhere on her toes, looking hopeful. I gave her a few coins and she called them *my money.* She wept if they got muddy, although she enjoyed being muddy herself. She insisted that Mahler watch when Miss Turner bathed her. She'd stand shining and fat in the zinc tub, lifting her arms and turning around so that Miss Turner could be thorough.

"You're getting quite clean," Gustav remarked.

"It's my *bath,*" she insisted.

If I came in, she slapped her hips and shouted, "Noooo, Papi. *Papi.*"

"I can't see you too, dumpling?"

"When I'm *dry*," she explained.

But when she was dressed she ran from her father to me and stood glaring, holding out her damp hair in both hands, until I told her she looked pretty. Then she was satisfied and went off with Miss Turner.

I'd loved the idea of bearing a man's child – blood, sacrifice, all very Wagner – and I loved the idea of a baby with, for instance, Mahler's genius and my beauty and strength. But I thought children ought to be like songs. You conceived them in ecstasy, revised them a bit, and you were done. The fact is, from girlhood until the day I died, I had a real horror of being a mother. I didn't want to be like Mami. I didn't want to do all those dismal squishy chores. It was such a relief to find that Miss Turner was going to take care of all that. She attended to the feeding and the napping and the playing and the messes, and just before supper she took Putzi away, and when I saw my daughter next she was tucked up in bed, brushed and shining, as if lying in state. A woman of my time and class didn't see her children much, and that was fine with me.

But sometimes I worried that I was a bad mother. In fact, I often felt as if Putzi were Mahler's daughter and not mine. So one evening after her bath I told Miss Turner, "Just leave her with me for a bit."

"As you say, ma'am," said Miss Turner, confused. "Shall I... You can just ring for me. Of course," she said, and fled.

Putzi remained, standing with straddled legs, like a little Colossus of Rhodes or a little Mahler – just as he did when it was time to lecture or reprove. If she'd had a waistcoat, she'd have hooked her thumbs in it.

"Well," I said. "How have you been getting along?"

She looked at me as if I were mad.

We went on like this for a while. It was wretched, just wretched, but I was ashamed to call for Miss Turner so soon. At last, not knowing what else to say, I said, "Would you like to see some pretty things?" and took her to my music room.

Putzi stopped when we got to the door and looked keenly about, as if for enemies. Then she ran to the piano and pushed both hands against it. It didn't move. She reached up and touched the edge and looked at me inquiringly. She tried to walk along the curve of the piano while stroking her hand along the edge, but this was difficult and she sat down. Next the pedals interested her, and she crept underneath and pushed at them with her hands. "That's my piano," I said, like a halfwit. "Your Papi has his piano up in his Häuschen, and I have my piano in here, and in the parlor we have one that we play together. You've heard us make music together, haven't you?"

"No," she said. The pedals were also difficult.

"Well, we do," I said. "I suppose we haven't for a while." I lifted the lid of the piano and said, "These are the keys."

She slapped them, making a splashing noise.

"Oh, no," I said. "That's not the way. You must press them correctly."

She thought about this and slapped them two-handed.

"Slap slap," I said. "You're not minding me."

She grabbed at the keys with both hands and jumped up and down.

"You're an arrogant little thing, aren't you?"

She grinned.

I sat down on the bench, hoisted her up on my lap, and took hold of her little right forefinger. Gently, I used it to press middle C. "There," I said. I had her press it herself a few times, and then I started dancing my fingers around her middle C to make different chords. Then I began explaining about the black keys, and how they'd squeeze in between the whites and make things more interesting. She was quiet now, thinking. It seemed so strange to me, having this little person in my lap, with her own opinions. I thought she might like a song, so I began to play *Ach Du Lieber Augustin*, but then I stopped, because that wasn't right. I felt she ought to have a better song, a really good song. So I began to play my favorite – I began to play, for this little two-year-old girl, Isolde's Liebestod, which she sings over her lover's corpse.

Well, Putzi liked it. First she started slapping at the keys again and kicking her heels excitedly against my shins. But when she saw that was spoiling the music, she quieted down. At last she just laid her hands lightly upon my forearms, as if she were holding reins. I sang, *"Can it be that I alone / hear this wondrous, glorious tone?"* I thought Mahler might come and complain about the noise, but he didn't. I played slowly, as the aria ought to be played. It was a long time for a little girl to be so still. It was as if she really understood the music, and I had a notion, very vague and confused, that maybe she wasn't just Mahler's daughter. Maybe she was mine, too.

When I was done, she kicked her heels discontentedly.

"Well," I said, "we'll make music again sometime. Would you like that?"

Putzi understood she'd been dismissed, and slid down from my lap, all dignity.

Then she rushed at me, clutched my skirts with her little fists, and ground her face into my legs as if she were trying to grind her way back inside me. "Why, look at you – look at you fight!" I said.

She gave a shout and ran off to Miss Turner. She didn't bounce up and down, as a small child does, but ran deftly, and was gone in a moment.

So little by little I began to get used to my life, and to see a few good things in my marriage. For instance, Mahler used to like to talk about us as Hans Sachs and Eva from *Die Meistersinger*. The old mastersinger in love with the young beauty! I adored this. He used to row me around the lake tirelessly. When he was in Salzburg once doing *Figaro*, I scored the *Alles vergänglich* chorus from memory and sent it to him. He wrote back, *What a dear letter! What an astonishing facility! I have corrected only a few trifling details,* and he came home dragging a whole crate of Salzburg marzipan potatoes, because he knew I liked sweets.

Once we were leaning on a marble balustrade at the Hofoper, and when he felt that the marble was cold, he slipped his arm beneath mine, so my arm wouldn't rest on cold stone. And once at the Bösendorfersaal, an enormous ox-faced lout was hissing Schönberg's *Pelleas und Melisande.* Mahler marched over and cried, "I must have a look at this fellow who's hissing!" It wouldn't occur to him to be afraid of an unintelligent man. He'd have gotten a beating, but Moll came and thrust his big body between them, and then after the recital Mahler strode to the front of the dress circle and clapped loudly until the last of Schönberg's enemies had gone. Then he shyly asked me, "Did you like it? It seems so willfully ugly. But I'm old, and maybe my ear isn't sensitive enough." And he helped the younger man with money.

One night he came down to my bedroom clasping the note-book in which he was sketching his Sixth. He lit the lamp, seated himself beside me, and pointed. "Here to here," he said. "This will be the principal theme of the first movement. It's meant to be a portrait of you."

Well, it was marvelous. It was like some vast fierce swooping bird. It was a first-rate motif, and I thought maybe I'd gotten to be a bit of a muse after all, although the woman in the music didn't seem terribly nice. "Oh my," I said, "I'm not sure I'd care to be the husband of such a theme. It's very fierce."

He said, "I wanted to do your portrait. I don't know if I've succeeded. Anyway, you'll just have to put up with it!"

When my next daughter came I didn't get so sick. I felt like I knew what I was doing. I felt that my body knew how to make beautiful girls, and to ease my pains, Gustl read Kant to me until I sent him away. The baby didn't cry, but only whimpered when she was laid on a pillow, because of the strangeness of pillows. We named her Anna Maria, for our mothers, and called her Gucki, Little Peeper, for her big curious blue eyes. Afterward Mahler woke me by dangling a huge stag beetle in my face. He'd caught it in the park. He was frightened of insects, but his own face was all hope and jollity, and he cried, "I know how you love animals!"

"I dreamt," I told him, "that I married a fool, and that he waved bugs at me."

"You're exhausted from your labor," he explained. He dangled the beast before his own eyes and squinted. "In fact, its back is a very fine color. But I'll go now and return it to nature."

"It looks like you," I called after him.

"Now, I think, you are being unkind. But I can't be angry at you! For the only thing more beautiful than my new Anna is my Putzi, and the only thing more beautiful than my Putzerl is my Annerl, and the only thing more beautiful than everything is everything else, and you are the most beautiful of all. Except for your daughters."

"I was only joking," I mumbled. "I've borne you two children and I think I've got the right to make a little joke."

"You have the right to the sun and the moon, and I will never wave bugs at you again."

"No – come and sit with me a little bit."

"You have the right to that, too."

"I just want a little more sleep. But sit with me a little."

"Yes, yes," he said. "I'll sit here and think of all my daughters."

I slept a little, woke a little. When I woke for good, it was dusk and the room was dim. Mahler was in the chair beside me with our new daughter in his arms. They were both drowsing, with their mouths open. The shadows made their faces very simple and pure. My God, it looked like such a nativity.

IN THOSE DAYS we thought of America as a barbaric half-wild place, and if we thought of the Metropolitan Opera House, which we didn't do much, we figured it must be a tent in a field somewhere. It was actually a big baroque lump on Broadway in New York City, with thirty-five grand-tier boxes for the thirty-five stockholders of the Metropolitan Opera and Real Estate Company. These were the Vanderbilts and some other wealthy Americans who'd built the place because they couldn't see why they shouldn't have an opera house too. In 1903 they hired an old German impresario named Heinrich Conried as manager. Conried knew all the best people in Europe, and he was instructed to start shipping them back to New York, like J. P. Morgan buying altarpieces. He booked *Parsifal* and Strauss's *Salome*, he hired Caruso and Fremstad and Knote, and then he started wooing my husband with fiery telegrams.

We started hearing from Conried a lot in the spring of 1907, just when Mahler's troubles with the Hofoper were getting unbearable. The latest squabble was about his scenery master, Roller. Alfred Roller was a painter who'd never designed a stage set before Mahler hired him, but he hated the old painted backdrops, just as Mahler did, and Mahler adored him. For *Don Giovanni*, Roller built two great turrets that changed their nature in each scene through ingenious electric lighting. For the finale he rolled black velvet over the stage as the Don is swallowed up by darkness. This was just the sort of advanced thing Mahler loved, and so when Roller said he wanted to choreograph his own ballet, Mahler said he'd have everything he needed. Roller called a rehearsal in his office just when the ballet master had scheduled one of his own, and the ballet master wound up with an empty stage. Prince Montenuovo sent for Mahler and said, "In the ten years of your service, this is the first time I've known you to be careless of your duties. To employ your word, Herr Direktor, this is slovenliness. And you, of all people, can least afford it."

By the time they were finished, they'd begun talking about Mahler resigning.

"I don't even know who said it first," Mahler told me gloomily.

"Whoever said it, it's an excellent idea," I said. I was furious. I was going to run down to the Hofburg and give the Prince a talking-to. "Vienna doesn't deserve you. You've had nothing but quibbles and sniping from these wretched little functionaries. Not *one* of them has the greatness of soul to see what you're after," I said, forgetting that I usually didn't like his stuff either. "What do you need with these little pipsqueaks? We've got fifty thousand florins in the bank. And what about Conried?" Because Conried had cabled to say he was coming to Berlin.

So Mahler and his aspirin got on the train to Berlin, and in a few days he wrote me that Conried had offered him equal billing with Caruso. He closed the letter like so:

      kiss   kiss

4 years & 6 months à 125,000 crowns
making 1/2 a million crowns
or an annual guest visit of 6–8 weeks
50,000 crowns fee
making 200,000 crowns in four years

      kiss   kiss

Mahler's resignation was accepted, and in June we went to Maiernigg as usual. We were so excited we could barely swallow our food. We were just delighted at the thought of a new life. But we'd been there only two days when Putzi wandered into my parlor, bunching up the hem of her dress in her hands. She was letting out one big honking cough after another. She sounded like a fat middle-aged man whose phlegm is stained with cigars. After each cough she looked pensive and troubled. "Putzerl!" I said. "Come straight here."

"Want soup," she said.

"You don't like soup," I said.

"My neck is biting me. It's biting me *inside*." And another goose honk. She laid her arms across my lap and raised one knee as if she were climbing, to show that she wanted to be lifted. I lifted her. She was heavy.

Anna had followed Putzi in and was standing by the door. She was three years old now, a fair, lovely girl, quite thin, with a trick of darting around and then going still. She was a worrier, always waiting for a calamity, and we'd done well to name her Little Peeper, because she was always watching everything with those enormous blue eyes. Now she pointed at her sister and said, "She's making a noise," and then waited for me to say everything was all right.

"And you've got a rash," I told Putzi, with terror and disapproval. Her breathing was loud and rough. She climbed around in my lap and wouldn't be still.

In came Mahler.

"You're holding her upside down," he said.

"It's *good* this way," Putzi said. "A little."

"Putzerl," he said, "why are you that color?"

And then she coughed.

So we sent for Blumenthal. He saw Putzi alone in our sitting room with Miss Turner and then closed the door behind him and asked me, "Where is the Herr Direktor?"

"In his study. I'll fetch him."

"Let's leave him be. Your husband is… a bit nervy? I'm afraid I must speak seriously, Frau Mahler, and I require you to meet my words with a woman's courage."

"A cold," I whispered. "A cold and a rash."

"I'm sorry. Scarlet fever and diphtheria," he said. "She's got to be opened up."

"Got to… *what?*"

"Open her up," he said, and flicked a big forefinger across his Adam's apple.

I gripped his sleeve. "You're going to cut my daughter's throat?"

"A tracheotomy, Frau Mahler. You understand, a false membrane has formed. The child can't get any air. We need to make an incision, just a bit of an incision beneath the thyroid isthmus, so we can get the tube in there. Have you a room with north light? And a sturdy table. Ordinarily I'd give her a bit of castor oil in beer foam to – you know – clean her out a bit, but I don't believe there's time. I'd like to ask for your help with the chloroform. Children don't tend to like the mask. And if you, the child's mother, were willing to help us with the mask? we might not have to – I realize I'm asking a great deal."

"She's a child," I cried, "a little child!"

"Frau Mahler," he said patiently, "can you hear me?"

All Putzi's arrogance that I loved was gone. She'd become a small red beast with a great useless open mouth. Her blue eyes were twisted small now and saw nothing but tormenting shadows that wouldn't let her breathe, and she tried to slap us all away. Mami came and helped move Putzi into my room. Mahler crept up to the door, sobbing wildly, then ran off to escape the dragging sound of her breath. I told the gardener to stand outside Mahler's room and keep him in there, and told the cook to take Anna to the village so she'd be out of the way.

"I'm *sorry!*" Anna cried. She was clutching her hands together and weeping. She thought it must be all her fault, and that's why I was sending her away.

I said, "Now, now, there's no reason to cry." Her tears terrified me. I was afraid in a minute she'd fall down sick, too. "Now, now, now, Gucki, don't cry. You mustn't cry." I was babbling. "Get along, now. For God's sake, Cook, take her away."

Then I went to my room. It smelt of carbolic. They'd put our pantry table there and covered it with a sheet, and we laid Putzi down in the middle of it. Beside her on my dresser lay a stack of towels, a tray of knives, and a jar of catgut in ether. It looked like dirty old linguini. The nurse began washing her neck with a brush and green soap. They brought me a basin of water so I could wash, too. The doctor took up a hooked metal tube and started cleaning it out with a feather. I noticed they'd spread an oilcloth to protect the rug. I went to stroke my daughter's hair but Blumenthal said, "Ah! Mustn't get septic!" and I yanked my fingers away. Under the table lay a steel tank of chloroform and one of oxygen. They were attached to a black cone with a stopcock on the side, and Blumenthal put this in my hand. It had a big flabby rubber bag hanging off the side, and I could see Putzi didn't like the looks of it at all. I leaned over her and said, "Dumpling? Can you hear? We're going to make you well. We're going to give you some medicine, some special medicine that you breathe from a little tube, and then you'll sleep. And then you'll be much better. But you have to lie still and breathe in the medicine." He nodded and I began to lower the cone toward her mouth, very slowly, as if maybe she wouldn't notice that way. But she wrenched her arms from the nurse's hands and struck it aside, crying *no, no!* without breath. "It works best if you lie still, Putzi," I said, in a horrible jolly little voice. "Very still, and I'll be right here. I'm right here, Putzi! It's all right! I've got you!" It was astonishing how strong she was. She kept fighting and twisting around until we were afraid she'd wind up on the floor, and at last I was mashing her flat with my full weight, crushing the mask down over her mouth and nose and eyes and shrieking, "I've got you! I've got you!" as my tears dripped onto her freshly washed throat. Blumenthal opened his mouth, then shut it again and began to twiddle the stopcock. The nurse called out, "Do you know your numbers, Putzi? Count backwards, dear."

That night Gustav, Mami, and I slept all together on Gustav's bed. We were trying to hide from the terrible *ock ock ock* downstairs, like some contraption smiting itself to bits.

Next day she died. She was four and one half years old and lay in the center of my bed. I lay down beside her. The bandage at her throat was black with blood. The loose threads of gauze were black. Her face was smooth and cool. One eye was a little open but I shut it with my thumb.

Blumenthal prescribed a sedative powder for me and Mami, then turned to Mahler. Mahler was weeping and looking wildly from side to side. "You don't suppose –" he said. "You don't suppose she knew she was – Oh God! Oh God! While you're at it, Doctor, would you mind...? My wife is always complaining about my heart."

I smoothed my raw cheeks and began to laugh. *Ock ock ock!* I couldn't stop. "Like the last girl at a ball to be asked to dance! By all means, Doctor, don't leave poor Gustav out."

But Blumenthal, his ear to Gustav's chest, the beard tangling in the vest buttons, said, "A heart like that, you know, that heart's nothing to brag about!"

IN DECEMBER we left for America on the *Amerika*. My husband, they said, had a hereditary but compensated bilateral contraction of the heart valves and must be trained to walk – this man who loved to scamper up mountains and wallow in icy lakes – walking first five minutes a day, then ten, with a pedometer to count his steps. Mahler always took any doctor's warnings very seriously. He got out of the cab at Cherbourg as if he was afraid his feet would shatter on the cobbles.

We set sail at night. The ship was like a mountain of little lights, way across the dark harbor. When Anna saw it, she said, "No."

"Why not?" we asked.

She thought for a while and said, "It's too big."

The sea was choppy all the way across, and Mahler tried to prevent seasickness by lying stiff on his bunk like a stone cardinal upon his tomb.

I suppose New York would have had a great effect on us in any case. But seeing it then, in our grief, it was like a dream: an island city where the buildings go up and up, and everyone is kind to you, as they sometimes are in dreams, and the streets all have numbers so you can never get lost. We were weak and feverish, and little things like the street numbers had a great effect on us. It really did seem like a new world, and just then a new world is what we wanted.

We installed two pianos in our suite in the Hotel Majestic and went to lunch with the great god of the Metropolitan Opera. Conried granted us an audience reclining on a divan with a fringed canopy and barley-sugar posts. Behind him stood a suit of armor, which could be lit up from inside by pressing an electric switch. He explained that he'd continue to control the Metropolitan's dreadful settings. He explained that he'd made Sonnenthal and would now make Mahler. Mahler kept nodding and nodding. In fact, Conried was dying, of the success of his great rival the Manhattan Opera House and of consumption – he already had the characteristic symptom of euphoria. In two months he'd retire, and Mahler was his last great idea.

On New Year's Day 1908 Mahler made his New York début. We were hurrying to the lift in the hotel when he stepped on the train of my best gown and tore it. It made a noise like breaking wind. He wouldn't leave me behind, but I couldn't go with him until I'd mended my dress. When the telephone rang, we were afraid to answer. I said, "It must be the Opera, wanting to know what's become of you."

"An excellent question," he said.

"Gustav, you'll be late. *Please* go without me."

"Make bigger stitches," he said. "I've already been parted from too much."

Mahler lay in bed all day to spare his heart and only left his room when it was time to conduct, with the pedometer strapped to his ankle beneath his dress trousers. He forbade me to wear mourning – "We mustn't play to the gallery," he said – and he never let me speak of Putzi. He had rules for grief, just as he did for everything else. It was a dreadful winter. I didn't like English and I learnt little. Among Americans I was like a child that doesn't understand her elders' talk. I wore only my favorite clothes and rolled on a satin comforter. I got to know the sadness of comfort. I believed God was punishing me for having borne a bastard child. In two days, I'd empty another bottle of Bénédictine, sip by sip, and lick the insides of my cheeks and sob. I napped all day, and at night when I couldn't sleep, I'd go out and sit on the back staircase and wait for some sound of life.

Gucki was even worse off. She'd been quarantined for six weeks after Putzi died, and she still thought it was because she'd somehow killed her sister. She used to go from room to room, peeking in at Mahler, peeking in at me. I'd lost heart for daughters and treated the poor girl like a ghost, and Mahler spoke so kindly to her, with such pity in his eyes, as if she were about to die next, that she'd run back to Miss Turner. Once while Mahler was revising in bed on a board held against his knees, she said, "Papi,

I shouldn't like to be a note. You might scratch me out and blow me away!"

She was proud when we laughed, but it wasn't a joke to her. She was frightened.

One day we went to Philadelphia for a guest performance of *Tristan*. Mahler had led us all to the moment when the lovers are lying on a bank of flowers and Tristan is singing: *So let us die / and never part.* At this moment in my favorite music, I felt the orchestra rise up and interfere with my blood. I felt I was limping through a slanting field of crickets. They were ormolu insects with the faces of pocket watches, and they made a very cold noise. When Mahler peeked round at me, as was his custom, he saw an empty seat, because I'd collapsed and been carried off by Professor Leon Corning, the inventor of spinal anesthesia.

Corning was the brother-in-law of Heinrich Knote, who'd sung Tristan, and whose famous tenor voice I'd heard as bugs. He carried me to Knote's dressing room and went to the chemist for sal volatile. When Mahler flew in after the performance, mad with dread, Corning said, "Herr Mahler! Your wife is a sensitive woman!"

"I didn't know where she was," Mahler whispered. "I turned around and her seat was empty. Like that! I suppose we'd better get a doctor."

"I am her doctor. She needs strychnine and a month's bed rest. She abuses," he said, "her body with alcohol."

"I'm sorry," Mahler said. "Our daughter is dead."

"I'm well aware of that," said Corning. "When she's better, you'll come and dine with me."

The strychnine was effective, and a month later Corning sent a car for us, as he'd promised. He received us in his music room. He had three grand pianos there, standing in a row, and he walked up and down beside them playing the flute. His wife slid by, all in black, her face as hard as a crab shell. Dinner was served in a small square cabinet. Tiny candles smoked on the table. Corning was stingy, and in the middle of each plate lay a tiny bit of God knows what. If his wife opened her mouth, he closed it for her again with an angry look.

After dinner he showed us his study. There were wires crossing the room in all directions, and steps leading up and steps leading down, and an antique iron gibbet. He opened a door into a copper-plated cell in which patients were rendered unconscious by the breathing of condensed air. You had to stoop beneath the low ceiling. There was a pillowed couch inside, and a book lying open on the floor.

"That doesn't look so bad," Mahler said.

He stepped into the cell and lay down on the couch. "It's comfortable," he remarked.

Behind him I closed the door and spun the wheel. "It locks like so?"

Corning said, "A scientific couple! Yes. Like that."

In the middle of the door was a slab of glass as thick as honey. I could just see Mahler's amused eyes.

"Can he breathe in there?"

"For a time, Madame."

"Could we hear him if he shouted? Shout, Gustav! Shout!"

"I'm afraid he can't hear you."

"Yes. You're quite right. He can't hear me."

"Madame?"

"I believe, Herr Doktor, that I'd have made an admirable physician's wife. I cannot be heard. I'm not like some women, who are forever playing to the gallery. You'd have found me restful. Doesn't Gustav look rested?" I was trembling like a tuning fork. Gustav had risen on one elbow and was watching my face through the little window. "For how many minutes could he remain there?"

"Really, Madame Mahler, I don't –"

"Five minutes? Ten? Scientists should know such things."

"Much depends on the individual's pulmonary capacity and on the relative excitation or depression of his metabolism. A mature man of sixty kilos, after a heavy meal..."

"And this mechanism, this controls the evacuation of the air?"

"The Metropolitan would be cross with me, Madame, if I asphyxiated their principal conductor."

Mahler lay back and stared straight up at nothing. He wore his spiritual face, peevish and inward-turned, as if he were waiting for a sneeze.

"No one's asking you to asphyxiate any conductors," I said grandly. "The door opens like so? Ah, the lever. Thank you."

Mahler lay motionless for a moment or two. Then he rose and shook down his little clothes. He emerged smoothing his hair back with both hands and said, "Well, I see you decided to let me out. What were you asking me before?"

"I was asking you to scream," I said.

BY NOW it was plain: we didn't like each other anymore.

The next two years were bitter and dreamy.

We sold the house in Maiernigg where our daughter had died and rented a large farmhouse in Toblach in the South Tyrol. We spent Christmas back in New York with the soprano Sembrich. Her tree caught fire and we were all nearly burnt. I couldn't stop laughing, and Gustl couldn't stop saying, "You see? *You see?*"

In Paris, Rodin modeled Mahler's head, and I met Pfitzner again. "Unabashed chromaticism," I murmured. I crinkled my eyes. I had a second nervous collapse, and a third. Gucki and I went to the Sanatorium Luithlen to have our tonsils cauterized. Mahler wrote, *I've heard all about it – 24 incisions without an anesthetic! You have behaved* SPLENDIDLY *and I am convinced it will be of life-long* BENEFIT.

Louis Tiffany invited us to his house. He led us up a great

flight of steps adorned on either side with Sudanese native huts. Dana Gibson's wife showed me her mirrored bed canopy and asked me why I'd married such an ugly old man. Schirmer the music publisher hired a detective with a loaded revolver and took us to an opium den. The owner used to play women's parts at the Chinese Theater. He showed us photographs of American ladies and gestured that he'd been lovers with them. In February I had a miscarriage, and for a week I imagined that everything smelt of blood.

One evening our friend Gabrilowitsch came to see me and cried out, "I am falling in love with you madly! For Mahler's sake, help me escape from myself!" He clung to my bosom with both hands, as if he were climbing a cliff. When I thrust him back, he leapt for my hand, and then in came Mahler.

I wouldn't let go of Gabrilowitsch's hand. In a clear, consoling voice, I said, "Courage! That's the important thing."

"Who is it that needs courage?" Mahler inquired.

"Who doesn't?" I asked.

The disks of Mahler's spectacles were perfectly blank.

That night in bed he addressed himself to me very roughly. Leaving, he said, "Just read Tolstoy's *Kreutzer Sonata!*"

So I read Tolstoy's *Kreutzer Sonata*. It's about a man who stabs his wife.

Well, we couldn't go on like that forever. Late one night when we were back home in Toblach, Mahler collapsed outside my bedroom. I'd woken up to see a glimmer on the paneling in the hall, like the wake of the moon across the sea. Then I saw the glimmer dip to the floor. I went out and found him lying there, blinking. His candle lay upon the carpet. A curl of smoke went up from the woven leaves and cartouches. We gazed at each other, him upward, me down. My throat was dry from drinking Bénédictine, and I couldn't seem to swallow properly. The carpet began to burn with little spikes of flame and a foul smell, and

Mahler bit his lip. I stood there as the carpet burned, trying to see if I couldn't swallow a little better, and at last I patted out the flames with my slipper and went to the maid's room. Half her fat body was exposed, and she hugged a pillow with her knees, from loneliness. "I can't carry him by myself," I shouted. "Cover yourself, button yourself. Take the legs – you're young. Not to *my* bed. To his."

Mahler swung like a purse in our hands as we went down the hall. He was waiting. "Fetch Blumenthal," I told her, and smoothed the bedclothes across his breast. "You were right," I told him. "I don't love you enough. I don't love you. I don't love anyone."

My hand lay on his breast, as a cat pins some little creature with her paw. Gustav looked brightly up at me.

"Why don't you love me?"

"Don't bully me!" I cried, and he nodded. And then I muttered, "Your smell."

"Almschi?"

"The smell of your cigars, and just – you. It's sort of – it's sharp. I hate it. You don't smell like a healthy man. You don't come to me like a normal man. No wife could love a man who smelt like that. Why did you marry me? That horrible vulture theme, so cruel, and I've no music of my own, and no one pays any proper attention. Everything *smells!*" I nearly shrieked. "Why don't you and Gucki just go off and *live* together?"

My gasping alarmed him, and he reached up to feel my head for fever. I let my forehead rest on his palm. "Alma," he said. "You'll injure yourself."

I lifted my head and smeared at my wet face.

"My smell," he said. He smiled then, as he did when he'd figured out an error in his orchestration. "Do you know, I believe that's the key to a lot of things. You've been acting against your nature."

"Don't lecture me."

"No, I've lectured you too much."

"I've been a bad wife."

"This I will not permit. No one could have been better. But we've both ignored your nature and the result is this debility. I must admit, you're not a good color at all these days. Do you want to leave me?"

"Don't *bully* me!" I cried again, and pressed my cheek to his chest, trying to slip underneath the conversation and escape it. He stroked my hair. I listened as the old gate in his breast swung open and shut, open and shut, and I thought, *I can't think, I needn't think, no one could think with such a noise in her head.* "I do love you, Gustav, it's just I'm so ill all the time. It's just I'm so unhappy."

"You're ill," he said, nodding. "I'll speak to Blumenthal. He ought to know about spas. We'll send you someplace to rest up and take the waters. Before anything else, we've got to get you really well."

V

IN THOSE DAYS, illness was quite important. If you were poor it was another job, one you had to work at without pay. But if you had money, it was a great diversion, and people spent a lot of time at fancy spas. It was fine for a man to go to a spa and show how he was worn down by his important duties, and even finer to show he could afford to send his delicate wife there. You went to a spa for your nervous exhaustion, which was often a fine name for boredom, or for your fatness or your gout or, quietly, your inconvenient pregnancy. Tobelbad wasn't far from Toblach, in a bowl-shaped valley in the thick Styrian woods. It had chic and was fit for Mahler's wife, and we arranged that I'd go there with Gucki and Miss Turner for a two-month cure.

The specialty at Tobelbad was exercise in the open air. Barefoot, in a horrible nightgown, in rain or wind, we were obliged to make hoops of our arms and bow, or hop from foot to foot and clap. A maze of wooden bridges went out over the foul little hot lakes. Big red peasants in bathing costumes helped us down ladders into the boiling muck, then lifted us swooning out. Along the bridges there were small huts for fainting, with wooden benches and canvas-webbed cots and carafes of cool water. Then we put on dry nightgowns and went *slap slap* on boiled bare feet to the dining room, hoping for something good. The ceiling was painted with sturdy-looking angels, holding up scrolls and pointing at bright mountain peaks and sitting at the feet of white-robed physicians, listening to their wisdom. These angels were dressed the way we were, but I hope they were better fed, because we were on a diet of lettuce and buttermilk, and at night poor Gucki would cough this up on her comforter.

But there was also a ballroom at Tobelbad, and my physician decided that dancing might restore me. On 4 June 1910 he introduced a young architect named Gropius to be my partner. And that's how I met Walter. He was prescribed for me, like salts.

Walter was a Berliner and a fine-looking fellow: tall and slim, with steep-sloping shoulders and powerful hands. He liked to keep his dark hair swept back, and the tip of his nose was elegant, a little wolfish. I had myself a good long look at him. I was in a highly suggestible state. For a month I'd been forbidden to drink or wear my corset, and the nightgowns let the breeze circle about your body, which made me feel I was dreaming, one of those dreams in which you wander the Ring *en déshabille* and everything is permitted. Walter was just twenty-seven years old. It seemed a joke that such a strapping boy, with such marvelously clear skin, was having a rest cure. I decided he was a perfect Aryan type. One, I felt, of my own sort. And I also thought, without quite noticing I was thinking it: *If I made a baby with that man, it wouldn't die.*

When the physician had gone, Walter said, "I will never trust that man's judgment again. If I'm to be your partner for as long as I'm sick, it will destroy my desire to be well."

He was trying to be bold.

"But Herr Gropius," I said, "you came here to recover your strength, and you seem a young man of determination. Are you so easily dissuaded?"

For this he hadn't prepared any witty sayings. It stumped him. "Well," I said quickly, "you men of affairs never care properly for your health. My husband, now – you know my husband's work?"

"Who doesn't know Herr Mahler's work?" he said, bowing in alarm.

Well, he didn't. He knew Mahler was famous for something or other, but just then he didn't care about fame. He was hoping for a glimpse of my calves. Or an adventure, about which he could brag to himself. I had the ankles of a woman one might have adventures with, and here we were all dressed for bed.

The taste of buttermilk left me. My tongue was sweet in my mouth again.

I said, "Shall we walk? We'll discuss the details of your treatment," and we started making big loops over the terraces and the sloping lawns. Walter told me his mother was a Scharnweber, descended from French Huguenots, and that his great-great-grandfather had been a parson in Helmstedt, and that his great-granduncle created the Gropius Diorama, which was three twenty-meter landscapes by Schinkel, improved with colored lights and clockwork automata. At school, Walter had built a model of Caesar's bridge across the Rhine. He'd translated Sappho's *Ode*. In the summers he'd hunted hares on his relatives' estates and been happy. He was accepted into the Fifteenth Hussar Regiment at Wandsbeck. He was the best high-jumper there: 1.1 meters, he said, without a takeoff. His horse was named Devil. He got an inheritance from his grandaunt and sailed off to Spain on the *Albingia*. Everyone was seasick but him. He came home and went to work for the architect Peter Behrens. Behrens was the first true functionalist, but they quarreled, and Walter left to open his own office in Neu Babelsberg. Then, troubled by overwork, he came to Tobelbad and met me.

Next came a ball, and maybe the physician wasn't such a fool, because with the first crimp of whalebone around my waist I was fully cured. Walter looked very well in evening clothes. We were permitted punch, and he was attentive about filling my glass. When we danced, he moved us across the floor as if each spot in the world were as easy and pleasant as the next. I looked up into his sleek Huguenot face as a woman, I felt, should have to look up into a man's face, and we sailed out through an arch worked with plaster scrolls and onto one of the lawns over which we'd strolled and discussed Walter's talent as a jumper. At noon one smelt the inside of one's hot nose, but now it was black night and in the deeps of the lawn one smelt grass. We found our way between some slender trees and limped along a riverbank, our uphill legs too long, our downhill legs too short, stirring the punch in our bellies from side to side. A little stream ran invisibly past our toes. "In America," Walter said, "things are possible."

"Only there?" I said.

"I've been collecting photos of grain silos. They've cooked up a sort of new monumentalism. The Sears, Roebuck catalog sells houses by mail – factory-built, like a tractor," he said wistfully. "You know, I never finished Hochschule. They just teach you how to make new buildings look old. You spend all day doodling anthemions and antefixae, labyrinth frets and treble guilloches, and the thing is, I can't draw."

"I'm sure that's not so."

"I get a cramp and break the pencil point. I used to come to class with a hired draftsman."

"An architect who can't draw and a musician who can't hear! I'm a bit deaf—"

"No!"

"Measles. I was a child. But my father said I needn't mind."

"It was Onkel Erich who taught me to smoke and drink like a gentleman."

"My father said you could judge any man by the angle of his hat."

"Onkel had me build workers' housing for his estate. You know, most places like his, the peasants live worse than the horses – after all, the horses are noble-blooded! But they'll *work* better, the peasants, if they've proper light and ventilation. If one's *surroundings* have nobility, not this bogus Greek stuff, but correct proportion, fitness for use... I dream of vast buildings like crystal mountain ridges."

"I dream of a secret garden full of white studios and canals."

We were both panting like steam engines.

"I once found a little pamphlet," Walter murmured. He shaped a pamphlet with his hand and let me see. "About Bau-hütten – masons' lodges? Those fellows who raised the cathedrals. They'd pitch their huts right in the nave and live there until the work was done. For generations! *That's* worship. You know, you can diagram the forces that animate any structure. It's like holding a bird in your hand and feeling the heart beat. There's such *possibilities*, sometimes I think my head'll fly off. Take this business of light. Shouldn't all roofs be made of glass? Why treat our flowers more rationally than ourselves? Construction could be based on a few basic modules. Aluminum shutters would provide regulation. Happiness is a function of flow."

I halted, and he swung round to face me. I smelt the strong roots of the trees. I was a little tipsy. Here was a gorgeous rattle-headed boy who meant to tear down my lovely Ringstrasse and put up a greenhouse. It was my turn to be the elder who instructs – I'd have to teach him everything. I moved up against him and closed my legs around one of his. Looking up into his eyes, I heaved my *os pubis* against the blade of his hip, once, twice, a sufficient number, and then shut my eyes, for I was a god and Walter was no longer necessary.

When I opened my eyes, he hadn't moved.

Drowsily I said, "Good night, Herr Architekt," and strolled back to my room.

When Mahler met my train in July he was delighted to find me so well. My color was excellent and my gait was full of indolence and satisfaction. I'd learnt again the lesson of my young woman-hood, that several men were preferable to one, and now I had both a bed-husband and an art-husband, and it seemed that my requirements would in future largely be met, and I smiled upon Gustav in sincere love, for he was an important part of my excellent new arrangements. In this smile any porter in the station, had he been my husband, could in a glance have seen grounds for divorce. But not Mahler. Mahler was accustomed to believe himself the cause of everything.

I came home with him and rented a post-office box. The next day Walter sent me a letter filled with pleasant worship, and the next day another. The day after that, a letter arrived at my house addressed to *Herr Direktor Gustav Mahler, Toblach, Tyrol*. I put it on the music rack. When Mahler went to the piano for his letters, I heard him cry, "Almschili, what is this? This gentleman makes no sense at all. He seems to be asking me for your hand in marriage!"

My face went hot and then cold. Walter had written another pleasant letter full of besotted suggestions and had mailed it to my husband.

"Who is this mad gentleman?" Mahler cried.

The gentleman was mad, of course. There was, in Gustav's incapacity to suspect, cause for rage.

I was trembling, but I said, "Why, that – that gentleman? Why. That is my lover."

THAT WAS the beginning of a peculiar time. We didn't fight. Mahler didn't reproach me. We just went silently about our business each day – not much more silently than usual, in fact – thinking over what had happened.

I couldn't make up my mind about it. Sometimes it seemed I deserved someone strong and beautiful, like me, and then I felt Mahler had been cheating me. And then I'd remember his face when he found out, as if his bones had turned to knives inside him, and I wouldn't feel so good about it anymore. And then

sometimes I'd think, It's just two young people enjoying life –
what's it got to do with old Mahler?

I'd read my books, eat my lunch, and drink my schnapps, and
if I felt like music I'd play my piano, even if he was working. He
never said anything. I didn't enjoy it much, anyway. If we met on
the stairs, he'd step back and I'd force myself to climb steadily
past him. His eyes would be lowered in shame, but I never knew
this, because my eyes would be lowered, too.

One night I woke and found him standing stock-still by my
bed. It was dark. I didn't think he could see that I was watching
him. He seemed taller, and there was only a bit of light across his
forehead. I couldn't imagine what sort of face might be in the
shadows beneath it. And one afternoon he stepped into the parlor and then seemed to bow, very slowly, like a drop of honey
lengthening from a spoon, until he hit the rug with his shoulder
and cheek. I carried him to the divan, chafed his hands and feet,
and gave him beef tea.

In the afternoons we took long silent walks over the lanes of
Toblach.

"It's not surprising," he sometimes said, to the silence.

He said, "I have no right to be surprised."

He lay on the floor of his study, to be nearer to the earth, and wept.

Walter now wrote properly to my post-office box and begged
me to summon him. He wrote, I want to justify myself before you
both and to clear up the mystery! But I didn't want him clearing up
any more mysteries and I didn't reply. So one evening at dusk
when Mahler and I were out walking – I held his folded jacket
over my arm, in case it got cold, and he carried a lantern – I saw a
young man, hesitating in the shadows under the railroad trestle.
My God, I thought in a panic, he's come for his answer.

I pointed, and said in a thin false voice, "Who is that?"

"You don't know who that is?" Mahler said.

"Yes," I whispered. "I know who that is."

"I'll go and fetch him," he said.

The three of us walked home together. Mahler held the lantern in one hand and his cap in the other. The fields seemed to turn slowly in the dusk until they revealed our lighted windows.

We climbed to the first floor, Gustav moving carefully because of his heart, and went to the parlor. "I have the honor," Walter said, "to love your wife."

"Yes," Gustav said.

"This, of course, cannot excuse... cannot conceivably excuse..."

"No."

"She has long found her marriage to you insupportable. I ask that you release her."

"She wishes to be released, then?"

I was examining the fringe of the shawl covering the side table. "Almi?"

One tassel hung lower than the other. I felt that if I were just permitted to straighten them, I might be able to gather my thoughts.

"This choice, I think, cannot be mine," Mahler said. "If you like, the girl will make you coffee. And there's kümmel in the sideboard. I will be in my study."

Mahler closed the door carefully, and we listened to his footsteps bumping away toward the back of the house.

Now we were alone. Walter rubbed his hands over his face and then dropped them to his sides. I remembered those hands very well. The skin was taut and fresh over them, like the skin over a colt's flank. He took a step toward me and stopped. "So that's the 'feeble old Jew'!" he said, trying to laugh. "He's strong as a demon."

"You could kill him with a blow," I said. "I could do so myself. At this moment, we could both be killing him."

"No. He's strong as a demon. For God's sake, come with me. Now."

"Let's discuss this," I said.

"*Discuss.* I love you. I adore you."

"Yes. Walter, why did you send that letter to my husband?"

"It was a mistake," he said. "I've been half mad. I can't go creeping about like this. It's against everything I've been taught."

"We're back to your education, are we? Walter. Gustav collapsed on the parlor rug the other night. He'll never trust me again. Everything was going so nicely until you decided to make some sort of gesture."

"It wasn't going so nicely for me," he cried, and embraced me.

Well, it was already too late. Poor Walter should have embraced me right away. I was getting angry about him popping up like this and making a mess, but more than that, I didn't like to see a man take a step toward me and stop. It wasn't, I felt, heroic. And my whole life, I always liked a man to be heroic. So I discovered that I'd made my decision. I decided I'd been a good wife to a brilliant man until Walter came along, and I wasn't going to run off with some youngster who didn't know how to address an envelope. I lay my head against Walter's chest, to sort of rest up for whatever I was about to say next, and asked him, "Do you know *Die Meistersinger?*"

"You know I've got no ear for music," he said impatiently.

"Yes," I said. "I know. But it happens to be our favorite. There's an old mastersinger named Sachs. And a pretty girl named Eva. And a handsome young knight named Walther. Now, Walther knows nothing about music. *Nothing.* Hans Sachs has to teach him everything. The regulations of the singer's guild. The names of all the notes. *Short, long, overlong, writing-paper, black ink, hawthorn blossom, straw-blade, short-lived love.*" I felt like a young miss again, who torments her suitors. I felt elegant. I felt I probably knew what I was doing. "*Pewter, lime-blossom, calves, departed glutton, lark, true pelican, brightly gleaming thread...*"

Walter thrust me away and muttered, "I'm going mad."

"But Sachs tells Eva she ought to go with Walther. He gives her up. Because he's brave – and noble. And doesn't think of himself. And only thinks of what's best for her. And of music."

"You've changed," he cried.

"No," I said sadly. "I'm the same."

"I adore you," he said.

"I adore you, too. But Walter? You should have been more careful."

I turned and went down the hall to Mahler's study. He was at his desk. His face was white and calm. He set aside the cover sheet of his Tenth – he'd scrawled something across it. Later I found he'd written: *To live for you my Almschili, to die for you! My God, my God, why hast Thou forsaken me?* "I shall not question your decision," he said.

"I am your wife," I said.

"Yes?" he said dizzily.

"I am still your wife."

"You love this man. This much is clear. Once before," he said, "once before this, you denied, denied your own nature...."

"Oh, Gustl," I said, "for heaven's sake be quiet."

We went back down the hall. Walter was pulling on his coat. But the last train had gone, and we tucked him up in the guest room. In the morning Gustav shook Walter's hand with a little jerk to show things were finished. I left for a walk with Gucki. I felt too shy to talk with my husband. I felt like a newlywed.

When we returned, I heard my own lieder being played. There was Mahler with my manuscript case, which had been shut for years, open beside the piano. His thumbs were smeared with the dust of its catches, and there was a smear of dust on his cheek, and he was crying, "What a fool I was! It's good! It's really good!"

ON 7 JULY 1910 Gustav turned fifty years old and got homage from the entire musical world. But his mind was on other matters.

When I woke up each morning I found notes upon my bed-side table: *My darling, my lyre. Come and exorcise the spirits of darkness, they claw hold of me, they throw me to the ground. I lie alone and ask in the silence of my heart whether I can be saved or whether I am damned.*

He insisted we keep the doors to our rooms open all night, so he could hear me breathing. I often woke now to find him watching over me. He begged me to come visit him when he was working. He had his publisher publish my five best songs and implored me to write more. He bought smart waistcoats and beautiful shoes and ate knucklebone with horseradish to build up his strength for his young bride, but he was too frightened to do much, now that he had to come to me while I was awake, and the next morning I'd find another note on my night table. *Breath of my life!* he'd write. *I have kissed your little slippers a thousand times. You had mercy on me, but the demons punished me again because I thought of myself and not of you, my darling Almi.*

Almi, he wrote.

Almerl.

Almschi.

Almschl.

Almscherl.

Almschili.

Almschilitzili

Almschilitzililitzililitzili

He worshiped me. It was the worst thing the poor man could have done. I was appalled he could be so easily humbled, and I started thinking twice about Walter.

Meanwhile, I told Mahler he ought to consult the famous alienist Sigmund Freud. Freud was then in Holland with his family. He was unmusical, and wouldn't even buy a piano for his parlor, but genius can smell genius and at last he said he'd interrupt his vacation if Gustav came to see him there in Leiden. So Gustav and his aspirin took a train to Leiden, and the two men strolled along the canal for four hours, smoking cigars. Freud was a sharp-featured little fellow with the jaw of a schnauzer. Like Mahler, he was capable of great calming vowels. He said, "Your wife's name struck me: Alma. 'Soul.' A pungent name. But I believe your mother was named Marie? I was presented with this notion: Why didn't the man marry a Marie?"

"My wife's middle name is Maria," Mahler said with suspicion and pleasure, "and when we were first married I liked to call her that."

"Even though, if you'll pardon me, you have some difficulty with your r's?"

"Would that be significant, under your system?"

"Well, it's a daunting, a tongue-thickening business, isn't it? Calling one's mother by her name. One takes quite a lot upon oneself."

"One takes a lot upon oneself to call a wife by her name," Mahler said wearily.

Mahler explained that his mother had been the gentlest of women and that his father had been a brute. Freud said, "And perhaps when you come to execute your conjugal duties, you feel some reluctance to be... a brute? Meanwhile, this nervous young woman, what does *she* want? Of whom was she once cruelly deprived? An older man, a man of artistic attainments, of – forgive me – modest physical stature and imperfect health. You know, it wouldn't surprise me if she decided she prefers you over this 'healthy young man.' "

Mahler stared straight ahead, puffing and striking the gravel path with his heels, *tup! tup! tup!*

I'd heard that a course of psychoanalytic treatments took years, but this one little chat actually gave Mahler some relief from his terrors, and he was able to be my husband more successfully. He was so happy that he ran to get the proofs of his Eighth Symphony and dedicated it to me, sitting barefoot on the edge of my bed. It was the first time he'd ever dedicated anything to anyone. Over the next few weeks he kept writing to Universal Editions and giving Hertzka an awful time over the design of the dedication page. When he went to Munich to rehearse the Eighth's première, he took my wedding ring and put it on his own finger. He wrote me a new poem every day and telegraphed it. *Almschili*, he wrote, *if you had left me then, I would simply have gone out, like a torch deprived of air.*

They'd just built a new Exhibition Hall in Munich with an enormous stage, but it wasn't big enough for Mahler's Eighth and they had to extend it. It had to accommodate twenty-four first violins, twenty second violins, twelve double basses, four mandolins, a celesta, a children's choir of three hundred and fifty, and a pipe organ like the golden plumbing of heaven. In fact, the work required over a thousand musicians, more than any one city could provide, and Mahler had to rehearse this part in Leipzig and that part in Vienna. Now everybody was gathered in Munich and everybody agreed that this "Symphony of a Thousand" would be either a vast triumph or a vast catastrophe, except for its author, who was at last pleased with the size and style of my name on the dedication page and calmly sat himself down each morning – he now conducted from a comfortable armchair – and called out to his choir, "*Good morning, children!*"

His one anxiety was that I should be pleased. When I arrived at our hotel I found he'd filled our rooms with tuberoses, although they obliged him to sleep with his face wrapped in a dampened handkerchief. He went around telling everybody that *there* – he pointed – was the soul of his new symphony. My name, he instructed them, meant *Soul*. He decided that Justi was unfriendly to me and sent her away, saying, "Alma has no time for you!" He laid his head on my lap and muttered, "I've planted a great field. But you must shine upon it."

The autumn chill was persuaded by Mahler's confidence to

relent, and the night of the première was warm. I was too nervous to sit there on display in our box – I'd been imagining what
a failure might do to him – so I went and stood in the stage
wings, where I could hide in the darkness and smell the thick
ropes looping up into the shadows. At the first sight of Mahler
the audience rose up and didn't stop applauding until he'd taken
his place at the conductor's desk. Then he held up his hands,
with his wedding band on his ring finger and my wedding band
on his pinky. He stretched out one opened hand to me, where I
stood behind the choir. And the first great chords came forth, as
if all the air had become great chords.

Above us there seemed to bloom vast arches. These halved
and became wings, and more wings – Gustav was fathering a
race of great birds. It was a civilization of warrior-birds and it
rose to be mighty, but then there were wondering voices and the
crawling dreams of sick children, and maze-games, and dynasties schemed against dynasties by the excellence of their mecha-
nisms. But *then* the great slumbering voice was lifted up. It was
the *schäumende Gotteslust*, the *raging desire for God*, and called for
Heaven's Queen, for the *Highest Mistress of the World*, that she should
Come! should *Come!* and *sublimely command*. And she came, and
the realm was restored to us. The music was about ninety minutes long. But when it was done, everybody looked around as if
they'd lived with their neighbors through a stirring and difficult
long life. And then they all rushed to the stage, mad with joy.
There were thousands of them, stumbling forward, blubbing
and working their hands like swimmers. My husband and I were
only spared because the kettledrummers stood in front of us and
thrust back the crowd with powerful arms. Gustav's spectacles
hung from one ear. His nose was shining. He clung to a cellist,
crying, "Alma! For God's sake! Tell me!" I started to say, "Oh,
Gustl, it was everything –" But instead I just took a breath and
roared in his ear, "It was everything, Gustav. It was everything."

The next evening there was a celebration for the Soul of this fine new success at the Hotel Vier Jahreszeiten. It was arranged by Mahler's old Hamburg friend, the physicist Berliner. He presented me with three baroque pearls on a gold chain, and Mahler tried to buy them from Berliner so he could give them to me himself, and then stood around muttering, "*Pearls. Of course. I'm a fool.*" I'd made Mahler drink whiskey against the returning chill. His face gleamed like wet slate and his waistcoat was black with sweat. He pointed once more and shouted, "Any merit the work possesses resides on the dedication page," and everyone said, Yes, Gustav, we know, the dedication page, please sit. Thomas Mann gave Mahler a copy of *Königliche Hoheit*, in which he had written: *This must weigh as light as a feather in the hands of the man who embodies the most sacred artistic will of our time.* Prince Montenuovo begged Mahler to say whether anything could persuade him to return to the Hofoper. And so it was some time before I could leave and meet Gropius at the Regina Palast Hotel, as we'd previously arranged to do by letter.

Because I'd decided I ought to have Walter, too. I couldn't see why my sincere new love for my husband should deprive me of my first satisfactory coitus. It wasn't sensible to treat Heaven's Queen that way. All that was needed was a little prudence and no more mad tricks with envelopes. Walter latched the door of his room and kissed me. As always, he seemed to be in uniform. I found it easy to forget Gustav, or to remember him only as great chords, which in any case I seemed to create within myself when Walter embraced me. It seemed like a proper conclusion to the wonderful music. Afterward he rested, and his Adam's apple was like water flowing quickly over a stone. I kissed it and thought, This is so good, this is the good time. Later comes the bad time.

IN OCTOBER my husband and I made our last trip to New York. Mahler had a new post I was very excited about. A club of wealthy ladies had made him a brand-new orchestra, which they called the New York Philharmonic, and told him it was his to use just as he pleased.

But Mahler told me, "They want the Mahler of ten years ago, who could do anything. The man they want is dead."

Mahler was old. Caruso drew one of his caricatures, and it's a good thing Mahler didn't see it, because it showed a crumpled little fellow with a face like an intelligent camel. When he tossed snowballs at me in Central Park, they turned to powder in the air. He'd invite friends to our suite and entertain us lying on a divan. Then he'd say, "I'm going to bed now, and you and Alma can be merry. I'm no good for that anymore. If you get too merry, I will throw my boots against the wall."

The soprano Gatti-Casazza wanted to do one of the lieder I'd published at her next recital. Mahler tried to get her to sing all five and then insisted on rehearsing her himself, and each time he corrected her phrasing he turned and asked me, "Is that all right, dear?" He had his thumb tucked into his waistcoat, and the knuckle was so sharp it frightened me. It seemed indecent to see someone's bones like that.

I mumbled, "Please, you know far better than I."

On 9 December, Mahler had a concert in Buffalo, and we made a side trip to Niagara Falls. It was bitterly cold. The railings on the promenade were clogged with ice. A sort of lift took us directly beneath the water. The greenish light hurt our eyes. The earth seemed to be breaking before us, and I had a feeling I never forgot as long as I lived, of being way high up amongst the might of the world, of living amongst final things. Mahler was half frozen, so I took him into a little restaurant heated by an iron stove and smelling of galoshes. Even there, the floor trembled like the floor of a speeding train. We were surrounded by newly-weds, all snuggling away. Mahler gazed at them and murmured, "Almi, you're not vexed with me? There's a lot I've kept you from, that a young woman has a right to expect.... I wouldn't like to think you were vexed with me."

He came home with forty degrees of fever.

Soon after we got back, the Chairman of the Philharmonic Society sent for Mahler. This was a Mrs. Sheldon, a most imposing female. When he arrived at her house, he found all his rich ladies, what he called the Committee of Millionaires, sitting around one of those enormous American rooms full of Italian, Greek, and French bric-à-brac – plunder. It was already the same old story. They'd brought him there to complain about his tyranny. They said the choirmaster was in a fury, they said the viola da gambist was in tears, and then, at a signal, an attorney appeared from behind a brocade curtain, holding an instrument for Mahler to sign. It stipulated that the Chief Conductor's authority would be circumscribed. A Program Committee would select the music. It was all freshly written out on sheets of yellow foolscap. The ink was still shining.

Mahler came home sweating, as if some cruel woman had made him drink whiskey.

"They were all very vexed with me," he said.

We'd gotten friendly with a doctor named Fränkel. He'd come from Vienna as a young man and slept in a closet piled with old clothes. Now he was Chief of the Montefiore Hospital. He had a theory about ears: They were the only part of the body free of conscious control and therefore revealed an individual's Truth. We were both very fond of him. He took one look at Mahler and said, "Now there's a septic throat." He thrust his fingers into Mahler's collar, counted silently, and asked me, "Can't you make the man be sensible?"

On 20 February, Mahler conducted his last concert. Fränkel begged him not to, but Mahler had been a sick man for longer than Fränkel had been a physician, and so we wrapped him up as carefully as a gilt icon and delivered him to Carnegie Hall. When he got home, his temperature was good and he was jolly about conducting himself back to health. But by the end of the week his fever had returned, and soon everybody knew things were serious. The traffic policeman in Grand Army Plaza started asking me, "And how is Hurr Maller today?"

The chambers of every heart are lined with wet satin, delicate as a skin on boiling milk. To this the blood brings every sort of evil. We did not permit Hurr Maller to leave his bed. He couldn't bear a hired nurse, so I nursed him myself. I bathed him in alcohol, applied hot and cold frictions, and slept in a chair beside his bed, as my Mami used to do for me. We were parted for just one evening, when he packed me and Fränkel off to Mendelsohn Hall to hear the first public performance of my work.

Gatti-Casazza was in good voice, and everyone was very kind, but I couldn't seem to get comfortable. I kept dragging my fingers across the velvet seat, making little pale trails and smoothing them over again. I felt I ought to be with Mahler. My lied was ten years old and I was quite deaf that evening, and I almost didn't recognize it when it began. I thought it sounded like student work after the fashion of Schönberg. Then I heard a vague crushing noise – applause – and then the next song – no, it was my song again – an encore. I wondered why Mahler had to be sick now and spoil things. I kept telling myself this was the beginning of my true life as an artist. A functionary in a dinner jacket came over and started murmuring. He had a mole on his neck. I stared at it. Fränkel felt my wrist and said, "Have I got to keep an eye on you both?" It occurred to me that maybe I had no more music to write.

I came home and told Mahler, "I don't know how it sounded. I was too agitated to hear properly."

He nodded.

"They wanted me to come before the curtain and speak. I couldn't."

"They've no business," he grunted, "asking for anything but your music."

When I told him the audience had called for an encore, he said Thank God.

"Thank God, thank God," he said, sinking down between his pillows like Faust entering the underworld. "Thank God, thank God, thank God, thank God," and at last Fränkel insisted we have specialists.

Dr. George Baehr was a very young man then, and he lived to be very old, but one does not forget Mahler, and fifty-nine years later he gave a good account for the *Transactions of the American Clinical and Climatological Association*:

In February 1911 Dr. Emanuel Libman was called in consultation by Mahler's personal physician, Dr. Fraenkel, who suspected that Mahler's prolonged fever might be due to subacute bacterial endocarditis. Libman was at that time Chief of the First Medical Service and Associate Director of Laboratories at the Mt. Sinai Hospital, and the outstanding authority on the disease. He confirmed the diagnosis clinically by finding a loud systolic-presystolic murmur over the precordium characteristic of chronic rheumatic mitral disease, a history of prolonged low grade fever, a palpable spleen, characteristic petechiae on the conjunctivae and slight clubbing of the fingers. To confirm the diagnosis bacteriologically, Libman telephoned me to join him at the hotel.

On arrival I withdrew 20 cm of blood from an arm vein with syringer and needle, squirted part of it into several bouillon flasks and mixed the remainder with melted agar media which I then poured into sterile Petri dishes. After 4 or 5 days of incubation in the hospital laboratory, the Petri plates revealed numerous bacterial colonies and all the bouillon flasks were found to show a pure culture of the same organism, which was subsequently identified as Streptococcus viridans.

As this was long before the days of antibiotics, the findings sealed Mahler's doom. He insisted on being told the truth and then expressed a wish to die in Vienna.

ON OUR LAST MORNING in New York, Mahler dressed himself and was ready long before it was time, sitting motionless as a perched bird. He waved away the stretcher and walked to the lift on Fränkel's arm. The lift boy turned aside so that Mahler wouldn't see him weep. Gucki tried to cling to my skirts, but I was rushing back and forth, and at last she went over and took hold of Fränkel's coat. When we got down to the great lobby, we found the management had emptied it so that Hurr Maller wouldn't have to suffer the stares of strangers. On the boat back to Cherbourg the captain set aside a corner of the foredeck for Mahler's use. Each day we carried him up there and laid him on a chaise beneath a canvas awning. From Vienna he was taken to the sanatorium at Löw by ambulance, and before him went an automobile with myself and Mami and Moll and Montenuovo, and behind him came an automobile with reporters.

At Löw we had a big room with a veranda. On the bed sat a basket of white flowers from the Committee of Millionaires. We could scarcely lift it down to make room for the patient. The reporters stood in the hall from dawn to dusk like petitioners. Each day the *Neue Freie Presse* published its account of the patient's treatment. Professor Chantemesse of the Institut Pasteur returned early from his holiday in the Auvergne to examine Mahler's blood. He set a microscope on the table and called, "Frau Mahler, come look at these threads – like seaweed! Even I have never seen streptococci in such a marvelous state of development."

Mahler hummed from his Eighth: *Infirma nostri corporis virtute firmans perpeti.* Endow our infirm bodies with everlasting strength. He joked about his little bugs, which were always dancing or sleeping. A swelling came up on his knee but vanished after the application of radium bags. He read without stopping. The last book was Eduard von Hartmann's *Das Problem des Lebens*, The Problem of Life. This was his usual thing, a difficult work of epistemology, and he tore the pages from the binding as he read them because he didn't have the strength to hold the whole book, so that by the end it was gutted and he said, "My life has all been paper!" At that time a lot of people were afraid of being buried alive. To prevent this, you ran a steel needle through the heart of the deceased, and Mahler asked that this precaution be taken before his coffin was closed. But in the next minute he'd say, "We'll have more daughters. Many daughters. We'll have" – he was struck with this fine idea – "*sons*."

"What will become of Schönberg?" he'd say. "If I go, he'll have no one."

"I'll take care of Schönberg," I'd say.

"You'll have to take care of Schönberg after I go."

"I will."

"My skin," he'd mumble, "feels as if it would tear at a touch."

Once while I was trying to feed him his soup he said, "Well, you're young. Beautiful. You won't be alone for long. Now, to whom shall we marry you off after I go?"

"A man who knows when to be still."

"Not Klimt, I'd think – you've had enough of old men. Gabrilowitsch? No, a bit on the twittery side, and besides, hasn't he wed that Clemens girl? Perhaps our handsome Herr Gropius! Now there, from all accounts, is a man of real ability! And a manly, straightforward fellow. In spite of everything, I did quite like him, you know."

"I am accustomed," I said unwillingly, "to the society of artists. The Herr Architekt is a technician."

"Not Herr Gropius! Herr Gropius not good enough either!" Mahler cried, his spectacles aglitter. "Then perhaps I'd better not kick the bucket after all!"

I shut him up with a spoonful of soup.

"We'll have to keep on with this, this feeding, when I'm well," he murmured. "It's very pleasant."

I already looked at him a bit historically. There's my first husband, I'd think. My first husband had a bad night. His hair was very black and his face was white. For the first time I noticed how beautiful he was – Rodin had called his head a cross between Mozart's and Frederick the Great's. I fed him, I cleaned his messes, I did everything he couldn't stand to have the nurses do. I was very impressed with myself. I kept thinking, *Why, I'm not giving myself a thought!* A few times I carefully bestrode him. I adjusted him within me and let my skirts fall. They almost hid him. I opened my bodice so he could clutch at me, and brushed his lips with mine, and let him breathe my young breath. I had a fever myself, because I slept in his room and he wanted the place either overheated or freezing, with all the windows open, and my feelings were the same way, either numb or over-clear and exaggerated. I felt like an angel of mercy, I felt like a vampire. I thought, *We're united in our illness.* I thought, *Oh, Walter, come save me from all this Jewish hullabaloo.* I had the most vivid visions of Walter's body, very clean and young, and it seemed to take away the taint of death. I wrote to Walter every day – there was always a half-finished letter in my bag. *Thank you for your warm, soft, dear hands, I'd write, and for your picture, which I keep secretly in my room. I literally haven't undressed for ten days. I have been nurse, mother, and housewife. I want a child by you. Our two perfections must create a demigod. Remember that I'm your bride.* I'd keep rocking patiently back and forth, and at last Mahler would cry out and close his eyes.

Moll often helped with the nursing. He'd long ago grown to love Mahler, and though he understood the music no better than before, he now went around telling everybody it was excellent. He'd clamp the oxygen cone over my husband's jaws with delicacy and regard. "Gustl, darling maestro," he'd say, "a little breath? And now another little breath?" Every few days the doctors had me go off and rest, and so it was Moll and not me who sat by Mahler's bed as he gasped "*Mozartl! Mozartl!*" and died. I was kilometers away, in my old Hohe Warte bedroom. I heard great thunder, as on the afternoon of my father's death, and then the church bells at Löw started ringing. They rang without stopping, and then across Vienna another church did the same, and soon all the churches in Vienna were ringing, and I knew. It was 18 May 1911. It was, I remembered, Walter's birthday. Through my tears, I decided that this was a good omen.

They said I was too delicate for my husband's funeral, and so all the work was left to Moll. Moll talked to the reporters slouching in the hall. He took Mahler's death mask, and Klimt and Roller praised its beauty. About his funeral Gustav had been precise: He was to be buried in our daughter's grave at Grinzing, under a modest stone, cut with the one name only, MAHLER, and he wanted no mourning, speeches, or music – just flowers. It was up to Moll to commission the stone from Hoffman and see that everyone was properly silent. About the flowers he didn't have to do anything, because they came of themselves, vast hills of flowers, and Schönberg brought his paints and painted them. It rained. This didn't matter to the great silent crowds, but it made the coffin shine as it sank. And Moll sighed and went home to bed, because he'd done everything he'd been asked to do. He'd even gone to the undertakers to see that Mahler got the precaution he'd wanted and was buried with his misshapen heart pierced.

VI

EVERYBODY MOURNED my husband. Even the anti-Semitic press honored him on their front pages, and *Die Musik* and *Der Merker* published special Mahler editions. Everybody talked about how he was dead after his Ninth, how Beethoven's curse had finished him, or how maybe his young wife had. I obeyed Mahler's instructions and wore no mourning, and everybody talked about my heartlessness. They made guesses: Walter? Maybe many Walters. Some people considered me odious because I had betrayed the sainted genius Mahler, and some people considered me odious because I had married the degenerate Jew Mahler, and there were a few people who expressed both opinions at once, with great force and eloquence.

What surprised me was how badly I felt myself. I'd expected to feel free. I'd been all ready to upbraid myself for my lack of proper sorrow. I'd forgotten that for ten years my whole life had been Mahler Mahler Mahler, and now there'd never be any Mahler again. I lay in bed at Mami's house all day, cuddling a picture of him, which I told myself I couldn't be parted from, and working my toes against the bed linen until I was queasy. The maid would leave a tray by the door, but I'd just lie there with one thing and another going through my head like shapes in the fire. I'd try to guess how long Mahler might have lived if he hadn't found out about things. I'd try to sketch some new lieder. I'd pinch my jaw to see if I was getting old, and then I'd pretend Walter was telling me how a love like ours justifies everything. I'd peer in the mirror and decide that my eyelids looked dark and tainted. I'd think, *He died betrayed.* Once I dreamt my arms were splintered old sticks, and when people saw them, they shouted, "*It's appalling! How do you expect to get anywhere with those?*"

Meanwhile, of course, poor Gucki was downstairs with Mami, waiting for a little comfort from her mother. I'd hear her clopping back and forth, and then I'd hear her pleading with Mami, and then she'd start wailing again. I knew I ought to go to her, but her sorrow terrified me. It was as if we were both drowning in the middle of the sea and she was going to grab me round the neck and drag me under.

Well, that's how it was with me all my life. I'd take good care of you when you were dying, but otherwise? You were out of luck.

When a month or so had gone by, I decided it might finally be proper to go see Walter. I was positive he'd make everything all right. I brought along a new hat in which I had great confidence, which I'd had the maid wrap up in mauve tissue paper, and I sat on the train thinking, *After her husband's death she was disconsolate, and she flew to the arms of her lover.* But the visit wasn't a success. When I got to Berlin, Walter took me straight off to meet his mother. She looked just like him, the same narrow face, with no room for doubt, and it wasn't hard to see what she thought of me. I was an idle southerner, an older woman, a Catholic. I was a Jew's widow, whom people gossiped about. When I asked for schnapps, a white spot appeared in the middle of her upper lip. I was miserable, and sat there braiding the fringe of the tablecloth until Walter finally took me to a hotel.

Afterward, I held him close with a leg, so that he couldn't get away, so that if I was guilty he wouldn't escape his share, and started chattering away like a schoolgirl. I said, "He was so weak at the end, Walter. Even his hands had no strength. He lay with them *here*, like a nursing child, and said, *When I'm well, we'll go to Egypt and see nothing but blue sky!* But he couldn't look at me while he said it."

"Hands?" Walter said.

He took his hands from my hair.

"Walter," I said. "He was my husband."

"He was no longer your husband. He was never your husband. I am your husband."

"Oh?" I said, and pulled up the covers. "You don't seem very glad to see me."

"When he was dying? With a dying old man?"

Walter's father had died in February. Death offended him. His long nostrils were pinched.

"It didn't cost me so much."

"And this, how much does *this* cost you?"

"The price," I said, "seems to rise by the minute. Walter, you don't know how awful it's been. I'm not sure I can ever compose again."

"Alma," he said, "don't change the *subject*." He sighed. "I've waited so long for this. I've waited so long! But now I'm here, I find myself overtaken by a sense of shame. Was I blind to cloak my love in so perfect a form? First of all," he said, and gripped his left thumb in his right fist, "there's the loss of honor that follows the breaching of any vow. Then there's the violence done against the idea of chastity itself. Next, the pain we caused Mahler." He gripped his forefinger, then his middle one.

I cried, "For God's sake, stop counting on your fingers!"

I'd thought Walter would be glad to have me to himself, like a hero who'd taken what he wanted. I thought he'd be like Tristan, who didn't care who he had to kill or if Isolde was promised to some other fellow. I hadn't bargained on this Lutheran sermon. "Perhaps I'm too much the idealist," Walter said.

I thought, What a boring man.

He went to fetch his trousers from the chair, saying, "I've got to think. I've got to think."

In a panic I said, "For God's sake, what do you have to think about?"

He canceled the visit he was going to make to Vienna, and then he canceled my next visit to Berlin, and eventually his conscience got so refined that he wouldn't even write to me.

So all of a sudden, I didn't have anybody at all.

I sold the house, rented a flat in the Elisabethstrasse, and started looking around for something to do with myself.

The first thing I did was take an unpaid post assisting a young zoologist named Paul Kammerer. He was an amateur composer who'd worshiped Mahler, and he offered me this position as an act of homage. Paul had forthright black brows and a sort of pouncing look. He said, "You can accomplish more in a single glance than I can in an entire day. Here's a box of mealworms. My lizards could do with some dinner. No, you've got to *scoop* them out, with your fingers – there's no harm in a *worm*." And he stuffed some in his mouth, to reassure me.

Next I started a little salon, like Zuckerkandl's. I called this salon my Sundays. I had a hostess dress sewn from cloth-of-gold and sent out invitations in my awful handwriting. I was Mahler's widow, and still very good-looking, and Mahler had left me a hundred thousand crowns to make everything nice with, and all sorts of people showed up. Klimt came, of course, and Zemlinsky brought Schönberg. Burckhard came, though he was old and ill and used to open a window to cool his head. Pfitzner, Schreker, Klemperer, Ochs, old Reininghaus, Moser, even Fränkel came, all the way across the sea. I liked to shoo the young people from the best chair so that Hermann Bahr could sit his big stomach down and be happy. I liked to say, "We do things simply here!" and fill all the glasses myself. I'd play piano and sing and drink, the way I did when I was nineteen, and think how good it was to own a piano with a nice firm movement, and to wear a new dress, all slippery against my arms, and to have a long smooth throat from which came songs. My new music room was done all in red. The divan was port-wine silk brocaded with scarlet chrysanthemums. Along the bookcase were some geckos Paul and I were keeping an eye on, flopping around in glass tanks. When they escaped, he was very adroit about catching them. Bahr used to call me *Dearest Majesty*, and Peter Altenberg called me either *Madame Freia of the Apples* or *Eaglet*, which was pretty good, since I was twice his size. Paul would be off in some corner, looking hopeful and smelling of formalin. There'd always come an hour late at night – a little hush – when everybody who was still there looked round and thought, *What a rare little band we are.*

Gucki would still be wide awake, kneeling on the divan and watching everybody over the back. She was six years old now and very beautiful, with my coloring and Mahler's hard thin physique. She loved these parties. She liked men. They were always happy to see her. She'd go from one to the other, leaning a bit against their legs, silently, as if she hoped they wouldn't notice, and when they stroked her shining hair or cupped her cheek, her huge eyes would narrow sleepily and she'd look content. The only thing she didn't care for was the lizards, and one night after everyone left, she shouted, "Why do you put those awful things up there? I don't like it here, just the two of us. Why can't we go back to the house? If we stay here Papi will never find us."

"You behaved so well this evening," I said rather desperately. "Everyone admired you." I made my voice so tender that I was nearly in tears from it myself. I said, "Gucki, you mustn't be so hard on your poor Mami. It's very difficult when you've got no man."

This wasn't what I'd planned to say at all, and then I did start crying.

She flung her arms around me, and we wept together. I smoothed her hair and thought, Maybe I'm not such a bad mother after all.

AROUND THIS TIME everyone was talking about a young painter named Oskar Kokoschka. He'd made a big name for himself at the 1908 Kunstschau. This was an enormous show that filled forty-five pavilions on the Schubertring, and they invited scores of artists, even foreigners like Matisse, Gauguin, and van Gogh, but Kokoschka got a room to himself, even though he was just a young Kunstgewerbeschule student who hadn't even been painting a year. According to one story, while they were hanging the show, Kokoschka locked himself in his room and started shouting through the door that he wouldn't open up unless the jury promised all his works would be shown just like he'd hung them, no matter how peculiar or unsavory. Klimt was chairman of the jury, and he thought a lot of Oskar. He was also anxious to get home and take off his frock coat, which is uncomfortable when you're used to a monk's robe. So at last he said, "All right, then. Let him be torn to bits by the press. Let him learn."

Oskar always told this story wonderfully, and it's become famous. Of course, I remember his room at the Kunstschau – number 14. You entered through an archway. There was no door to be locked. But it's certainly a wonderful story.

Oskar was a dreamy boy from a family of gold workers. His grandfather made the chalice in the Cathedral of Saint Veit. His father married a young Styrian peasant and lived by fixing watches. He used to send Oskar to the museum of ethnography to improve himself. Oskar's favorite exhibit was a head from New Mecklenberg. It was decorated with shells and shark teeth and had blue nerves painted down its cheeks. Oskar told me how he'd walk round and round admiring it – and now, of course, if I want, I can see him do so. He's fourteen years old and his eyes are shiny and hard, like big blue marbles you can see clear through, but it doesn't get you anywhere, because they're just marbles.

He was fidgety when he attended Realschule and sneaked in classics in the cheap Reclam editions, which he read secretly, holding them under his desk. "That's why," he said later, "my intellect resembles the Tibetan desert, with just a few pagodas here and there."

Then he got a bursary to attend the Kunstgewerbeschule, which was run by Mahler's old scenery master, Roller. Kokoschka wanted a certificate to teach drawing, so he could get a little money for his family. He got sick at his first dissection. The air entered the knee joint with a hiss. The head lay beneath the marble slab in a pail, with its eyes open. He was eager for the money and drew like any boy that sat next to him, who might know tricks, but finally he did a few good sketches of some circus girls from his own district. At the Fledermaus he performed a shadow play called The Speckled Egg with puppets he'd made of sheet metal and painted paper. When it came down to it, his fingers shook and the puppets wouldn't dance. He fell in love with his friend Erwin's younger sister, who was blond and well-off and confused him with the brightness of her red frocks. She came to his studio and slept under a veil.

"A veil," Oskar would explain. "You know, a veil."

He didn't touch her. She expected her boyfriends to be amusing, but Oskar frightened her, and in tears he wrote to Erwin: Dear God, I want so much to be happy and travel anywhere with 100 negroes.

He painted one self-portrait after another, all of them sneering or pointing to their bosoms. He signed each with a big O.K. He made a terra-cotta bust called The Warrior and painted blue nerves down its neck. There was an open-air theater at the Kunstschau, and there he staged a Drama-Comedy called *Murderer Hope of Women*. The actors were art students dressed in rags. Oskar daubed them with veins and nerves and handed each one a bit of paper scribbled with the necessary oaths and shrieks. The hero is a man called Man. Woman wears a red frock. She desires Man and is therefore branded on her breast, so she stabs Man in his breast – it's a difficult play for breasts – but Man kills her, and then kills the chorus of Warriors and Maidens, and then he strolls away as the sun is rising and feels much better.

Oskar claimed that the audience fought each other with umbrellas. He claimed that Bosnian soldiers charged the stage with drawn swords. He claimed that visitors threw rubbish in the *Warrior's* open mouth. He claimed Roller took away his bursary and that he, Kokoschka, therefore shaved his head to show he was a man marked by destiny. All this is stories. It's true that the critic Hevesi called him Öberwildling, Chief Savage. The *Arbeiter Zeitung* said, *His daubs shimmer gall-yellow, fever-green, frost-blue, hectic-red, and seem bound by carbolic and asafœtida. They have a certain significance as manifestations of an epoch in decay; judged artistically they are massacres in paint.* The Archduke Franz Ferdinand stamped round the room, flung out a finger, and roared, "Pig turds! Pig turds! Someone should break every bone in that young man's body!" And it's true that some witty citizen left a candy wrapper between the *Warrior's* open lips.

But the architect Loos admired it. "This terra-cotta fellow with all the nerves..."

"They represent," Oskar said, "sensations felt under the skin."

"Ah? Well, I wouldn't mind owning him."

"Mind you, I expect a good price."

"I offer you one cigarette," Loos said.

"Done," Oskar said. "I never haggle."

"I see they're selling your postcards out front. What are you doing painting postcards for the Werkstätte? Their big idea is, let's replace all the old gingerbread with new gingerbread. Knickknacks. You're wasting time."

"I'm young."

"No more knickknacks, there's a good fellow. I swear you won't lose by it. I," Loos said, "will guarantee your income."

Loos had designed the showrooms for the Emperor's tailor, Ebenstein, and he made Ebenstein sit for Oskar. As payment the tailor dressed Oskar in fawn-colored Harris tweed, which Oskar wore with great arrogance and dash, his red hands dangling from the glorious sleeves. Loos was friends with Karl Kraus, and they took him to Kraus's famous table at the Café Central, where Oskar peddled his drawings to get liquor money. Then they'd all eat goose-liver pâté at Piovatti's Jewish restaurant, to get something on their stomachs before drinking. They took him to brothels and tried to cure him of his virginity. They sent him to the Sanatorium Mont Blanc on Lake Geneva, where Loos's mistress was an inmate. She was a phthisic English dancer named Bessie and she introduced him to all the wealthy consumptives. Oskar painted the Count of Verona, the Duchess Rohan-Montesquieu, and Bessie herself, who looked like a lewd child and would be dead in a year. She told him, "Loos said you're interested in structure. But I'm going to keep my stockings on because Doctor said to keep warm. There. How do I look?"

"Cold."

She said, "Oskar, are you weeping?"

No one paid him for his portraits.

"Switzerland was a mistake," said Loos.

Next they tried Berlin. It was a big new place, famous for liveliness and ugliness. The Prussians were still excited from their victories over Austria and France. Officers ordered civilians out of their paths. "What fills the Germanic heart?" Loos asked.

"Sentimental bloodshed," Kraus answered. "Over such hearts Oskar must rule."

They sent Oskar to work at a journal called *Der Sturm*. Oskar shared an attic over the offices with a *Sturm* writer named Blümner. He and Blümner lived on dry rusks and strong cigarettes. For *Der Sturm* Oskar was reporter, janitor, messenger, proofreader, deliveryman, and critic. Each week he took up a pen and scratched out a drawing for the title page. The line broke and shivered, for soon it was winter, and the attic was unheated. Out his small window were roofs, chimneys, and a dim courtyard stuffing itself with snow. The gas meter gave an hour's light for a groschen, if there was a groschen, and when there wasn't, he and Blümner crept into bed and lay there in the dark, back to back for warmth, dreaming aloud of food and love-making. They invented a girl named Virginia and raised her together from childhood. They argued under the blankets for the right to be her father, each glaring at a separate wall, their buttocks pressed tightly each to the other's.

The art dealer Cassirer showed Oskar in his gallery and had him paint his new wife, the actress Durieux. "I have been painted by Renoir," she said, "and I think I'm entitled to say that that's not my nose."

"No, Madame, it's my nose. My nose my eyes my hands my tits my *mouth*." He scraped it down with a few swipes of the knife. "And now it's no one's."

He rushed out, leaving his canvas, brushes, and paints behind, which he often did when defeated by shyness or rage.

But things had started going Oskar's way. Soon he could afford to warm himself in the brothels. He went back to Vienna and Roller made him an assistant drawing master. Oskar hired half a dozen models to do Greek dances naked on the stand. "Round is old-fashioned," he said. "Angular is new. Dreams are law." He was paid 150 crowns a month. Riches! For his sister he raised a dowry of 10,000 crowns and was in debt again. He wrote to a lawyer's wife: *Truly, you should not imagine that there is any other dog who remembers what you are like better than I do*, and he sent best thanks to her husband. He experimented with narcotics and stirred powdered amber into his coffee. He read history and talked about world production of coal. Loos took away his paintings to keep him from painting over them for want of new canvas, and got him subjects to paint.

One of them was Moll, and Moll came home very excited and told me, "I've found the most brilliant young portraitist. A Czech, you know, and a bit of a roughneck. But really, you ought to sit for him."

Oskar came to see me at the Hohe Warte house. Mami was always overjoyed at the thought of anything new, and she nearly carried him into the parlor in her arms and then ran off to see about luncheon.

I was thirty-two years old. Oskar was twenty-six. He was tall, with dainty little ears, and his head was still almost shaved. His beauty so upset me that in my memoir I wrote he was dressed in rags and coughed blood into a dirty handkerchief. In fact, he wore Ebenstein's splendid tweed suit, which was just a little frayed at the cuffs. But he walked sloppily, as if he was shoving himself forward, and then halted and stared at my breasts.

"I don't have any small talk," he announced.

"Don't boast," I said.

"It's true. I don't know how to talk to people."

"You are talking to me."

"Usually," he said, very large, "I have two friends sit on either side of me as I work, quite silent and still, to give me courage. Sit over by the window, please. I'll need daylight across your cheeks. Ideally it ought to be three o'clock."

"It will be. Don't you want any lunch? I thought we'd work after."

"By the window, please," he nearly sobbed.

We had a word in those days, *malerblöd*. Stupid as a painter.

He told me my shoulders ought to be parallel to the wall and held up a big finger to show me where to look, and then he pulled some ordinary office stationery from his portfolio and started scratching away on the backs. The cheapness of the paper offended me. He moved his elbow like a lunatic. I didn't see how he could be drawing the tranquil lines I admired each morning in the glass. "You're a pig," I said. "Look at my face. What did you come here to draw? Are you employed by a corset maker?"

"It's still all you, isn't it?" he mumbled.

"I'm not comfortable in this chair."

"Where," he said savagely, "would you be comfortable?"

I didn't know what to do. I felt life, what I thought of as Life, flooding back into me, madly prickling, like blood rushing back into a sleeping foot. I got up and went to the piano, and my hands found the opening chords of Isolde's Liebestod. I began to sing in a muttering voice. Oskar came up behind me and placed his left hand gently against my throat, as Zemlinsky once did to demonstrate the breadth of different notes. The right fingertips sank lightly to rest in the valley of my bosoms. It was like closing an electric circuit: the prickling went everywhere. I kept playing, and when the song was done, I cupped my hands in my lap.

"I have no small talk either," I said.

He rushed from the house, leaving his drawings and portfolio behind.

The next day I got his letter.

My dear friend, I know I am lost if I continue in my present unclear way of life. If you can respect me, and are willing to be as pure as you were yesterday, when I knew you in a higher and better sense than all other women, who only want to make a ruffian of me, then dare a real sacrifice for my sake and become my wife, in secret, for as long as I am poor. I believe in you as I have never believed in anyone but myself.

Well, he'd gotten my attention. The following night I brought him to a Schönberg recital promoted by the Academic Society for Literature and Music in Vienna. Oskar tried to have opinions, he mumbled, "Quite...," he mumbled, "I found it very..."

But I gulped sherry and cooed at him: "Widowhood purifies. I have taken up the study of science. We are all the products of our thyroid essences. The iguana's pineal mount is indistinguishable from the lark's. I have suffered greatly. I, too, am an upstart – not culturally, as you are, but financially. Pfitzner, Gabrilowitsch, Charpentier. They all saw the worth of my music and tried to rescue me, but Mahler crushed the life from my songs like a great wheel. Any other woman would have fallen prey to drink, or taken lovers. Where do you sleep?"

He said, "With Mami and Bohuslav, in Liebhartstal."

"And where else?"

He kept a folding cot in his studio in the Hardtgasse.

Off we went. Oskar had painted the walls black, as he did with all his studios. I looked around and decided the *Arbeiter Zeitung* was correct to call his paintings massacres. They possessed all the terror and splendor of lost battles, and I knew I wasn't wrong in my judgment. I had Oskar undress and lie down upon the cot, and I rode above, because the sheets weren't clean and besides, Oskar was just becoming O.K., while I'd been Alma a long time. He tangled his arms beneath my shift. I took it off. He blinked. Like Loos, he had a taste for starved girls, ortolans one crunches up in a mouthful, and he was surprised at the strength of my legs. He shut his eyes. I dragged my breasts across his blind face to punish him for having touched me between them.

"That'll teach you," I said.

He fitted his mouth into the cusp of my collarbone and cried *mü* like a lost calf.

We fell slowly and clumsily to our sides, and gently came disentangled as we fell. I lay there admiring the joining of his limbs. It was boyish and lax. I seemed to have wrecked him with pleasure. I liked him. He had a wonderful head, like an anvil, with so much chin, and his eyes were large and beautiful and set close together, almost comically so. He was a gnawer and had left my breasts sore, as if I'd been nursing. He'd been very quick and clumsy, grabbing for everything two-handed. I thought, If we do this again, I'll have to explain a few things. I tightened my legs around one of his and brought myself to an acceptable happiness as he bumbled around, half asleep, wondering if something was expected of him. Perhaps, I thought, I won't see him again like this. It's too laborious. He makes wonderful paintings, though. I'll certainly bring him to bed again if the portrait's a success. It's lovely to have made him so happy. My thoughts were very supple and quick just then, and it would have been nice to have him awake to talk to. But the privacy was also nice. I thought the best thing just then would be him lying on me, so that I could feel his weight, but it wasn't worth the effort to arrange it. It wasn't worth anything if you had to arrange it. I thought I might be falling in love with him, maybe for a long time. I'd sleep a few minutes and then get up and go home. I got ready to give myself up to sleep. It's lovely, I thought, to give yourself up to things. I'll have a better idea where we are in the morning.

VII

BUT IN THE MORNING I had no idea where I was, or even quite who I was. I heard a man slowly rubbing his shaved head with both hands. So, I thought, I'm awake. I must have spent the night here. Quite a little adventure. My shoulder fit just so beneath Oskar's arm, but his bed was narrow and I was glad to get up. I strolled around the little studio, still nude – I was impressed with myself, strolling around like that. There was a swatch of swan's skin on Oskar's worktable, and a celluloid pattern for making fans. Along the mantelpiece sat a row of small bright senseless things. Everything was painted black, even the windows. I knew it was morning, because the scratches in the paint were shining like comets and stars.

I pointed and said, "Stars."

"You circle about me like the constellations," Oskar said.

"Be quiet," I said. "I'm looking at things."

"The Big Dipper. The Big Knockers. The Big Pink Bottom."

"I should go home."

"Big big big pink pink. You should be brought fine things in a silver bowl. Candied orchids. Cut with an amaranthine knife. Amaryllis. Amber. Amply. Umpty ump. You should be worshiped like a Bengali cow."

"What's this on the mantelpiece?"

"I can't see."

"A bit of crinkled silver paper, a cockleshell, and a red wax flower. Squashed."

"That's my landscape. It travels with me everywhere, to help me forget the wicked city. Bring me my cigarettes?"

"I thought *you* were to bring *me* things. In silver bowls. As if I were a cow."

"But I'm so comfortable," he said.

Eventually Oskar got up and took me to a café for breakfast.

I said, "You take all your women here, I'm sure."

He said, "No, I can't afford it. This is the good place."

The waiter spread a white napkin on the round marble-topped table. Then he noticed it had a ragged hem and took it away to get another.

"He knows he's got to take care of us," Oskar whispered, "because we're so happy."

From all the nudity my clothes felt strange. I buttered a bit of roll. Oskar put four lumps in his mélange. "I like it sweet," he said.

"Is it good like that?" I tasted it. The heat went into my belly and made me perspire. "It's terrible. It's too sweet."

"You've eaten up all the bread."

"Yes," I said. "Get me some more."

He counted his coins. "I'm going to have an omelet, like a gentleman."

I took my time with the second basket of bread. Oskar ate his whole omelet without offering me any and went into the WC. When he came back he leaned close and said, "Alma, I just had the most *wonderful* shit."

"You horrible man."

"No, really, and now I feel so pure. Look into my eyes – don't they look pure? Alma, you're not looking."

"I should go home soon."

Instead, we took a walk. With a man of Mahler's size a

woman like me was a bit comical, but Oskar and I looked well together in the glass of the shop windows, and I enjoyed walking with him as long as we stayed in districts where I wouldn't meet people I knew. He jingled his big fists in his trouser pockets. He pointed to a necklace in a window. It was made of red glass beads and shone deeply.

"That's the sort of thing you ought to wear about your beautiful white neck. However," he said grandly, "I am poor."

"I'm not," I said, and went into the shop. When I came out, I tore the beads from their paper and fastened them round his throat. If I tucked them well into his shirt, no one could see. His neck was as white as mine and looked well in red beads.

I kissed him and said, "You, you are the one who is beautiful."

"Ah," he said. "If that's the way it is, maybe we should go home."

We went back to his studio with the black windows. In the familiar darkness he pretended he couldn't find his way and blundered about to amuse me. He latched the door and grasped me by the sit-upon. "You'll kill me," he groaned, and put on the light. He put a big hand to my cheek, pressed my face aside, and examined my neck. "Pale," he said. "Smooth. Turn *around*. You have the hind end of a gazelle. An insinuating gazelle. Your walk is insinuating, you always seem nude. And with that long sleek secrets-keeping nose, and those big long Persian eyes with the blue blue pupils – that's all you ever wear: two cornflowers. Bismarck's posies. For God's sake sit down."

"Like so?"

"No, astride the corner of the bed, like Boadicea. As if you'd killed it. Conquered it." He was already at his easel, smearing out the face of a meager brunette. He turned her upside-down. She clutched her knees in panic. "God *damn* you don't you move."

Scrfff, *scrfff* went the brush. The room blossomed with the familiar greasy perfume.

"Careful of your shirt," I said peacefully. "I'll bet it's your best one."

He took it off. The necklace glittered wildly on his chest.

"You're pretty, with those beads," I said.

He took those off, too, and fastened them round my neck. He tugged down my bodice to expose me.

"Now I do feel like a cow. Careful. You'll tear it," I said.

He stood and examined the effect, and I examined him. The teats of his chest were tiny and set close together. I reached up and pinched them gently until they grew sharp. I stood and lifted my bosoms in my hands and pressed the teats to his.

"Now we're the same," I said.

I licked his hard white breastbone. He groaned, fell upon my bosom, and began to suckle. "I thought we were going to get a little work done," I said.

He tried to thrust his head up inside the necklace, with mine. It wasn't long enough.

"Stand up," he said. "I'm going to faint."

He stood behind me, twisting the necklace gently round my throat. I felt the hard red beads and, at my back, the great red lever. He steadied my breast with one hand and attempted to wind the necklace around the teat. He pressed me down on the bed and bound my wrists with it. He flung up my skirts. "I forgot you don't wear anything," he said. "Oh, you whore. Why did I live before I met you? This is how you ought to be posed. Remind me." He undid his trousers and prepared to complete the act.

I whispered, "Oh, slowly. Oh, I *hate* you."

With Walter I'd always felt like a fine vessel being filled decorously with pleasure, but Oskar muddled me, as if he were stirring me up with a cooking spoon. I knew I must be making noises.

"I *hate you*," I screamed.

He fell across me, hurting my nose with his shoulder.

"I hate you," I hummed. "You whore. You promised to paint my portrait."

He didn't reply. I began to feel the wrinkled bedclothes beneath me. I felt his body very clearly, all knobs. Even within me he was still knobby. I was afraid he was going to cause me more sensations. I said, "I should go home."

He didn't reply.

"Up," I said softly. "Up, up," and I patted him on the shoulder. He worked himself up on his elbows, very slowly, rolled off of me, and lay still. I got up and went to fetch the contraceptive apparatus from my purse.

"That's an unsightly thing," Oskar said, sadly watching.

I smiled at him and filled the rubber pouch at the tap. There was no way to warm the water and it was uncomfortable.

WE WERE TOGETHER every day that week, at his little studio or my flat, and I'll say one thing about Oskar: He put you to work. He drew me as a calm Madonna, as a supplicant on my knees, and as a strict saint with a jabbing finger. He started a canvas where my arms are folded Gioconda-fashion. He told me Leonardo's *Gioconda* had been stolen from the Louvre and that it was up to him to make another. All Oskar's girls had been paltry little things, and somewhere along the way he'd decided that women's faces were all triangular, like cats' faces, but for me he had to learn a curve or two. He kept coming back to my eyes, making them bigger and more faceted. He drew with lunges and flinches, shuffling his big feet, squinting tenderly, and at last came the arrogant lift of the chin when he decided the drawing was good. Then he'd throw everything on the floor and reach for me.

I spent the whole day being admired and stared at. I liked attention, but Oskar nearly sucked the marrow from your bones. At about eleven each evening, I'd go home or pack him off to his.

I'd already stayed one whole night with him, and I thought that was enough for a while.

Back then I had a friend named Lili Leiser, a wealthy woman who came to my Sundays. She'd once tried to kiss my shoulders, but I'd explained she ought not to do that. I must have been pretty persuasive, too, because we became friends. In fact, she became my *dame de compagnie*, someone I could travel with – we both liked to travel – so it wouldn't be scandalous that a single woman was on her own. Ten days after I met Oskar, I went with her to Paris. And this is how little I knew: I couldn't see why Oskar should mind.

In Paris we visited our dressmakers. We ate mussels and roast chicken and watched a cabman cut a burr from a mare's mane with his pocketknife. After supper she'd come to my room, brush my hair, and bicker with me, the way disappointed suitors do. It was a nice ordinary little visit, but Oskar went off his head and started writing me twice a day. In the first letter, he wrote: *Yesterday I was still relatively calm, but today I've been searching like a beggar in every nook and cranny of my damned life for a trace of you. Any word in French now strikes me as remarkable. I've looked at Paris newspapers to find out if the sun's shining. My poor mother is suffering very much at present from my electricity, which must be discharged if I am to keep lucid control of my nerves. I'm not used to being thwarted by an external difficulty. Alma, I now believe, stronger than anyone on earth, that you must bind yourself to me.*

I read it aloud to Leiser as she did my hair. I was showing off, but I also wanted to know what she thought. She massaged my neck and said, "I don't see what you're grumbling about. I wish someone would write to *me* that way. Do you know what your problem is? You're not used to pleasure. Pleasure isn't comfortable. You're like a big cat, you want comfort."

"I'm not sure he's entirely sane," I said, boasting a little.

But I was nervous, too.

The result of this trip was, from then on, after he left each night, Oskar would march up and down beneath my window like a sentry. He'd march until two or three, then give a whistle so I'd know he was going home to sleep. He wanted to be sure nobody came and took me away again.

It really shook him up, my going off like that. After that, he was on the lookout for more betrayals, and he kept on writing those letters. I invited him to the première of Mahler's Ninth at the Vienna Festival and he wrote: *I can't come to you in peace so long as I know that another man, dead or alive, inhabits you. Why have you invited me to a dance of death, to watch in silence as you move for hours, a spiritual slave, to the rhythm of a man who was and must be a stranger to you?*

I went to Scheveningen with Gucki so she could play in the waves. Leiser accompanied us, hoping to see me in a bathing suit. Cunningly Oskar wrote: *Kraus tried to tempt me with a Malayan snake dancer, but I gave her to the porter to look after.*

On my way back from Scheveningen, I stopped in Munich. He wrote: *Should you have a darling child by me, great, good nature is merciful and will extinguish all terrors.*

Oskar was welcome at my Sundays, but pretended he wasn't. He wrote: *I passed your house at 10 o'clock and could have wept with rage because you can endure to surround yourself with satellites, while I stoop in some dirty corner. And if I had to take a knife and scrape from your brain every antipathetic notion others have about me, I would do it before sharing with you a redeeming joy. I will not tolerate any other gods before me. If you can withdraw, my dear, good woman, a time of torment will ensue for you that I would not wish. Alma, I would have loved you with uncommon strength.*

I went to his studio and said, "You're to write no more letters about knives and gods. That's the end of everything, if you're ever so ugly again."

He bowed his head. "When I was little, my mother gave birth beside me. The blood made me swoon. Since then, I've been unable to get along properly with people."

"Maybe," I said, "but don't do it again."

My birthday was 31 August and Oskar made me a fan of swan's parchment painted with gouache. On it he painted a story of Oskar and Alma. First we're floating in two boats, ignoring wild beasts and each other. Next, everything is ripe fruits and we're riding up a red Alp on a flaming horse. We're happy but the horse has doubts. For Christmas he gave me another fan upon which we embrace in flames and there's a young son with Oskar's big face. He gave me a miniature portrait of himself. I was to hang it over the hotel bed whenever I traveled, to spiritually protect me. I brought this to Nice at the end of January and to Paris in May.

Gucki shouted at him, "Can't you paint anybody but Mami?"

He gave her her own chair in his studio.

On Friday after his life class I'd meet him at the gate of the Kunstgewerbeschule and drive him someplace nice for the weekend. I always paid. He had a lot of debts and I lent him money. This vexed him. I introduced him to a critic named Grünfeldt, who began writing the first book about Oskar. This vexed him too. He kissed each of Mahler's pictures on the face to exorcise his jealousy, but I can't say this was effective.

One evening I had him to supper with Leiser in my flat. She circled around him on her long legs, like a mating bird kicking up dust, and said, "I've decided you're quite mad." Oskar smiled briefly, then held still so that she could go on admiring him. He lowered his head and stuffed in the food. She was fascinated. At eleven I told him good-bye, and Leiser watched with little eyes as we kissed. She gave Oskar her hand and he kissed that, too. Then he left. I told her to stay.

"Well?" she said. She was examining her kissed hand.

"Wait a bit. Now. Go to the window."

"There's a man down there."

"No," I said. "Only Oskar. See? He wants to make sure I'm safe. When he's satisfied, he'll whistle."

"Satisfied? *Whistle*? That boy frightens me. I'm not going down there until he leaves."

I went to the window myself. There was Oskar, tiny and upright, marching up and down the Elisabethstrasse, swinging his arms militarily. If I stood just so, he seemed to march along my windowsill like an insect creeping along a stick. He marched until he vanished behind the linen rosette that secured my curtains on one side. Then he marched back into view and vanished into the rosette on the other side.

"Gucki," I said wearily, "bring us a deck of cards and get yourself to bed."

My daughter crept up with the cards, bright-eyed, and then crept down the hallway, out the door, and down the stairs.

She slipped out the street door and leaned against it, clasping the knob behind her back and being a *femme fatale* over her shoulder. She took a lingering step down, then another. Then she got bored and trotted up to him, all business. "They're fighting about you up there," she said.

"With their bare knuckles?" Oskar asked politely. "With pistols? With swords?"

"Yes," Gucki said. "They've both got big long swords."

"Well, I'd better go and break it up," he said.

She led him inside. Halfway up the stairs she sat down on a step and faced him. "You're making her cross," she said, caressing the marble step beside her with a thin, nervous hand. "You'll spoil everything if you keep trying to make her mind. She never minds. And she doesn't like it when other people fuss. She calls it ill-bred." She pointed at him and said, "A word to the wise." Then she got up and led him to our flat and into the parlor, saying, "I found him."

"Hello, madman," Leiser said. Oskar bowed.

I examined my cards.

He sat himself on the divan, one knee here, the other there. He cupped a big red hand and put the other big red hand in it. He shook them together a few times, looking about. There stood Gucki. He saw no one else who was pleased with him. He pulled a leaf from the *Presse* on the table and folded it across, very neat, and then the other way, and a few times more. He dragged Gucki over by the arm and said, "Here."

She considered and put it upon her head.

"Why have you put that boat on your head?" he asked.

She took it off and said, "Let's go to the river!"

"Why would you put a hat in the river?"

"You don't make *sense*!" she shouted.

Oskar stood. "Well, so long. I'm going back down."

"Guard me all you like," I said evilly. "Lili is already inside."

Leiser glared, and Oskar looked puzzled enough to weep. "What? I don't want to be interrupted again," he said, and left.

I went to the window and peeked down at the curb. When Oskar saw me, he saluted.

Leiser sat beside me and pulled my head down upon her breast. "My poor girl," she said. "How they martyr us."

Her fingers were skilled upon my neck. I smelt her female odor prowling about inside her dress. I said, "We're hurting him – he imagines there's some mystery. We should bring him along next time we travel. We should all go someplace warm and simple."

She hesitated, then bravely said, "Perhaps we can all be happy together."

"No," I said. "I haven't got what you want. I'm sorry."

"Well," she said, rising in a temper, "he may find you haven't got what he wants, either. I wish you all a good night."

So Oskar and I went to Italy alone. It was a three-week trip, and very happy. Now that he had his wish – he had me all to himself, every minute of the day – he was lighthearted and courtly. He bought a prism to study the spectrum with and passed it over my skin to make more colors. He led us into the woods in Tre Croci and fed the wild colts walnuts from his palms. They polished their long heads against his shoulders. We crossed the Dolomites to Venice and got on board a vaporetto which couldn't quite start, and after this Oskar could always make me helpless with laughter by making popping noises with his mouth. I remember a stone Venus broken off at the thighs. Her legs plunged into a stone half-shell like a plump hand thrust into a purse. We sat on a terrace and I took his dictation. "The silhouette... of Venice..." he said slowly. "Is the calligraphy... of the Italian Renaissance." To save time, I left out all the vowels. It didn't matter. No one could read my handwriting anyway.

Next we went to Naples. Each morning the women sat down on their doorsteps and combed their hair to the side, like a picture by Blaas. Before us Vesuvius hung in the blue sky. Since Klimt, I'd thought of Italy as the land of kissing, and I walked around all day with my lips gently parted. We went to the aquarium and to the Teatro San Carlo, which Oskar painted on a third fan and gave to me. He made the theater very fine and tall, with gold columns and a gold octopus climbing up the wall to fight a gold shark. In the middle we lie peaceful in each other's arms. My face is gold with sleep. His is plum-blue.

"You're being so lovely these days," I said.

"I'm always lovely," he said. "Won't you put that bottle away?

It's wicked to drink alcohol. You should drink plain cold water, like me."

"If alcohol's wicked, you're the wickedest man I know."

"Yes, but when I drink water I enjoy it so. Isn't it better now, without that atheistical Hebrew crowd of yours? Isn't it good, just the two of us?"

"Yes."

"Aren't we doing what's important now? Only what's important?"

Oskar claimed to be impractical but could have my corset off in half a minute. Then he'd rub his face against my creased belly in what I considered an unsuitable manner, saying, mmm, mmmm, mmmmmm. The physcial act made him talkative, as if he were a woman, and afterward he told me how he worried about his young brother Bohuslav, who was whimsical. Whenever he came home they dug together for fossil ammonites and flints of the La Tène period. Liebhartstal, he told me, was a maze of gardens. Hot water for washing came in a big cart like a brewer's dray. Oskar looked out for the cart when he was small and was given a four-kreuzer coin. Nearby was Galitzinberg Park, and two well-to-do little girls used to come there with their mother. They invited him to have tea in the English manner, but he spilled cocoa on the elder girl's skirt. "I didn't want to play the gallant," he said, "however many crowns her mother had embroidered on her handkerchief."

One afternoon there was a great storm. All my senses were exaggerated down there in Italy, and I had to get into bed, quite dressed, and roll myself up in blankets.

"Alma?" said Oskar.

I said, "No."

"Alma, come look," he said. "You can't be afraid of anything so beautiful."

I'd hated thunder ever since the afternoon of Papi's death. It seemed to get right inside you.

Oskar climbed into bed and spoke with his lips near to mine. "You mustn't be afraid."

"Go away," I said.

He lowered his head and gently tried to butt me out of bed, like a goat. I clasped his neck in the crook of my arm and murmured, "Don't."

We realized at the same moment that he couldn't get up: I was stronger than he was. "Aha," he cried in fright, and I quickly let go. He scrambled to his feet.

There was a silence. Then I pressed my face to the pillow and said "Go away" again, so we could start over.

"Come on, Alma," he said. "Stand up. Take my hand."

"No," I said, but this time he pulled me to my feet.

"Thank you. And my other hand? And now," he said, and turned me round like a flamenco dancer until my back was to his chest and our arms had twisted tight around me. He murmured, "I've got you, see? And now here we go," and he walked us *bup bup bup* out the French windows and onto our balcony.

"No! Oskar, I'm afraid," I said, and then, stupidly, "We'll get wet!" We were already sopping. Oskar licked my ear and said it was like drinking a glass of water. He slid my wet dress to my waist. "Someone will see."

"There's no one but us," he said.

It was true. The storm had emptied the city and the harbor. It spun above the bay and stirred the sea and sky until they were all one thing. This one thing gushed from a crack in the plaster parapet. It lapped our feet. It bubbled on the limestone balls at the gateposts below and flooded the steep gutters – where two streets joined, water folded over rushing water like the fingers of two entwined hands. There was a single sail in the harbor and the rain made it hang, gray and dirty. It ran down our lips. Our clothes were so wet that clothed and nude were also one thing, and then Oskar lifted my dripping skirts from behind. Our balcony sailed like a boat over a drowned Vesuvius.

"It's a *boat*," I cried, and gripped the edge.

"Our boat," he said between his teeth. "And now you love me."

I cried out to God, and that I loved him.

"And now you're mine," he said.

I stared back at my wet legs.

He grasped my upraised rear as if leaning upon a lectern. I closed my eyes and didn't look at anything for a while. At last he jerked and went still.

I stood up slowly, undid my torn dress, and let it fall. Then I wore only the red necklace. My legs felt drunk. I wandered inside and took up the contraceptive device.

Oskar ran in shouting, "No."

I stared at him, a little drunkenly. Then I said, "Oskar. I have to."

"You mustn't," he said.

"Oskar," I said. "Please don't spoil things."

"It's that, that *thing*, that spoils things!" he said, towering over me, and then he sank down on his knees, touched my belly, and said, "Please don't kill the spirit we've created." He tilted up a face full of rage and a little entreaty, so I could see how serious he was. He looked like a boy ready to smash up an anthill and then cry.

"Oskar," I said. "For heaven's sake, get up."

I think I was in some ways more like a man than a woman, because everything got very clear for me after love, clear and a bit shabby. I could feel the floor very distinctly under my toes. My wet hair lay heavily on one shoulder. I looked down at Oskar's twitching face and thought, He's a beautiful boy, but his eyes really are awfully close together. I wonder if there isn't something wrong with him. I asked him to get up twice more and then turned away and went to the washstand. Oskar knelt there in the middle of the floor, watching me. There was still a little thunder left, but I found I wasn't afraid anymore. I kept thinking, If only he wouldn't spoil things.

138   WHEN WE GOT HOME, Oskar's painting was very different. He no longer frayed the canvas with his palette knife. Now he painted with thick, generous strokes. He'd been to Venice and could arm himself with Titian's reds and purples. We were both very pleased with our good trip and his good new paintings, but our conclusions were opposite. I thought it was time for a little rest. He thought it was time to get married.

By this time, Oskar had fought with Loos over me, and the two of them no longer spoke. He'd fought with his family over me, too, and with the rest of his friends. Now I was the only one he had left, because he'd given up everything for me, as he kept saying, and I just had to marry him, that's all. He got Moll's blessing, and Mami's. He convinced my friend Erika Tietze to plead his cause. He wrote his dealer Walden that he was going to be wed and must therefore become internationally known. He proposed each time we met, and when I sent him home, he sat down and proposed by letter. He signed himself *Alma Oskar Kokoschka*. He'd decided that from now on it was going to be Naples all the time.

But I was tired of being fussed at. I'd started daydreaming about calm, sensible men. I felt that we'd reached our high point on the balcony – I could be pretty realistic sometimes – and thereby improved Oskar's paintings, and now he shouldn't be greedy, because it was time for something else. I had that old feeling of having gorged on sherbet. You can't eat sherbet forever. In my diary I wrote: *O.K. must work! He was put on earth for that purpose!* LIFE *holds no interest for him, but I am ready with my own evolution –* AS OF TODAY I CANNOT LEARN ANY MORE! *If only I had climbed Mont Blanc! But what a lunatic idea! Where is my own truth?*

Mahler had left me a plot of land in Breitenstein, and I decided to build a house out there. I was thinking of a place all to myself, where maybe I could escape once in a while. But this just got Oskar more excited, and he put all his hopes into the building of our house, and discussed the drawings with Moll until poor Moll was frightened. He was getting more peculiar all the time. He covered the black walls of his studio with runes in white crayon. He lit one room with a red lightbulb and the other with a blue one. At last he shouted, "You still don't know who I am! You won't listen! Well, you'll listen now, because I got your birth certificate! by tricks! and used it to publish our wedding banns, and there's an end to your nonsense! Now, what do you say to that?"

"I?" I said. I was mad with rage. "I? I say that you'll now be put to the trouble and embarrassment of withdrawing them. And I say that you are a donkey. And I say that from now on I shall see you only every third day."

I'd gotten the every-third-day idea from Goethe's Wilhelm Meister.

He got so upset that Frau Kokoschka wrote to me. She explained that it would be my fault if Oskar failed to attain his great destiny, and gave me until a certain date to release her son. After that, she said, she'd shoot me. On the appointed afternoon a little peasant woman came and marched up and down beneath my window. It seemed to be a marching family. One of her arms swung militarily and the other was thrust into her purse. The purse bulged. The strings of a lace cap were knotted beneath her jaw, tight as a tourniquet. I telephoned the Kunstgewerbeschule and said somebody better go get Oskar. At last he ran sloppily up, elbows and knees, like a newspaper blown by the wind. "Mami!" he cried. "What's this?"

"I'm going to shoot her, Oskar," Frau Kokoschka said happily.

"Just let me take a breath, Mami," he said, "and then I'll shake you until your head chimes."

I flung up the sash, daft as a she-goat eating tin. "Pranks!" I screamed down at them. "Pleasantries! I'll never marry you. You're a child."

"A child," he called up, "does not paint as I do."

"You scratch on the backs of invoices with pencil stubs. What sort of husband would you make?"

"What sort of wife kills all my children?" He began to weep. "You and your rubber bag! Never once will you let me prove myself."

"Then prove yourself. I'll marry you when you've painted a masterpiece."

"I'm going to shoot her, Oskar," his mother said.

There was room in her little round head for just one idea.

"Mami, what do you mean by all this shooting? It's all right now. We're going to be happy." And he took hold of her elbow.

Proudly she brought out from her purse a sweating empty fist.

SO OSKAR STRETCHED a big new canvas and finished it with rabbit's-foot glue. He felt he'd made a good bargain. He'd been planning to paint masterpieces anyway. He began to paint a half-circle of sea, illumined as if by Bengal fire. Then a water tower, mountains, lightning, and the moon. There was a man and a woman. She lay with her cheek and palm upon his chest. They twisted together on a flying boat of clouds or a giant cockleshell or a hotel balcony. The weight of Oskar's feet seemed, as always, a torment. I was asleep. He called it The Great Boat. It was full of magnificent red flames and the purples he'd learnt from Titian, but everything grew darker and bluer as Oskar saw me only one day in three and began to doubt, and one night, the way Oskar tells it, the poet Georg Trakl came to the studio, dressed in mourning for the death of his twin sister. Trakl stepped through the door just as Oskar made the final strokes, and at once improvised a poem called Die Windsbraut, gesturing with pallid hands, his eyes haunting and unforgettable and so forth, but this is more stories. It's true that Trakl went home and wrote, *Over black rocks, / drunk with death, / plunges the glowing Bride of the Wind.* Like all Oskar's friends, Trakl didn't like me.

But now the picture had its true name, *Die Windsbraut*, and it was soon finished. Oskar brought me to his studio and stood me before it, his hands on my shoulders. The effect was a little terrifying. He'd painted a great shock, running circularly through nature. The painting seemed an affair of muscular caves, like a dark heart. For a long time I looked at his painted face, and the chest upon which I'd laid my painted hand, and at my own painted face, with its enormous saintly closed eyes. I was almost as excited as Oskar. I knew what I was looking at. And I was very proud that this man who loved me – and whom I loved too, as well as I ever knew how to love anyone – had accomplished such a thing, and that he'd done so by means of my face and, I felt, my spirit. But at the same time, I was wondering what else he expected of me. Wasn't my job done now? Meanwhile, Oskar was waiting.

So I took his hands from my shoulders, put them on my stomach, and said, "I want your child."

A bargain is a bargain.

VIII

By SPRING the Breitenstein place was nearly finished, and Oskar and I went to live there. The house was pleasant, full of air and light, with fine big rooms and a fireplace made of granite blocks cut from the Semmering mountains. The electricity wasn't hooked up yet, so we lit the place with dozens of candles. The weather was mild. I was newly pregnant. The whole thing was a terrible idea.

I'd always thought I'd change Oskar's life, the way I changed Mahler's. I felt I'd shown Mahler what a woman's love was – which in a way, I suppose, I did – and then afterward he was never the same – which is certainly true, because then he died. But Oskar was used to changing things round, not being changed round himself. And when he moved in, he thought, I'm the man of the house at last, and now what I say goes.

He insulted all my visitors and forbade my Sundays. He painted faces and horns on the bottles in the pantry. They were meant to be guardian fetishes and he complained when they were emptied, for certain spirits had to be yellow-faced with oil or red-faced with wine. He spoke in a deeper voice, now that he was practically a father. He tried to teach me Greek, which he didn't know. When he couldn't think of a word, he bit his lip and waved his arms. He pulled my clothes from their places and sorted them in a system of his own invention, and threw on the floor those that were made in unlucky colors or unsuitable for a married woman, because now all my dresses had to be closed at the neck and the wrists, and he forbade me to cross my legs when I sat down. It was immodest. He hunted through our rubbish to see if I'd thrown out anything I shouldn't. He waved a withered pear and called me a rich girl. He said he wouldn't have made the parlor quite so wide. It was *arriviste*. I might have an eye for proportion, but it wanted development.

He said, "You must begin a new girlhood with me."

He said, "You must conduct your life nobly in order to remain an emblem for me."

He said, "You have lived worthily ever since you really learned to love."

We began that famously perfect summer of 1914. The weather cosseted you. I was furious as a child who's sick of cosseting. By now Oskar and I were having real shrieking fights. We sounded like one of his plays: *eeeee, aaaagggh, oooof*. Outside, I was storming around all the time, but inside, I was almost quiet. Inside, I was collecting his outrages like butterflies and waiting for him to finally go a little too far.

One day Mahler's death mask arrived in the mail. We were all still busy with the house. Mami was giving instructions to the cook. I was showing the servants how I wanted the draperies sewn, yelling over the clatter of the sewing machines. Gucki was eating chestnuts and watching Onkel Oskar paint a fresco over the fireplace. It was three meters wide and showed me abandoning him to death.

"Onkel Oskar," she cried, "you've painted yourself right in the fire!"

"In hell, Guckerli!" he said jovially. "Right in hell!"

He had me flying away to heaven, waving good-bye. This made sense to Gucki – it was what she was used to. It was Onkel Oskar with the fire-snakes she didn't like. It looked untidy, and as though it hurt. She was buffing the shell of a chestnut against her hip to make it glossy. Inside was a velvet sheath, which she liked to wiggle loose with her thumb. It was grainy and translucent, and she laid it upon the tip of her nose. Tipping up her nose to keep this adornment in place, she said, "*You* don't belong *there*, Onkel."

"A man in love is always in hell. Especially a man in love with your Mami!"

It was awful and it didn't mean anything. Or anyhow, it shouldn't mean anything. But she liked hearing it.

I came into the room then, wiping my clean hands busily on my apron. "What nonsense are you telling my child?"

"Hello, muse. Have you come to aid me in my labors? Flap your arms, muse."

"No, I'm expecting a package. What's this you're telling my child? Gucki, take that thing off your nose."

"He's saying he's in the bad place because he loves you, Mami!"

"He's in the bad place, Gucki, because he's a ninny."

"We don't disagree," Oskar said tranquilly.

"Ah," I said, for here comes the postman's toot. I went to the door.

"What's this?" Oskar said.

The death mask was packed in wood shavings, and I lifted it out with care. Moll had done his work well. One saw Mahler's fineness and strength, and the long vein along each temple that used to grow sharp when he got enraged.

When Oskar saw it, he went right straight out of his head.

"Always that dead man again!" he cried. "It's bad luck. Get rid of it. Put it in the cellar. I won't have it in my house."

I ignored him.

So he snatched the mask away from me, and when I tried to get it back, he gripped it by the cheeks and thrust his own face against it, baring his long yellow teeth like an ape. He shook his face back and forth, gabbling, "Leave her alone, old man!"

Gucki was in tears, her little hands in fists. "*Leave Papi alone!*"

"You lunatic," I shouted. "You'll spoil it." I took it away from him. "I won't have it in my house!"

"*Your* house? You dirty brat," I roared, "I found you in a chicken coop and that's where I should have left you."

It was a real imbroglio. I called him a halfwit and he called me a whore. He said there was no light in my greedy fat heart. I said his nails were dirty. I said he wasn't the first *genius* to mistake me for a serving girl, and where was Mahler now? And I flourished the mask, like Judith with the head of Holofernes.

He grabbed my arms and gasped, "Are you *threatening* me?"

"*Leave Mami alone!*" Gucki screamed.

"Your house," I said. "A painter's wife. Am I to slop around in some old kimono then, washing out your brushes?" I shook his hands away, got a hammer from the workmen, and went to the foyer.

"You witless cow!" he cried. "Don't you know anything about powers? I don't want a child with a dead man's face!"

My heart was humming and humming, like the sewing machines upstairs – oh, I was in a frenzy. There was a fine spot in the middle of the hall that got light from the glass transom and I drove in the nail myself, crooked, and hung Mahler from it. He looked very well there. "You won't have it in your house," I said. "You won't have it in *your* house. Oskar, you've made a mistake."

And I went to the spa at Franzensbad and got an abortion.

I was pregnant a lot in my life, and this wasn't the first time I'd gone to get it fixed, but it's not the sort of thing you ever get used to. They took me to an eight-sided pavilion behind the steam baths and led me through a heavy door. Then I was led through another, quite small, and then a third, which swung open very lightly. At first, it made me feel safe to be so hidden away. I thought, *They'll never find me here.* Then I thought, *No one will ever know what became of me....* The floor was freshly mopped. I heard, very faintly, the noise of drumming from the bandstand on the back lawn. They spread my legs and bound them in place with a long canvas strap.

"What if I have to get up," I whispered.

On a tray by my hip lay a row of tools: scalpels, little forceps, curettes. The doctor took up a gadget like a pair of pliers with long, curving tips.

"I'd better get up," I said.

A nurse held a basin near my face.

"It's not that," I said.

She said, "Done before you know it, dearie."

There was that laboratory smell. I thought of Kammerer's lizards. We'd pin them to a plank with tacks. When you opened them up, the hearts were like mushrooms, stubborn little knots, cool and gray. I started weeping. There was a wet coarse scraping noise from inside me, and pain, not so severe as childbirth, but quite bad. I heard something wet dropping into a steel bowl, and then a bit more, and then the last little bit.

AFTER THAT, I was through with Oskar. I blamed him for everything. The fights, and Gucki's tears, and the fact that I had no peace, and the horrid scraping noise, because if he'd been a sane proper fellow one could marry, I wouldn't have had to sneak off to Franzensbad to be butchered. When I came home, he took a bloody cotton pad from my wastebasket. "This," he said, "is and will always be my only child."

I thought, I've got to get this maniac out of my house.

A few weeks later Oskar's most enraged critic, who had recommended the breaking of his bones, was shot to death in Sarajevo. It seems he had a critic of his own. This was a Serbian zealot named Princip, who was upset that Austria had annexed Bosnia, and he scampered up to the Archduke's automobile with a begging look, as if asking directions, and fired a bullet into Franz Ferdinand and one into his lady. So now the heir to the throne was murdered and Austria declared war on Serbia. Everybody was jubilant, because an Austrian can never remember a defeat. There are too many.

They put up proclamations everywhere, on the train stations, on the municipal buildings, on the gazebos in the Prater. Each bore a big scarlet KRIEG. They looked like announcements of a concert in the open air. Everywhere you looked you saw flags and military bands, and after them came regiments, marching, with polished brass helmets and blue cockades. They marched very well. There seemed no reason they couldn't just march across France. I knew there'd be battles too, of course, where horses rose up on their hind legs like orators – I'd often seen this painted – and each cuirassier displayed a gleaming sword horizontally above his head, and the air was adorned with little bright starbursts, as if someone had hung lanterns for a festival. Well, maybe this wasn't quite up-to-date. Now one read of trenches. It seems the French hid in them. Need one fear Frenchmen squatting in ditches? At Demel's they sold chocolates shaped like cannons. In Berlin, Crown Prince Willy stood on the reviewing stand in his tennis flannels. He saluted the departing troops with a wave of his racquet. Everyone said the war would be won by autumn.

But Oskar looked around and saw poor boys herded off with loud music to die. "Oompah," he said. "Oompah. Simpletons. It'll be Russia next – do they think Moscow's forgotten Belgrade? And then their music won't be quite so peppy. And here I sit, all snug, while Bohuslav bobs about the Adriatic like a rat in a fish tin." Bohuslav was in the navy.

"I should miss you greatly if you enlisted," I said dreamily.

"Enlist?" Oskar said.

"But I shan't be selfish."

"You built this house," Oskar reasoned, "so you could live with me."

"I shan't be selfish," I said again, and my voice was like a shovel on stones.

It was all very clear to me. Oskar must go and fight. They'd give him a sword, and make a man of him, and he'd come back with medals and find some nice girl, and I would no longer have rotten pears waved at me in my own house. Everybody agreed that the war was a new beginning – *a moral cleansing*, as the orators said, *a bath of steel* – they did make it sound a bit like a spa. Each of us had to contribute something. I would contribute Oskar.

Oskar repainted the fireplace mural so that my face was kinder and his beseeching arms were longer. He painted new Alma-and-Oskar fans and left them on my bed. He made our faces the same. But he couldn't change my mind by enlarging my chin, and I closed my door against him each night. I wouldn't show him a moment of tenderness. I talked about nothing but duty and the war and kept asking if he'd heard from Bohuslav. It was unwise of Oskar to have made so many pictures of us, because now I considered our love a work of art, and finished.

When Loos heard that Oskar had decided to fight, he offered his help, and it's a good thing, too. Oskar was too weak for the infantry, too bad at maths for the artillery, and too poor for the cavalry. But Loos still knew all sorts of people, and he arranged for Oskar to be admitted, not just to the cavalry, but to the Fifteenth Regiment of Dragoons at Vienna Neustadt, in which the sons of the imperial family were accustomed to serve. Oskar sold *Die Windsbraut* to a Hamburg pharmacist named Winter for four hundred crowns and used the money to buy a uniform and a cream-colored mare. The mare was named Minden Ló, which is Magyar for All Horses.

Before he left, he gave me one last fan, the seventh. It shows cannons gushing flame and soldiers sinking in waves of ultra-marine smoke. In the middle, a horse flings open its jaws like a choirboy. Oskar lies beneath it in the golden dirt with his hands crossed on his breast. An older man with a statue's big gray face pierces Oskar's ribs with a lance, and I kneel down on the lance with my big pink knees to keep the point in place and kiss the old man's cheek. Oskar gave me this fan for Christmas.

I thanked him.

Then I saw him off at the train station and went home, quite relieved. The truth is, I liked loving Oskar, but I preferred to remember having done so.

AFTER OSKAR LEFT, I was ready to start being free and enjoying myself. I ate marzipan and stayed up late reading cheap novels. I spread my best lieder over the rug and examined them. I lay in bed late, sweetening my mouth with schnapps. But somehow I wasn't happy the way I thought I'd be. I had that feeling you sometimes get after you've taken a tumble, when you seem to be off at a little distance from yourself, not quite trusting your legs or your balance, and if a voice reaches you it sounds hollow and dull.

I started up my Sundays again, but talking to all these people seemed like work. They struck me as trivial, and I wondered why the men weren't off fighting. Gucki would always be huddled in a corner, missing Oskar, and I was afraid that any minute she'd come to me for consolation. When she didn't come, I thought, That girl does not love her mother.

Oskar's training took seven months. He wrote me a letter a day. Everyone, he said, used a comradely du, but for all their friendliness they were eternally separate from him because they were aristocrats. They took him for a Futurist. They'd ridden from childhood and swore at his clumsiness until evening. Each day he exercised upon four strange feet and a wooden saddle, rushing back and forth over a great snowfield edged by mountains. It was frozen hard as a skating rink, and the horses skidded and fell at the rate of one per minute. The captain wore sideburns and armored gloves. Each time he stopped screaming, the ravens settled back into the bushes.

I answered Oskar's letters as if doing lessons. I thought, *I'm being bullied.*

One day I went to Vienna and saw my first newsreel. It was all about the war. There were big holes in the ground, as if they were digging up water mains, and the soldiers looked like laborers. Their smiles were frightened. The barbed wire was very ugly, and I could imagine it tearing at my face. Even the flickering gray light seemed disreputable, like a peep show at the Prater, where you dropped a coin into an oily slot and saw train wrecks, big-game safaris, Jenny Lind singing without a sound. I wondered if the war was such a good place for Oskar after all, and I started to feel very lonely.

It was around this time that I began hearing about Walter again. Berta Zuckerkandl with her procuress's eye wrote to tell me that he was becoming a noted young man. He'd redone a shoe factory in Alfeld-an-der-Leine to give it walls of glass. The corner staircases appeared to float. This was, apparently, a good thing, and the Deutscher Werkbund had made him their youngest director. He designed the pavilion of new machinery for their big show in Cologne and displayed his own designs for automobiles, parlors, and railway sleeping compartments. I wrote to congratulate him and he replied that he hoped I was well. His manner was a bit formal. He'd seen a nude double portrait of Oskar and me and it had given him quite a jolt.

When Germany entered the war, Walter was sent to the Vosges. Berta mailed me stories, cut from the newspapers with her father's old copy shears. As patrol leader, he was always first to jump into the enemy trenches. They'd given him an Iron Cross Second Class. He'd been made a lieutenant. She circled the word in red.

She took me to lunch and said, "You're looking a bit seedy."

I was pleased. Other people told me how well I looked, which was annoying. I smiled bravely.

"I thought you'd be jollier," she said, "now your lunatic's gone."

"I gave him everything I could," I said sadly, but in a well-practiced way. "We would at length have devoured each other."

"Yes. You're both –" She swushed tea round her mouth and frowned. "Strong personalities. Your Walter's been cutting quite a dash."

"I'm afraid he's not 'my' Walter anymore."

"Why not? Think he's found himself some mademoiselle? I'd imagine he's too busy. Now, there's a thing I wish you'd explain to me. Why didn't you two make a go of it? Looks, talent, good family, tall, ambition – there's a proper match for you."

"We quarreled," I said, and let my head hang limp over my tea.

Twitching her wide lizard's mouth, Zuckerkandl examined me. "Quarreled? What the hell's that? You always were a dolt. You've got all your father's charm, but unfortunately you also got his brains. Write the Herr Lieutenant a letter."

"I did."

"That's the spirit," she said. "Write him another."

When I went home, I was very excited. I started thinking about my quarrel with Walter in a new way. In the novels I read with my marzipan, soldiers were always going off to war with bitter hearts, and then pretty soon the misunderstanding was cleared up and the reconciliation was reliably quite splendid. I remembered one of my favorite lines from *Zarathustra*: *Man should be trained for war, and Woman for the recreation of the warrior. All else is folly.* I did a lot of this thinking in the middle of the night, when many things seem suddenly true.

On New Year's Day a fifteen-centimeter mortar grenade exploded next to Walter and he woke up with the mud above him instead of below. In hospital he got my note: *People who have experienced something so unusual and beautiful should not let it slip away. Will the time ever come when I may take you here, where you measured my floor with your steps?*

He responded: *I don't know what will happen. It doesn't depend on me. Everything is topsy-turvy, ice and sun, pearls and dirt, devils and angels.*

"I've hurt him so much," I told Zuckerkandl proudly.

I collected Leiser, my traveling companion, and off we went to Berlin to start the wooing.

Walter met us at the train station. I remember an attendant walking backward along the track, raising and lowering a great paddle with a single glaring yellow lamp. Then up limped Walter through the drifts of steam. Twenty paces away, I could see that his temples were scooped out like saucers. His hair was awfully black. He'd been let out of hospital for three weeks' convalescent leave and looked like a disapproving corpse. "You certainly do like the handsome ones," Leiser muttered. "Even if he is ready to croak. How they ever let him out like that – I don't know what I'm doing here. *That* is an unforgiving man."

"Don't be ridiculous," I said nervously. "If you knew what he'd forgiven me already."

"Don't *you* be ridiculous. That sort permits everything – a gentleman, you know – but *forgive?* Oh, I don't know what I'm doing here. Tell him – oh, as if *you* ever needed to be told what to tell a man." She hurried off, and then up came Walter.

He put out his hand so that I wouldn't kiss him. All right, I thought. I took it and held it with both hands, keeping my eyes lowered, prayerfully. And then I raised them. I gave him both blue eyes.

He only said: "Hello, Alma. Is your friend unwell?"

I began to be a little frightened.

"Hello, Walter. She thought it'd be better if we could speak alone."

"Why? We've nothing to say that can't be said before your friends."

"Are you so sure?"

"Reasonably sure."

Yes, I was frightened.

I told him I'd had a filthy trip and wanted coffee, and at once he was gentlemanly. "Of course," he said. "There's never anything drinkable on these trains. Let's see. There used to be quite a decent place. Down by the east gate, I think it was?"

"Oh, it doesn't matter. Let's go anywhere."

"No, let's at least go someplace decent."

"What do you mean, at least?"

He didn't reply.

"Why did you agree to see me," I said. "If you're going to be like this."

"It was a mistake, wasn't it?" he said.

He took me to the café, and pulled out my chair for me, and asked about my daughter, my health, my daughter's health. I was going crazy. At last I said, "Walter, why are you *being* this way? You needn't be jealous of Oskar anymore. I believe it's over. Anyway, he's in the cavalry now. We got him into quite a good regiment, you know. A dragoon! I believe it'll make a man of him."

"A man?" Walter said in a fury. "*A man?*"

Well, it was the wrong thing to say.

The little cords in Walter's jaws started jerking. I didn't know he was capable of such a face. "Neatly done, by God," he said. "Pack him off to the front. Make a man of him. Well, the French give you a proper education, I'll grant you that. I thought I had some clever notions about death – you know, from school. But the death out there isn't so fine and philosophical. It's just something you step over, like horse turds. Not much time for burials,

you see, and besides, the shells stir everything up, like a stew, and up float the bodies like carrots and leeks. After a bit, the lining of your helmet smells of corpses, the water in your canteen – everything. Some of the horses can't get used to it. We have to send them home. I'll tell you who enjoys it, though: the lice. They lay eggs in the seams of your uniform. The only thing that gets them out again is a gas attack. Oh, it makes a man of you, all right."

My eyes filled with tears. "Oskar has lice?"

"You're ignorant, that's all. I've got to keep reminding myself how much you don't know."

"Aren't you a soldier?" I asked, weeping. "Don't you think it's *good* he's fighting for us? Walter, you've changed."

"Probably not enough," he said.

By this time I was absolutely in a panic. I couldn't believe Walter – or, really, any man – didn't want me anymore. I figured I must be getting old and ugly. I figured the world must be ending. Well, I thought, maybe I *have* been unkind to Oskar, but can't I make it all right by being nice to Walter, who's probably a better soldier anyway? I was all at once desperate for Walter to like me again. I wanted be back on the side of everything brave and noble and well-bred.

I went back to the hotel exhausted, but a part of me was thinking, Oh ho. Alma's desperate. Walter better look out.

Leiser went home, and for the next three weeks Walter showed me round Berlin as if I were his maiden aunt. We went to the Chinese Teahouse at the Sanssouci. We rode along the Unter den Linden in silence, the springs creaking, our knees jiggling to the same rhythm. It displeased him, as if he'd been tricked into making a concession. He took me to a little patisserie near the

Parisier Platz and got me éclairs. "You've still got your sweet tooth," he said.

I said, "I don't want us to be enemies, Walter."

"No. Let's not be that."

"It's cold."

"You don't like Berlin, do you?"

"No. I'll always remember it as the place you hated me so much."

He said, "Why did you come here."

"I'm sorry?"

"Why did you –" he said loudly.

"Yes – sorry. Oh, I don't know. I knew you'd suffered terribly. I wanted to – comfort you."

"It doesn't comfort me to see you."

"You won't let it. You'd rather watch me suffer. You're an unforgiving man."

"That's a new one."

"You drove me away just because I was a wife to my husband when he was dying, and after that I suppose I was meant to dig a hole in the garden and bury myself, but when I tried to find happiness with another man, you weren't having any of that, either. And now you won't let me – be nice to you. You won't stop being the wounded hero long enough to kiss me."

"It isn't that. It's just I've got to look after myself," he said.

"What a horrible thing to say."

"It's true."

"Come back to my hotel."

"I can't. I know you mean every word you say. But tomorrow you'll mean something else. And I can't – You'll just turn away again. I've got to look after myself."

"Come back to my hotel. Let me look after you."

"I can't."

"Oh, God," I said.

We were silent.

"Well, at any rate," I said, "you look a bit better now. At least you let me make you eat."

"Well, at any rate," he said, "let's not be enemies."

On his last evening in Berlin, Walter took me to Borchardt's restaurant. He drank from a tall pilsner glass rimmed in gold, and scraped the foam from his new mustache with his bottom lip. It was early. The restaurant was empty. A workman was trimming the brown edges from the potted palms by the door. The good food lay sadly in our stomachs, and beneath the high yellow ceiling, the air was full of snipping. This was our last meal. "Well," Walter said when we'd done eating. "It's nice, after all, to have a nice dinner with a pretty woman – a friend – and wear clean clothes. Do you know, I believe I mind all the dirt more than I mind being shot at. Thank you for helping me forget things, for a while. Well. I've got a train to catch."

He paid with a rattle of coins and I went with him to the station. On the step of his train he bent down to embrace me. I kissed the well-known mouth. It was our first kiss in three weeks, and our first happy moment. Then the train began moving, smoothly and heavily, and Walter, still blindly kissing, all at once mad with resolve that he should not be prevented from kissing, that his – who knows? – his last kiss shouldn't be interrupted, hoisted me from the platform with an iron arm across my back, then carried me down the corridor so as not to obstruct the other passengers, kissing, kissing. "An abduction!" I cried. My heels scuffed the paneling. "But I've got no nightdress!"

He said, "You'll get no opportunity to wear one."

In August he got another furlough and we were wed.

THE LAST I SAW of Oskar was a postcard I found at a tobacco kiosk in the Nachtmarkt. By then he was a noncommissioned officer. They wore light blue tunics with white facings, red breeches, and brass helmets, and Loos had had postcards printed up of Oskar in this uniform and put them on sale throughout Vienna, as if he were a Burgtheater juvenile. I bought the postcard, stuck it in my diary, and pretty much forgot about him. I didn't know what became of Oskar until many years later, when we all wound up here, where there's nothing you don't know.

When Oskar heard I had another fellow, he asked to be sent to the Russian front. He fought in the western Ukraine under von Bosch. It was a calamity. They came prancing up on their parade saddles, and the blue tunics and red breeches that made such admirable targets, and the Russians lay in ditches in field gray, the way the Japanese had taught them, and killed Austrians at their leisure. Eleven days after I married Walter, Oskar was leading some horses across the River Bug, near Luck, when Minden Ló was shot through the heart and Oskar beneath the ear. They fell into the reeds together, and Oskar was bayoneted by an old Cossack who'd been sent round to kill the wounded. The blood rushed into his lung, he wrote later, with the sound of a choir.

He lay in the mud for two days until the burial detail came by, saw he was alive, and packed him off to the Palais Palffy in the Josefsplatz. The palace was now a hospital. It reeked of iodoform and was littered with bits of straw from the mattresses. Oskar's eyes were yellow and his lips were purple. He'd lost eleven kilos. He couldn't close his drawing hand. But he told everyone who'd listen how his horse had been killed and a bearded elder had stabbed him in the ribs, just as his seventh fan had foretold.

Loos came each afternoon.

"Loos," Oskar would say, "you're just in time to save me from this child."

He'd been befriended by the Countess Mensdorff-Dietrichstein, who was eighteen years old and a day nurse.

"You're looking fine today," Loos would say.

"Yes, I can tell. Because I feel so fine. The countess says I've got a touch of gray now. I imagine I look rather distinguished."

"A proper gent," Loos said.

"Appearances are deceiving," said the countess.

"Frau Gropius would be pleased to see me looking so distinguished. Hobnobbing with the quality."

Loos said, "Shall I bring her here?"

"So she can gloat?"

"So you can stop talking about her."

"No," Oskar said. "I wouldn't interest Frau Gropius now. I'm not like Praxiteles' stuff. It just gets more interesting when you knock off the limbs and the nose. But this child's interested. Aren't you, Countess? She's a shameless creature," he told Loos, "and puts her hands where she shouldn't."

"Was he just this bad," the countess asked Loos, "before the head wound?"

"Do you want to hear some of my play?" Oskar said. "I dreamt it up on the cart. They hauled me off in a farm cart. Seventy kilometers across the Ukrainian steppes. You can't imagine the sky. It runs over one's face endlessly, like a stream of cold... soup. There wasn't any roof to stop me seeing things, so that busybody Alma plumped herself down right there" – he pointed to the foot of the bed – "and we argued all the way to Wladimir-Wolhynak. Luckily for the art of poesy, I wrote it all down."

"That's splendid. I thought your hand was still bad."

"I wrote it all down in my head, and it's great stuff. I call it *Orpheus und Eurydike.* He goes to the land of the dead to save her, but she kills their child with a hatpin."

"All right."

"Tell you later. Going to get some sleep now."

"All right."

"Little slee'," Oskar hummed. "I was jealous of the wrong man. Should've kept my eye on the living one."

"I suppose I'd better go," Loos said.

"Please don't trouble, Herr Loos," said the countess.

"No?"

"See...? He's off now."

"He couldn't be properly asleep."

"Oh, yes. They go off like that, just awfully quick. And when Oskar goes off this way, talking doesn't matter. He speaks so well, doesn't he? Not like his paintings at all, and he does have a dear heart. It's a shame he's so ugly."

Loos took a creased postcard from his pocket. It showed the gallant dragoon of four months ago.

The countess's eyes filled with tears and she cried, "Surely not?"

Oskar half woke, and he too cried, "*Surely not?*"

Over the next year he was blown up twice more and finally discharged as hopelessly shell-shocked. He went to pretty Dresden to teach at the Academy. There he was given rooms by a Dr. Hans Posse, who lived in the Grosser Garten with his father the general, a manservant, and a young Saxon maid named Hulda. Hulda always called Oskar *Captain*. She'd come to his room and talk to him about Keyserling, as if she were a Posse and an intellectual. Tagore, she said, had been arrested in the marketplace for wandering around in his nightshirt! He was a philosopher and therefore had no pockets. She told him she liked onions, beetroot, and peas. It would be a happiness to cook these for the Captain, but one could no longer obtain them because of the war. If he left town, she wrote, *Hulda is still your obedient servant, but the sun shows itself rarely, probably because it is there with you in Vienna. Today I was in town and saw many girls who were also young and pretty. Don't you think, dear Captain, that perhaps they were all waiting for a tall blond man with the blue eyes of a child who hasn't shown himself in the Pragerstrasse for three weeks?*

One night the old general died, and Posse asked Oskar to

draw the body. Afterward Oskar went back to his room with chattering teeth, sliding both his palms along the wall. On the stairs he met Hulda.

"You've been to see the General," she said sadly.

"Posse sent me. I made a drawing, if you'd like to see it. The ears are wrong."

"It was wicked of the Herr Doktor. A gentleman like you shouldn't be troubled with so much death. You'd much better take my arm."

She led Oskar down into the cellar, where there was a barrel for her to bathe in, and turned her back and stripped and got into the water. Hulda's legs and buttocks were powerful. He thought of his dead cream-colored mare. Her waist was narrow and her hands small and foolish. She turned, hunching to make herself little, and cupped water over her head three times, saying, "This is on account of the dead man, so he won't trouble you in your dreams."

"You're kind," he said. If he looked only at her navel he knew he wouldn't fall. But a trail of gold hairs led one by one from her navel to a dark gold cloud, thick as smoke, and then he sat down on the cold floor.

"No man has ever seen me," she said. "But I know the Captain is an upright gentleman."

He nodded and reached up to touch the tangled hair. She was blond like me.

She whispered, "Dispose of me, sir."

"I can't do that," he said, with tears in his eyes and his thumb on her personal place. "But I would like to call you Reserl, in secret. I've always thought Reserl was such a jolly name."

He determined to be well again and every day ate boiled beef on the bone. To keep his wound warm he wore a close-fitting leather jacket with woolen sleeves. He refused to shake the hand of any ex-soldier. They had all committed murder and in normal times would be hanged. He went to Uppsala to be treated by Professor Bárány for shell shock and was strapped onto a stool and spun at great speed while he clutched a lead weight in either hand. He came staggering home and had an affair with a Swedish baroness named von Fock-Kantzow. She found him willful and wed a more docile man, a flying ace named Hermann Göring. He published his *Orpheus und Eurydike*. He published an illustrated poem called *Allos-Makar*. This is almost an anagram of our names – *Allma-Oskar* – and in Greek means *Another-Is-Happy*. He made oils, drypoints, and chalk lithographs, and every woman he drew looked just like me, and these Almas mistreated Oskar terribly. They squatted on his grave so he couldn't climb out. They rode him round the church like a donkey. They dragged out his guts with a spinning wheel, as if he were Saint Erasmus of Formio.

Finally, he hunted up a Stuttgart dollmaker named Moos. She was a fine seamstress and had once, they said, made a dress for Gustav Mahler's young wife.

Here began a long correspondence.

Yesterday, he wrote, I sent a life-sized drawing and I ask you to copy this most carefully. I only drew in the second, bent leg so that you could see its form from the inside. THE FIGURE MUST NOT STAND! *For the 1st layer (inside), please use fine, curly horsehair. Buy an old sofa or something similar. Then, over that, a layer of pouches stuffed with down. The skin will probably be made from roughish silk. And the foot, e.g., like that of a dancer: Karsavina perhaps. Can the mouth be opened? Get feathers. Color may only be applied by means of powder: fruit juice, gold dust, layers of wax, and so discreetly that you can only imagine them. The woman should be 35–40 years old. Please make it possible for the touch to enjoy those parts where fat or muscles suddenly give way to sinews, and where the bone penetrates to the surface, like the shinbone. It is better not to consult a book of anatomy but rather to examine the place on your own body, which you must move with your hand until you have the feeling of it warmly and distinctly. The parties honteuses must be perfect and luxuriant and covered with hair; otherwise it is not a woman but a monster. When shall I hold all this in my hands?*

After nine months, a packing crate arrived at the Posses' villa. The figure inside was bitter to Oskar's hopes. The eyelashes were twine. The mouth was an evil little V. The *parties honteuses* were horsehair dyed yellow and remained closed to his hopeful finger. But the Cossack's bayonet had taught Oskar discipline, and he carried me grandly to his room, and Posse's manservant kicked the packing crate and swore he'd give notice. Oskar had bought clothes and underwear. When I was dressed, I looked a bit better. He came downstairs and said everybody had to be quiet, because the Silent Woman was resting from her journey.

And in the silence Hulda said, "Of course, sir."

For the next few months, Oskar spent every day with the Silent Woman. He painted it, formal portraits and nudes. He took it on carriage rides past the Frauenkirche. He carried it into restaurants and demanded that a place be set for it. Only Hulda understood. She was one of those who are born bereft and she needed no explanations, and soon Oskar addressed himself only to me and to her. At home she assisted him in rituals. He gave her a frilly apron, black silk stockings, a magnificent new broom, and the red glass necklace I'd given him. With these, the drab Hulda was transfigured and became Reserl the accomplice, with the big doll in her strong Saxon arms. She grew skilled at producing the Alma-voice.

"Oskar," I said from her arms, "you daily grow more impossible."

He said, "Madam, I had a good teacher."

"Oskar, did I ever love you?"

"I think not."

"I bore you children."

"You singly and severally exterminated them."

"I bore you tadpoles, then. I didn't love you with the young horses?"

"You found me picturesque."

"On the balcony maybe?"

"Energetically not."

Reserl's own legs inspired her. In the black silk stockings they were more beautiful than anything she'd ever dreamt of. "I didn't love you like so?" she said. "Like so, maybe?" She stripped off a stocking so she wouldn't be distracted.

"Madam, you have the advantage of me."

"Oskar, you're a saucy fellow. You may kiss me." She put my arms around him and smoothed his sweating, jerking back. By now she wore only the necklace and a cowering look of pleasure. Reserl didn't ask him again to dispose of her, and he didn't. He disposed of me. She cupped her hands for his seed, and then Oskar slept.

In the spring, when he was getting tired of his lunacy, Oskar announced a party where his friends could meet his mistress. The war was over. The magnolias in the garden were blossoming. Oskar held his party beneath them, with tall torches and plenty to drink, and the chamber quartet from the Dresden Opera played in the fountain basin with their trouser cuffs rolled up. Posse's manservant expressed the weight of his contempt by handing round the soup plates with a white-gloved thumb in the soup. A Venetian courtesan kept calling for Oskar's mistress, where was Oskar's mistress?

At last I appeared in Hulda's arms.

Bravo! some cried, and others said, It's the Silent Woman! or, My God, so there really is a doll! and some said, But it's only a doll! Hulda was Reserl and said nothing. The red necklace shone around my neck. "Why would anyone make such a thing?" the courtesan snapped.

"Why else, madam?" Oskar said pleasantly. "To perfect my loneliness."

He wore a dinner jacket and was sleek.

She wanted to know if I was fashioned to resemble a former paramour.

"We fashion all our loves," Oskar said, "upon some impossible memory."

"And do they return the compliment?" cried an analytical chemist.

"Depend upon it, sir. If we are not fashioned by impossibilities, we remain unfashioned."

"You're an unfashioned fellow," called a currency engraver. "You won't give us anything to drink."

"We all drink at the one well of m-melancholy," Oskar said, but he could not say *melancholy* without sniggering like a schoolboy.

"Melancholy? Not you," said Posse. "I've meant to tell you what a pain in the arse you've been."

Everybody was very drunk. They passed me from hand to hand until my head was coming loose.

"Spin her on the stool!" Oskar roared, lurching now. "Spin her on the stool!"

But not even Reserl understood.

I was with consideration decapitated. The manservant intoned in Latin as he doused me in wine. Then he departed on hands and knees to vomit in privacy like a gentleman. It was the black hours. Reserl was Hulda again and slept beneath a table with her pink fist near her lips. Posse worked at a chess problem with the currency engraver. The courtesan sat in the fountain and suckled the chemist. My body lay by the fountain's stone rim, one arm soaking in the cool water. The red necklace hung from a wire in the stump of my neck. Oskar wanted to read an invocation over me, a Japanese *sutra* to comfort the spirits of broken dolls. He knew it was near the top of a left-handed page, but the torches were dying. He let the book drop in the water, detached the chemist, and took the courtesan to his room.

In the morning the police came. The postman had reported a headless body in the garden. Posse, ill in his bed jacket, was obliged to make apologies.

Then they tossed me, headless, purple with wine, into the dustbin.

IX

MY SECOND WEDDING WAS even smaller and plainer than my first, but I was pleased with it. Walter had gotten a two-day leave. We spent it in his hotel room in Berlin. The summer was unusually hot and Walter drained the carafe on the night table and then drank from the vase of peonies, and I told him he was just showing off, and he said *Yes* and grinned like a peasant. He touched my temples and belly with vase-water. This made me cool and flowery. Walter preferred to take a shower-bath, the way you did in the barracks bathhouses, and I sat on the closed commode after my bath and watched. He left the bath curtain a little open for my sake.

"What knees you have," I said. "Very hard and complicated and large."

He rubbed them with the loofah, humming. "In fact," he said, "they're killing me. I had no idea war involved so much walking. I thought we'd ride everywhere. And you see, I've always been a bit proud of my horsemanship. Besides, with a horse, there's always company."

"I'm keeping you company."

"So you are."

"Unless you'd prefer a horse? What a lot of steam. You're quite red. You must like the water very hot. Done already? Now you have to let me dry you."

"Dry me?" he said, laughing.

"Yes. Is this all right? You're very clean. But I'm clean already. It's as if you're my baby and I've bathed you. No, you mustn't do that," I said, pointing at it, "because it spoils things. You're my baby. I should carry you to your crib now and tuck you up."

"I'd like to see you try."

"All right. Mind, now." I crouched a bit and hugged him around the waist.

"Careful."

"You shouldn't laugh at me. All right." I stood with a grunt, and up came Walter.

"My God in heaven."

"And now I'm going to tuck you up." I left the bathroom with Walter in my arms. It wasn't really so difficult, just clumsy. Together we fell across the bed. "There," I said.

Never in my life had I been so proud of myself.

"My God."

"You ought never to laugh, you see. I'm taking care of you."

His organ had subsided with surprise. "That's better," I said. "Now I'm going to take care of your knees." I began to rub them, as I imagined a masseur would do. "Like so?" I asked.

"Ah. This is nicer than the Somme."

"Thank you very much. I bet the girls aren't this nice to you in the brothels."

"But I don't go to brothels."

"You shouldn't lie to me."

"But Alma, I never do. Not since I was a kid. I don't like those places."

"You're a liar. They're full of horrible women."

"No. They just want a few marks to live on, like the rest of us. I just don't like them. The furniture in the parlor's always so awful, with a long mirror over the sofa, and you always look so sad in it. Now what?"

I had fetched two silk scarves and was tying them round Walter's knees. "There," I said. "Now they'll keep warm."

"They look warm." Around his left knee was my mauve scarf, tied in a bow, and around his right knee was a black and red foulard that I'd never successfully worn. "Very nice. My feet hurt too, you know."

"Well, I've no more scarves." I lifted my shift and put his feet up under my bosoms. He wiggled his toes, rudely. His middle part was recovering from its astonishment, and I closed my eyes and lay down across his shins. "There," I said. "They ought to be good and warm now. Are they warm?"

I felt hard hands beneath my arms, and then Walter drew me up over him as if I were a featherbed.

All my life I remembered the texture of the bed linen against my forehead, against my nape, between my fingers and teeth. My tongue was sensitive, as if I had fever. It seemed quick and rough, like a cat's tongue. I bit the bedsheet, and afterward I was proud of myself for having done it. I thought, Now that I know about war, everything seems more real and exciting. When we were both too chafed to embrace anymore, we got dressed and found a magistrate to marry us. It was 18 August 1915. Afterward we went to a military equipment store to choose leather for his new riding boots. That was our honeymoon. The walls and ceiling were hung with useful-looking items made of leather, rubber, canvas, and steel. Above my head swung a bridle and bit. I imagined it around a horse's smooth neck, and the heavy bar across her tongue. "I knew," Walter said. "I always knew I'd be with you. I had to go through horrors and struggles, I had to be *tested*. But I knew we were destined to be together."

"I like to hear you talking like a fool."

"So do I. So long as I'm your fool."

"That's the chief thing, just don't go thinking you're someone else's fool. What a stench in here."

"It's marvelous." He filled his lungs.

"Breathe like that again. I like to see you breathe. Thank you. You breathe very well."

"Nothing like the smell of good leather. Hah!"

"You're my fool."

"And you're my wife."

"No, that's a secret. The people on the street didn't think I was your wife. They just saw a soldier and a soldier's tart. They knew. I want them to know, to know everything. Except that I'm your wife. I want them to know I'm your soldier's tart."

"Hardly that."

"Yes. Because now we've done things. No, don't look around. The clerk can't hear us. He's gone deaf from smelling the boots. You'll look very handsome in your boots, but I don't want you to buy them and go stamping around in the muck. You shouldn't have told me those awful stories, Walter, because now I keep having terrible thoughts. I see you all in pieces."

He set his thumb gently across my lips.

"Oh, now," I said, against his thumb. "You're not superstitious?"

"Well, it doesn't do any good to talk that way."

"I know, Walter, I'm sorry. It was wrong of me. But I'm frightened. I hate to think of you hurt. I hate to think of you with lice. It would mean everything was spoilt."

"It would mean," Walter said, smiling, "that I needed a bit of kerosene and a wash."

"No, you're just so clean, and everything would be spoilt. Oh, I'm only talking this way because of the stink."

"It's a fine stink. Everything's fine. I've got a beautiful wife, and soon I'll have a beautiful pair of boots. I'll have everything a soldier needs."

"You're my fool who drinks flower-water, and I'm your tart. But I'm getting a headache from the fumes."

He embraced me. "My wife," he said tenderly.

I said, "You're forgetting again," and went out to wait in the cab. A bookseller's cart was passing. I bought the latest *Weissen Blätter* and began reading a poem called *Der Erkennende*, The Seer.

> *One thing I know:*
> *Nothing is mine to own;*
> *I possess alone*
> *This awareness....*

It summed up my mood exactly. I set it to music – it was the first thing I'd written in quite a while. Later I made it the first sentence of my memoirs. And Walter went back to the Somme.

After Walter returned to the front I wrote to him that our heavenly wildness had made me tremble. I wrote, ALMA GROPIUS! ALMA GROPIUS! *Isn't that lovely? Do write this name in one of your letters. Want to see it written by you. Gropius – such a lovely foreign name. I am very sensual, want to suck you in from all sides like a polyp.*

I gave this to the maid to post and sat down to wait.

TWO WEEKS LATER, I celebrated my thirty-sixth birthday. I was still pretty exalted. I wrote in my diary: *My will is clear. Nothing shall deflect me from my new course.* I wasn't sure what my new course was, but I was certain I must be on one. For instance, it was time to make something of myself as a composer. I'd be like Walter, disciplined and bold. My songs were written carelessly, on papers of various sorts, and I bought fresh staff paper with a nice blue tint and began to copy them over, so I would have them good and tidy when I started writing the new ones. Then I made a cover sheet that read ALMA MAHLER GROPIUS: 100 SONGS. Then I began to design a monogram to put on the cover sheet. I tried an M and a G creeping up the sides of a great A. I tried an AM in the gullet of a great G. Then I put aside the staff paper and scratched out some more invitations to my Sundays, and that was that about my music for a while.

I'd never enjoyed my Sundays more. By now I was getting quite a crowd. All my old beaux came, of course, and so did a lot of new people with nice big reputations. The Bittners and the Alban Bergs came, and so did Count Dubsky and Countess Wydenbrück, and so did Rilke, Schnitzler, von Hofmannsthal, and Franz Blei, who published *Die Weissen Blätter* and was always bringing someone new. I always made sure the tabletops were shining and that there were cloisonné trays set out with good little things they couldn't get just anywhere, and I'd go round to see that everybody had what he needed. To the young men I was a mother and made them eat cake. To the others, ah! I was a pretty young woman – young! young! – who loved a young patrol leader with an Iron Cross. I got myself a new gold dress. When my belly began to swell beneath it, they gazed at me as if I'd accomplished a marvel. We all agreed it was heroic of me to make my home so festive. "Sit, sit," they'd say, but I wouldn't sit, and as I handed round the tortes I quoted *Zarathustra* about Woman and the recreation of the warrior. "All else," I said, "is folly."

In October of the following year I had a daughter. I named her Alma Manon Anna Justine Caroline Gropius. She had black hair and her nostrils were perfect, and so tiny that I couldn't see how she got any air. Each Sunday I led my flock into the nursery to admire her. They put gifts in her crib: a heron of folded silver paper, a Tibetan temple bell, which I took away before she could swallow it, a poem in which Manon rides off on a dandelion puff and visits all the clouds. Gucki was now a little teenager, and hopped around telling all the men, "I've been reading to her, to make her wise. Do you suppose she'll turn out like Mami? Mami and I aren't the same thing at all. For example, Mami sees nature on a large scale, and I more in detail. She recalls the music she's played, and I the pieces I've read. I'd never do a room all in scarlet. I think blue's more spiritual. We'll get a red ball and a blue one and see which Manon prefers."

It was the thought of Walter that made everything so fine and gallant, and I kept saying, *If only Walter could be here!* But inside, I knew it really wasn't his kind of party. He wouldn't have liked the little temple bell. He wasn't the sort of man who joins in merriment. The fact is, I was getting a bit restless about Walter. It was a year since we'd wed, and then two years, and I never saw him, and I didn't like being left all alone. The war was going on far too long to suit me. Walter's letters were full of upsetting and sordid news. Franz Josef had died, and no one much liked Karl I. As I poured out the tea I thought, All these men are endangering the baby.

One Sunday Blei brought along the author of *Der Erkennende*. His name was Franz Werfel. His book *Friend of the World* had been such a success that Kraus had paid him the compliment of hating him. He was a Prague Jew, and his clothes were untidy. "Blei says you once liked a little verse of mine," he said.

I said, "Yes, I set it to music."

"Sing it for me?"

"I am not prepared to give a recital."

"A fine way to talk to your artistic collaborator. We can discuss it after you've fed me. Have you any sandwiches?"

"I'm afraid I'm not prepared to offer you sandwiches, either."

"No sandwiches! But I did so want a little sandwich. I know just what sort I want. I can picture it in my mind," he said helpfully.

"But I've none of any sort. Perhaps you'd care for a bit of plum cake?"

"Cake!" he cried. "*Plum* cake! I knew you'd think of something."

Mahler had eaten his concoctions with scrupling little bites, and Walter's manners were so perfect that he never seemed to eat at all, but Franz chewed with a tranquil air, like a worker doing worthy work. He was twenty-seven years old. His blue eyes were clear. His hair was thick and dark blond, like mine, and rushed back from his round forehead and hunted through the air behind him. "This is excellent plum cake. There's another piece? Only one? I'd better eat it. It's an honor to eat the last piece of such plum cake. And otherwise it might be eaten by someone who can't appreciate it properly."

"I thank you for your consideration. Mind your vest. You're getting all plum sauce."

"Alma," called Bahr. "In a moment I'll be jealous. Neglecting us like this."

I called, "As if one could neglect *you*." I turned back to Werfel and said, "*Die Fackel* suggested –"

"You have to remember, Kraus was a champion of mine. But then he took up with the Baroness Nádherný. She called me Jew-boy, so I told everyone she'd once been a circus performer, so Kraus wrote, *Franz Werfel should be chased off Mount Olympus with a wet rag.* But he'd already said all those nice things, you know."

"You're not going to talk sensibly, are you?"

"I suppose I could," he said, confused. "Should I?"

"I'd hate to put you to the trouble. Let me introduce you round."

"But I already know everyone."

"That's right, Herr Blei tells me you're all soldiers together."

I meant this as a bit of a dig, because they were all propaganda-writers for the Military Press Bureau. In fact, Franz had been an artillery sergeant for a while, but he'd never fought. He'd stepped off a funicular before it reached the top and gotten dragged. After they patched him up, he went hobbling about Prague on two canes. The streets were all tangled with flags and every three steps someone asked him how he'd gotten his wound, and if he said he'd fallen off the funicular they got angry, so he said he'd pulled his captain from a burning wagon, and pretty soon he'd pulled everybody out and won the war. "They were glad to hear it," he said. "But Count Kessler likes my stuff, so he had me posted to Vienna with Blei here and the rest of the fellows. There will always be wars. The modern state is made for war as a cholera hospital is made for cholera. They've put me up at the Bristol, very nice, and I don't have to wear my uniform if I don't want, but how can I be happy while there is still one creature on earth that suffers?"

This I'd already heard from the lips of another egocentric par excellence, Gustav Mahler.

"My throat is dry," he complained, "you've let me talk too long. I'm done with my cake and now I want some little girls. Some beautiful little girls. You over there, what do you think you're doing? Spying on your elders?"

Gucki giggled. "You're not so old."

"You're far too good-looking to be a spy. You should be, what should you be? You should be an angel. Do you know what angels do? They fetch me cigarettes."

"You've made a conquest, Gucki," I said.

"Well, then, I guess I better go get the cigarettes," she said.

"That's not how conquests work, dumpling. But I'll explain later."

He pointed after her. "Mahler's child?" he whispered reverently.

"And mine."

"Bless you, Shorty," he said when she returned, although Gucki was taller than he. She lit his cigarette with a proud flick she'd practiced for guests and danced away. "Ah, now I'm smoking. Very well, Frau Gropius. Explain yourself. You have musical gifts, which you attempt to dissemble. You have a large angelic child."

"I pulled her from a burning wagon."

"In your gold dress. You *have* been busy. You've got a lot of explaining to do."

"Have I? I don't mind showing you my setting for Der Erkennende, but how gifted you'll find it I can't say. I've certainly had good teachers. Zemlinsky. Mahler himself, of course. Josef Labor – he introduced me to Wagner."

"Sing some? No? I never met such a woman for not singing. What's this, Shorty, a sandwich? You are better than an angel. You are an archangel and a divine light and a bunny rabbit." He ate. "That was a perfect sandwich, if it were a little bigger. Just you show me how you made that sandwich." In the kitchen, he sawed out great slabs of bread. "Beef," he hummed. "Mustard. Pickle. Madame," he told the cook, "I am invading." He'd found the sherry and poured himself a glass. His cigarette veiled his head with smoke. He blinked blamelessly. He set his cigarette on the edge of the chopping block, raised the knife, and said, "Un ladro son forse? Son forse un bandito? If you won't sing, I will."

As a child Franz had spent his allowance on gramophone records of Verdi on the Schreibender Engel label. Later, the prostitutes at the Gogo used to call him Caruso. Now he began to sing Se pria ch'abbia il mezzo and to wave my knife. Sparafucile has been paid to kill the Duke, but Maddalena says no, and Gilda loves the Duke and so comes through the door before midnight and is stabbed. Franz was upset about all these women. But it was fate, and it's lovely to be paid! He was small and stout, with powerful round shoulders, and had a really first-rate tenor voice. Soon everybody was pushing to be in my kitchen.

"Ebbene – son pronto, quell'uscio dischiudi," he sang, "but my throat is dryyyy."

"No," they cried, "more Rigoletto!" And Blei said, "Sing properly, now."

It felt marvelous to laugh like that. I said, "You look like a priest, with your wine and your bread."

"Oh, no," Franz said, shocked. "You shouldn't joke about the Eucharist."

Franz wasn't heroic or stern. He wasn't the sort of man a woman needed to make herself worthy of. This was awfully refreshing, and I began to see quite a lot of him. He became the chief ornament of my Sundays, and on Mondays he came back and we made music, and then he amused me with his stories, which were all about him. His father was Werfel of Werfel & Boehm, the big glovemakers. Someday Franz was supposed to be running the firm. "The gloves do have a lovely smell," he said. "I had to sew one as a journeyman-piece. I got the foreman to do it. So they packed me off to Hamburg to learn the export business and I put the bills of lading down the commode. There, I thought, now the freighters will have to stay at sea." He'd just gotten the galleys of his new book, but he couldn't quite get started correcting them. "I'm a lazy swine," he said. This was something new to me: a man who didn't want to work.

He really did have the most gorgeous voice. It was big for a tenor, with marvelous clarity of tone. Anton Kuh used to say, "It's not a solo instrument – it's like listening to a whole orchestra!" Deaf as I was, I never had to ask him to repeat a word. "*I'm weak!*" he'd cry, "*I'm weak!*" and it sounded like he carried all the strength in the world in that stout little chest. He'd lay his head in my lap and moan, "You don't understand. I'm a slave to good living!" By this he meant nice food, cigars, and the cafés – he went to the Central every day. It was full of an atmosphere of corruption, he said, worse than any brothel. And brothels he knew a lot about.

"She was quite double-jointed," he'd say, reminiscing.

"Sit up and behave," I'd say.

He loved to talk about what was wrong with him, which I considered a Jewish habit, but he was obsessed with the Church and knew a lot more doctrine than I did, and his vocabulary was quite Catholic. "I've polluted the body God gave me," he told me, with his head on my lap, because apparently masturbation was also part of what he called good living. "It's *concupiscentia* – morally disordered both *per ipse* and in intention."

"You ought not to be telling me such things," I'd say. "You ought not to be down there. For heaven's sake sit up."

"No," he'd say, "it's not a proper confession if we can see each other's faces."

I'd pinch him a bit to make him get up, and then harder, like he was Gretl. He'd lie there squirming around in bliss. At last I'd really pinch him a good one and he'd leap up, outraged. "See?" he'd tell Gucki, and show her his arm. "See how mean your Mami is?" Then, in a whisper: "She's *awfully* mean, isn't she?"

Gucki was in love again.

I was getting pretty smitten myself. He wasn't like any of the men I'd known. He was like me. He loved to eat and drink, he loved society and crowds and being admired, he was full of big ideas – I loved hearing him talk about the Church – he was talented and lazy. He was full of big vague ambitions. You could see how with a little shove he might go places. He thought so too, and he made it quite plain that he believed I'd been sent to him, in my gold dress, to give him his little shove.

We'd sing and bicker and snack, and after he left I was always a bit guilty to have had such a good time, when Walter was off somewhere in a hole. So for a while I'd picture myself welcoming my husband home and tending his wounds. But the wounds kept getting more heroic, and pretty soon he was passing away in my arms, and then I'd start picturing the mourning dress I'd wear. With a beaded yoke, maybe, and one of the new dropped waists.

It wasn't until Christmas of 1917 that Walter got a furlough to see his daughter for the first time. I told myself how happy I was, but from killing him so often in my dreams I was actually wild with guilt. My flat seemed like a waiting room in a clinic. I sat in all the chairs in turn, trying to find one in which I hadn't already sat and been agitated, from which the view didn't seem dismal, because soon my husband would be there, with his stern narrow head and his slightly stupid look of moral purpose, and then I'd live, not amongst plum cake and admiring glances, but at War. Walter traveled all night and arrived scented with chloride of lime, which the army used to kill corpse-smells. He was grimy, bristly, black as a murderer. When he saw the baby, he grinned.

I stood in front of the swaddling table and wouldn't let him near it.

"Almschi, can't I see my child?" He tried to joke with his weary face. "It's only soot. There wasn't room in the carriages and some of us had to ride in the locomotive. But I had a wash before I went to the station. There's no question of germs. Just a quick look, Almschi? And then I'll go and have another wash?"

At last I said, "Wash now."

THAT SUNDAY everyone gathered round Walter and asked childish questions. Is the fighting very bad? What do they give you to eat? They were like birds perching on a statue. Walter was patient and kind, and I was pleased with him again, and wondered how I could have been so mean to him. Eventually everybody left except Franz. I played *Meistersinger* and *Louise* while Franz sang and Walter tapped a cushion out of time to the music and said Bum-pa-dee, bum-pa-dee.

It was really snowing. "Just listen to it out there," Walter said.

"But it's so quiet," I said.

"Yes. You never hear this kind of quiet except in a snowstorm. With just a bit of wind, like this, and then you get the new snow against the windows. It's so nice. Like little fistfuls of silence against the glass."

"You ought to be a poet yourself, Herr Gropius," said Franz.

"And that's what my men are out in tonight. Ah, well. I suppose it won't be so long before I'm back there with them."

It was the small hours. When I was too tired to play, Franz sang alone and I cuddled close to Walter on the red divan brocaded with chrysanthemums. They seemed as big as cabbages. I liked to have Franz see me with a handsome man. I stroked Walter's neck. I felt I was showing Franz how I stroked a man's neck, some fortunate man's neck. One doesn't just want happiness – one wants one's happiness admired. When our heads were humming from all the song, Franz grew serious and recited his new poems.

> *The fools babble and the overambitious croak*
> *And they call manliness their old excrements.*
> *Just so that the fat women yearn for them,*
> *The chest full of medals*
> *Is vaulting into dawn.*

"That's right," Walter said, laughing, "you tell those soldiers. Bunch of medals and excrements."

"Present company excepted," Franz said with a bow.

"No, no, don't go excepting any company. He speaks his mind straight out, doesn't he?" Walter asked me excitedly.

"You're not shocked?" Franz said. "Opening your home to a pacifist?"

"Oh, I'm a pacifist myself," Walter said. "Here I am, and everything's peaceful, so I'm all in favor of peace. In ten days I'll be back at war, so I'll be all in favor of war. I'll be a war-ifist."

"I admire your flexibility."

"That's it," Walter said, "I'm flexible." And he waved a hand flexibly back and forth. Then he sat up, in order to be sober. "Would pacifism be a Jewish belief? If you don't mind my asking?"

"Ah, you're asking the wrong man," Franz said. "Am I a Jew? Truly? Sometimes, for instance, I think Catholicism is the only civilized system in a desert of materialism. Alma, don't make faces."

I smiled. "Mahler could never pass a country chapel without going in. Every Jew I know is mad for the Church. Maybe it's the incense. Maybe that's a good reason, too – myself, I'm a pagan."

"Oh ho," said Walter.

"You're just being shocking," Franz said. "No one's prouder of her Christianity than you."

"It's true," I said, laughing. "But maybe I'm just proud of the incense and the music. I do think I'm a pagan. I believe in this world. In light. In wine. In my own strength. In my children," I said, lifting my chin. "My husband," I said, and patted vaguely around for Walter's leg.

"You have the luxury of talking that way," Franz said. "You were born safe in Rome's bosom."

"I was born in the Mayerhofgasse."

"But look at this war," said Franz to Walter. "Isn't it the most obvious sort of spiritual emergency? Tearing at each other like rats, blind to God..."

"Yes," Walter said. "You put that very neatly. Blind to God."

"Are you a religious man, Herr Gropius?"

"Me? No. But we've certainly gone blind to something out there."

"Well, leave God aside. Isn't it plain that man has grown brutal, swinish, *degraded*? Crammed by the millions into filthy big cities –"

"Hear, hear," cried Walter.

"– we've turned abstract. We've forgotten there's an Above and a Below. No longer do you find the man driven by soul and spirit, the man of sympathetic emotion, capable of rapture, infused with holy grace – who, in the widest sense, is musical. Instead we see abstraction. That's the great Jewish weakness, of course. It's a legalistic tradition, preoccupied with *deeds*, as opposed to the mission of Christianity, which operates within the *consciousness* of Man. Perhaps I'd be happiest in a world closer to the time of primitive Christianity. Then Jewish and Catholic ethics were joined in one marvelous idea."

"So – you want to convert, then?" Walter asked, struggling on like a soldier.

Franz looked sad. "Even a Jew who regards Christ as the true, historically realized messiah cannot be 'cured' by baptism. He is as completely barred from becoming a Christian as he is from becoming a – a sparrow. An elm. A German."

"Oh, nonsense," I said. "It's just Franz will never make up his mind. He likes to talk."

"It's a form of prayer," Franz said. "I offer up my doubt."

Walter laughed. "You should come round often, Werfel. Do you know, my Alma's genuinely needed a musical friend. Don't worry, Almi, I won't start singing myself!"

It was three in the morning. Franz couldn't leave in all that snow. Since the girl was asleep, I made up his bed. He watched as I snapped a sheet into the air and let it settle, voluptuously, and then again in order to get it just so, and then Walter helped me lift on the feather bed. "You're both being very nice to me," Franz said humbly. In our room, Walter embraced me as I listened to Franz's snores. They sounded hoarse and warm. The gray ceiling seemed to be lit by the swirling snow. My husband's body was gray, too, and moved like a sheet snapped in the air. And his face was gray and shadowy, and I was happy and a little confused about everything, and I thought, Ah. *My husband is a stranger. Some fortunate man.*

Walter went back to the war just before New Year's Eve, just as Mengelberg arrived from Amsterdam to conduct a concert series of Mahler's entire oeuvre. The last of this series was Mahler's Fourth. It had had its première here back in 1901, just after Mahler and I got engaged. He'd explained it to me as a sort of primitive altarpiece with a gold background, but the critics had written that the Heaven of the finale was a Hell in which

Moslems prowled about and that the whole symphony had to be read back to front like a Hebrew Bible. Now, I thought, the world sees its mistake. But none of them had comforted Mahler then, as I did. They're applauding, I thought, in ignorance.

I examined the house through my opera glass. Franz was in a box across from mine. I was fond from comforting Mahler, and I turned this fondness upon Franz. He was in a group of young men from the Military Press Bureau. Their shirt studs glittered, their shirtfronts shone, white and splendid. He seemed a part of the music, the splendid evening, my own splendidness. We met at the interval and went back to my flat. We'd known each other three months. It was the longest courtship I ever had.

A WEEK AFTER Walter went back to the front, Franz left for Zurich to lecture on the war effort. Two weeks after that, I knew something was up. I locked my bedroom door and drew a calendar in my diary – in the back, you know, well away from the rest of my life. I began putting little W's in some squares, for Walter, and little F's in others, then tore out the page and burnt it over the washstand. I hurt my fingers and sat there sucking them, thinking, I don't even know whose it is.

I went to my Breitenstein house early that year. I usually didn't go till late spring, but I needed to think. Maybe one's will was sacred, the way Nietzsche said, but I still had to admit I was in a pickle. If it was Franz's baby, and people found out, that was it. I wouldn't be the patrol leader's heroic young wife anymore. I'd be some no-good slut, and people would stop coming to my Sundays, and worse, I kept remembering how I'd once made a baby out of wedlock and how horribly she'd died. I kept thinking, You can't cheat God. So the smart thing was to get myself fixed, but what if it was Walter's, with marvelous little Aryan nostrils? Except I didn't love Walter anymore. Or anyway, it was more interesting to think I didn't love him.

Meanwhile, Walter was writing me letter after letter. He'd limped away from an aeroplane crash. He was living on turnips and so-called liverwurst. He'd become a communications instructor and had to feed the homing pigeons and train new recruits of forty years old. In July I got a telegram telling me that my husband had been buried for two days under the rubble of an old *mairie* on the Soissons-Rheims line. He was the only one to survive the bombardment – he'd been buried near a broken flue, and that had given him a little air. They sent him to a hospital in the Semmering so he could be close to his pregnant wife, and when I went to see him, the poor man kissed me with cracked lips and called me his best medicine, but in my head we were having a whole different conversation. In my head he'd guessed everything and he rose from his bed like a prophet to call me fickle, shallow, vicious, lusting, and false, counting on his fingers all the while.

Franz was going crazy. He didn't know whether to stay there in Switzerland and hide, or run back and somehow marry me on the spot. He was afraid somebody would open his letters, and wrote them so discreetly that even I had no idea what he was talking about. Then he'd call me up and start whispering. "You've got to have it taken care of. I know a man. Of course you mustn't. It would be a sin. I don't care whose it is. I'll raise it as my own. It's a sign: You've got to marry me. He's no true husband to you, he doesn't understand you – it's merely physical. You've got to marry me. I've grasped the higher meaning of this child. It was *sent* to us, so that, through *it*, I myself could be reborn in *you*. I'm going to desert and come see you right away. You need me there."

"Work," I kept croaking, "you have to work."

I finally let him come see me in middle of the summer,. As soon as we thought everyone was fast asleep, he came to my bed. I was enormously pregnant, but he wasn't gentle with me. I didn't want him to be. I was half insane with the uncertainty, and I wanted things to happen, and I almost didn't care what they were. It was nearly dawn before Franz went back to his room, and when he'd gone, I lay there quietly and felt his love slipping out of me. It seemed to keep slipping out for a long time. The windows were getting light. I touched myself and held my fingertips up near my eyes. They looked black in the dimness, but I knew perfectly well they were red.

I wiped them on the sheet and thought, Now what? I wasn't scared, somehow. I felt far off and a little disdainful about this mess I'd made – almost the way I feel about me now. I didn't want to call for help yet, because I had a society lady named Redlich staying with me and I thought if anybody heard Franz's footsteps just before I called for help, they'd start thinking things. So I lay there bleeding and waiting for enough time to go by so I could call for help without making a scandal.

I kept gazing at the knickknacks on my dresser, which stood between me and the window. I could see the little black silhouette of my perfume bottle. After a while, I couldn't tell what size it was – it was like a great big urn between me and the light. Beside it was a deck of cards, the kind with the bicycle-spoke pattern on the back. I thought I could see the spokes in the darkness, and that they were turning, faster and faster, because the light from the window was getting all wiggly. I was cold. I began hoping I'd lose the child. It would make everything simpler. Maybe I could take my punishment all at once that way, and people would feel sorry for me, as they had after Mahler's death, and I wouldn't have to worry about whose baby it was – no one would think to ask – and I could start over on a clean page. I thought if Walter and I were both in hospital, we'd be even somehow. Or maybe it would be simplest and cleanest if I died too. And then I saw I'd waited too long, that I was about to pass out and die, so stupidly, and I opened my mouth and let out a yell.

It was a good strong yell, and everybody came running. The maid saw me lying there in a heap of bloody bedclothes and fainted. Franz went floundering off through the wet grass to find a doctor, promising God that if I lived, he'd give up smoking. Only Gucki kept her wits. She called Walter, and he climbed out of his hospital bed and got things organized. He made the army doctors tell him about a good gynecologist in Vienna, and he called the man up and got him out of bed too, and they arrived together in a truck the army used for transporting corpses and took me to the Löw Sanatorium, where Mahler died. I was carried from the house with my womb in the air so I wouldn't bleed so much. Everything was upside-down. I was looking up Walter's nose. The Semmering mountains were upside-down, very pale and sweaty-looking, and then we were in the hospital and I heard Walter saying *immediately* and *never* and *that won't be necessary.*

By then I was out of my mind from loss of blood. I imagined the doctors were running around dragging canvas hoses and metal hooks. I imagined that they split me open like an orange and found one monstrous baby after another in there, babies with ribs wriggling like spider's legs, babies with delicate little fins and flaps, babies with a sort of big smeary navel where the mouth ought to be, and that all of them were covered with a stinking slime, because the main thing I knew was that I'd spoilt all the purity in the world and so from now on everything would be filth. The sweat on my face was filthy. The blood in my veins seemed cold and filthy. The light from the window had a mottled, grimy look. After a while I thought I was dead and that my big private room was some closet where they left the corpses, and I thought I could smell myself rot, and the more my room piled up with flowers the more I knew it was true. For three days I lay head-down on an inclined bed, raving and bleeding, and then they cut the child out of me and laid it in a basket. It was a boy, tiny, dark-haired, and fine-featured. He'd been starved of oxygen for a week and then pulled two months early from my thirty-nine-year-old womb, and he wasn't expected to live. He moved like a sea creature, with little mechanical jerks, and had convulsions where his eyes gaped open and his throat closed up. Then he'd lie there, breathing quickly and shallowly, too weak to cry. No, I kept thinking, you can't cheat God.

On Sunday morning they decided my son and I might have visitors. Franz took one look and knew exactly whose it was.

They kept us in hospital for almost a month. The only way I could speak to Franz privately was on the telephone. "I've ruined all our lives," he told me one afternoon. "How does the heart bear such guilt?"

I shut my eyes and said, "There is no such thing as guilt."

Franz began to laugh, horribly. "He's the image of my father. You should call him Martin."

"Is that what you want?"

Here Walter came limping in with more flowers and heard me calling Franz *du*, like a dear one.

He was still pale from shell shock. You could see his whiskers floating beneath his well-shaved skin, like sawdust in skim milk.

I covered the mouthpiece and calmly said, "I am speaking to Franz Werfel. He suggests we name the child Martin."

Walter said, "Martin?"

"Do you like the name?"

He held the bouquet easily by his side, as if it were a pistol.

"Whose child is Martin?" he said.

I put the receiver back in its cradle and folded my hands in my lap.

Walter sat down in the visitor's chair and set the flowers on the table. "All right," he said.

I didn't say anything.

"All right," he said. "Yes. Why should I be any different."

"What?"

"Poor Gustav."

"Please don't say that."

He went over to the basket and rubbed the baby's tummy, looking down. It didn't smile or wiggle, and he took his hand away. "Yes," he said. "It's quite clear when you know what you're looking for. Poor little chap. Do you know, I believe I'm being punished for my conceit. When I first met you, I imagined I was seducing you away from your goodness. A proper married lady. But you are what you've always been. Someone who – You don't even seem to know what you've done."

"I know I've wronged you, Walter. I'm sorry. You have a right to be angry."

"That's what I mean. You really don't know. I go off to war, you've married me, you've *just* married me, and the first thing – Wronged me. Don't you know what you've done? Please tell me you know what you've done."

"I'm very sorry, Walter."

"No," he said wonderingly. "You don't know."

I honestly had no idea why Walter kept saying that. I thought, Haven't I said I was sorry? Can't he see I'm ill? I could understand why he might be angry, but I didn't see why he should look at me in that horrified, almost frightened way, as if I'd opened my mouth and showed him a set of fangs. I never stayed contrite very long, of course, and I was already beginning to get annoyed. I thought, Walter's behaving so oddly. He must still be concussed.

"You meet a man," he said, trying to reason it out. "And then you meet another man... Alma, people don't *act* this way. And all you have to say is you're very sorry. And you're a little angry, too, because you think I ought not to fuss so."

"I don't know what you want me to say, Walter. I really don't feel very well right now."

"And I brought you flowers," he said. "I brought her flowers. But Alma, really, don't you know what you've done?"

"Please. I'm weary. I don't feel well. I can't talk to you."

"It was only a couple of years." He was almost wheedling.

"You only had to wait a couple of years. And I was –" He pointed a finger at the window, then dropped it. "Flowers," he said. "Well, I guess you'd better get some rest." He got a look in his eye and started limping toward the door.

"Where are you going?" I cried.

"To see Werfel," he said. "No, no – what do you think I am? I'm going to tell him to take good care of you. I'm going to tell him it's his turn now."

SOON AFTER THAT, we lost the war. Then the whole business came apart quicker than you can imagine. In Kiel the sailors mutinied, and then everybody else thought, What a good idea, mutiny, and so good-bye to twenty-two princely houses. And in the empire of my childhood, everybody decided they'd had enough imperial glory, all the Germans, Czechs, Hungarians, Jews, Gypsies, Croats, Serbs, Slavs, Slovaks, Slovenes, Romanians, Ruthenians, and Poles. That's it, they all said. From now on we make our own nations and fight our own wars.

Karl I dissolved the Empire, as if it wasn't dissolved already. Then he abdicated. The Socialist chief Renner came to the Summer Palace and said, "Herr Habsburg, your taxi is waiting."

The war left everybody in the most awful shape. In the streets you saw all these mutilated young men, with shiny burn scars, with metal pincers or brand-new jaws made of flesh over hammered tin. People ate a meat made of stewed tree bark. If a book got printed, it was on gray paper with little flakes of wood that glinted like mica schist. There wasn't any coal and you stumbled through town in the dark. In the shop windows you saw little ziggurats of soiled velvet, empty, without goods. You saw dusty zinc basins without ice or fish, apple barrels without apples. If you had a fat little dog, you guarded it like a daughter, and the farmers only sold food secretly, at five times the legal price. So the government printed more money to pay the farmers, and the farmer found his big bundles of notes wouldn't buy him much, and next time he charged, not five times the legal price, but fifty, until at last a crown was worth a thousandth of a kreuzer and in Germany a dozen eggs cost four billion marks, which at one time would have bought every building in Berlin. Next came the Spanish influenza, which killed seventeen millions. It killed Klimt. Egon Schiele sketched him upon his deathbed and then died himself. The doctors had shaved Klimt's beard, and when I saw the drawing I wept, thinking, *I would never have kissed that strange man's face.*

On 12 November the Republic was declared. The weather was rotten, cold and slushy. There were hundreds of thousands of people in the streets, from all over Austria, and everybody was purple-nosed with cold and ready to start something. Franz and some of his Café Central friends ran around making speeches and causing trouble. They'd named themselves the Red Guard after the gang that overthrew the Tsar. From my red parlor I saw them tear the white stripe from the new Republican flag over the Parliament and hoist the red part back up. Then Franz made a speech in which he explained that feudalism was dead, and shot the Parliament in the door to demonstrate. The crowd panicked and two people died, and I sat there listening to the breaking glass, holding a revolver in my lap like a sewing basket. When Martin started crying, I went into the nursery and rocked him with the gun in my pocket. "Bubi Bubi Bubi," I sang. "Bubi Bubi." We called him Bubi, as if he were a normal child that needed a pet name. It was bad for him to get excited, and he began to twitch and retch against my shoulder, so I started smoothing the edge of my hand down his back, which he always seemed to like, until finally he lay silently against me like a sack of sand. I thought, The good days of youth and splendor, that's over. Everything's turning filthy and monstrous. I thought, Martin's a judgment. We've all lost our purity, and now we're going to pay.

After the riot, the Red Guard shoved their way into the offices of the *Neue Freie Presse* and printed a broadsheet to explain that they were unhappy. Franz brought this to me late that night, stinking of liquor and tobacco. "Almi," he said, "look!"

I was a Monarchist, of course.

"Lout," I said. "Animal. Child. Did you think you were still in the café? Consequences!" I screamed in his face. "You won't like the food in prison. Go to Breitenstein until you're called for. I'll have to speak to people, because of you."

"But Almi, at least look. I saved you a copy."

I smacked it to the floor. It left ink on my knuckles.

"If you had done something beautiful," I said, "you would be beautiful now." And I shut the door in his face.

Defeat was very bitter for Walter. He'd suffered a lot for me and for Germany. But now both his loves had betrayed him, so like a lot of people he decided we'd all been wrong about everything and became a kind of revolutionist himself. In April of the next year, the Grand Dukedom of Weimar hired him to run their art academy and their crafts school. Walter combined the two schools to make a place he called the Staatliches Bauhaus. He told me his new Bauhaus was going to reinvent art and industry. We were fighting over the terms of our divorce just then, and I simply said that I hoped so.

Like everyone else, Walter published a manifesto. His was decorated with quite a nice woodblock print of a cathedral made of explosions. *Together,* he wrote, *let us desire, conceive, and create the new building of the future, which will embrace architecture and sculpture and painting in one unity and which will one day rise toward heaven from the hands of a million workers like the crystal symbol of a new faith.* Another Gesamtkunstwerk. He was going to take a steel straightedge and sweep away all the lying antefixae and treble guil-loches. Bauhäuslers would study basic materials and forms. They would live in a Bauhaus community, he dreamt, and grow food in Bauhaus gardens, and be a laboratory to make products that were true to the spirit of the machine and the soul of the worker. The soul of the worker, apparently, was mostly circles and squares. Red and yellow were also very good. Bayer invented a special Bauhaus alphabet with no capital letters, because German was full of capital letters and now nine millions were dead. The inflation made the budget money worthless, and Walter got more by selling Napoleon's silver table service and personal linen, which had been acquired by his soldier ancestors. His nights he spent with excitable new widows. He wasn't used to a woman being nice to him, and he went a little bit nuts. He signed his notes to them *Your planet* and *Your shooting star.* He wrote, *I create* LIFE. *I am a* STING *and a dangerous instrument! I love* LOVE. *You wanted me and I gave myself to you, but: Ask for nothing, expect nothing! Be happy with your new universe.*

I didn't like Walter running around with all these ladies, and I thought his new ideas were the sort of horrid rubbish one might expect now the Empire had fallen. Beauty and nobility would be abolished so that everything would be cheap enough for street sweepers. And I noticed there wasn't much of a role for me in his new world anyway. This gang of his didn't want Heaven's Queen to light their way. They wanted a bare bulb with a tungsten filament. I only visited my husband's school once. The students admired Russian politics and Negro sculpture. We watched them play soccer in a field beside the school, scuttling about on the cold, patchy grass. They were children, with fanatical Adam's apples and peculiar hair, dressed in their old gray uniforms from the war. They ate uncooked mush roaring with garlic. You could smell a Bauhäusler from a distance.

"But it keeps the blood clean," Walter told me.

I thought, I'm glad I had him before he went queer.

Walter looked older now, with two hard creases joining his wolf-nose to his mustache. "It dawned on me," he said. "The old stuff? The old stuff is out. This is a teapot." He picked up half a steel sphere and stuck his thumb out to make a spout. "It's not finished, of course. Here are some splendid photos László's been making without film. Here's a house we're doing from the teak paneling and timber of an old warship. There's our wall-painting workshop. I apologize for the smell. Towers like this might one day replace newspapers – you never know. It would be fifty meters tall. The letters are meant to be mechanized."

It was a sort of electric Tower of Babel, spelling out immense Communist slogans and displaying pictures of hydroelectric dams and leaping athletes. "You've put the prizefighter upside-down," I said. "I suppose it's more modern that way."

"There's been no end of petty obstacles. We aren't exactly loved. After all, this is Goethe's town, and what's a mere Berliner? Pushing, loud, might as well be a Jew. To these good Thuringians the world is now a suburb of Versailles. To think internationally is to be a traitor. I want my daughter," he said. "You and Franz can keep Martin and start fresh."

Everyone had to be starting fresh.

"With you," he explained, "feeling extends only to the short time of passion and sexual fervor."

"When the feeling of limitless devotion to the other has ceased," I explained, "the marriage has ended. That is God's law."

"Well, it's someone's law," he said dryly.

"I see you've a number of women students."

"I think we've all done enough damage to our instincts, Alma. But you needn't worry. They're my charges. I want my daughter."

I was a nineteenth-century ornament. Walter had led his revolution against me.

EVERYTHING I WAS AFRAID OF for Martin came true. He had a short, hideous life. The first time the new Parliament met, his brain began to swell, and in February we put him in a clinic. They confined his huge head in a sort of bonnet, with four linen straps tied to the rails of his crib so that he couldn't roll his skull against the bars. They ordered a cephalic puncture, and then another, but he died in May of water on the brain while I was in Weimar, arguing with Walter about Manon. By that time, I was relieved, as if some terrifying growth had been cut away from me. But I still wept all day, because my Empire was in ruins, because I'd never make a healthy baby again, and because I'd never loved Martin the way I ought to do. However, none of this stopped me arguing with Walter, and I didn't come home. They had the funeral without me.

When I finally took Manon to visit her father, we arrived in the middle of the Kapp Putsch. Kapp was a little civil servant who wanted to kick out the Socialists and put the army in charge. Walter and I watched the workers rioting from the windows of his new flat. The dead lay about amateurishly, as if they were playing a children's game. There was a general strike all over Germany. The streets were dark and smelled awful, because the workers wouldn't let the students bury the corpses that lay heaped up by the cemetery walls. Walter put Manon in an inner room, away from the windows and the gunfire, and managed to get a bucket of water to make tea on his army field stove. In a corner was an apparatus of canvas straps and welded steel tubes. It was made by one of Walter's students and meant to be a chair. Once I'd figured out what it was, I didn't look at it again.

"That fellow's still lying there by the lamppost," Walter said, peering through the shutters. "Poor fellow. I thought I saw him move."

"You're not going down there, are you?" I said.

"In whose aid? To what purpose? Besides, we turned in our guns when we mustered out. They probably sold mine to one of those chaps down there."

It was dusk. Here and there in the street you saw a match flame drawing near to an invisible cigarette. Kapp's men stood without moving while the workers spit on them. On their helmets they wore a black cross with bent arms.

"An old Indian good-luck symbol," Walter told me. "The *svastika*, or *croix gammée*." And he wiggled his fingers as if they were once again cramped round an unhappy pencil.

X

OVER THE NEXT FEW YEARS, I started losing my looks. I still had the eyes, and my skin stayed good for some reason, but my jaw was getting soft and untidy, no matter how I raised my chin. My hair lost that nice bread-blond color. It was yellow now, from a bottle. I was getting stout, too, and I started having all my dresses cut from the same pattern, black and roomy, with full sleeves to hide my arms. But even if I'd kept my shape, the mollige Figur was out of fashion anyway. You were supposed to be a flapper now, like Anna. She was skinny, bosomless, tanned like a laborer, and she went around half naked, her legs all shiny with silk. That's what a beauty looked like now. I wasn't a beauty anymore.

In fact, both my daughters were beauties, though neither was like the other. Anna was blond, with slanting cheekbones and those gigantic blue Gucki-eyes. At sixteen she married a Breitenstein landowner's son. He had no idea of the technicalities and didn't touch her their whole wedding night, and she stopped eating for a week. Then she married the composer Křenek, a real cannibal, who covered every table and chair in my house with music paper. Then she went to Rome with a poor Italian nobleman and studied painting under de Chirico. It was one thing after another with her. Any minute now, I thought, she's going to make me a grandmother. Manon, on the other hand, was brunette and quiet and kept to herself. We called her Mutzi. When she was little, she liked to burrow around in my gowns and study the dressmaker's label for secrets. Later, she'd go out in the garden and lie there with her chin in the grass. If a deer wandered in from the woods, she'd stand still and it would dabble at her with its muzzle. She'd grown up during the Inflationszeit, when we were all eating barley meal and drinking a tea of boiled garden flowers, but she grew up clean and strong on this poor food. She learnt a new language as easily as another child might learn a new song. She said, "Mummy, I'm going to be an actress, like Margarete Anton."

I disapproved of ambition in women who weren't me. I said, "Don't exaggerate. You'd make a fine teacher of Italian."

I remembered becoming a woman as an endless, languorous business, but my girls seemed to do it awfully quick. In general, time seemed to go by faster and faster. From the beginning of one year you could see easily to the end. I couldn't believe life was made of these shabby little years. *Failing everywhere*, I wrote. *Right side of face asleep. My hands slow at the piano.* In fact, I was becoming an ordinary middle-aged woman, but this struck me as dreadfully unfair. I felt that, all my life, people had prevented me with a thousand horrid petty details from reaching the heights I was meant to reach. And now I was growing old, and it was someone else's turn, and I still felt like I hadn't properly begun yet.

Franz was still begging to marry me, but I wasn't so sure he was just what I wanted for a third husband. He lived like a little pig, dirty clothes everywhere, and manuscripts and galleys on top of the clothes, and cigarette ash on top of that. He lived like a child. He told me once that he'd dreamt he was a child in a velvet costume, playing with other children on a sort of stage. And where was I, meanwhile? Chatting with the *other adults* in the parlor. He called this dream *sweet and hot*. He liked it when I shouted at him to work. He'd say, "Now I feel quite serious." Then he'd make a real orgy of working, twelve hours a day, until

he was pale and nauseated. His health wasn't good, and I told
him it was from fiddling with himself. He puffed when he
walked quickly, and he preferred Verdi to Wagner, and I thought
there was something Jewish about the state of his finances and
his suits, and the noises he made while chewing. He was always
puffing a cigar or cigarette, too, because in fact Franz had all the
vices, except he didn't like to drink – no head for liquor. Since I
was always drinking, I resented this, too. I thought it was another
Jewish shortcoming. He kept talking about his Jewish friend Jano-
witz, who'd converted to Catholicism just before he died on the
Italian front.

I'd say, "Well?"

All Franz would say was, "The truly noble were exterminated
in the war. Only we, the brutal ones, remain."

Franz, brutal!

He had great socialist economic theories, this man who got an
allowance from his father until he was thirty-six, and I blamed
him and his radical pals for destroying my lovely Empire. He wrote
an ode on Lenin's death and I screamed, "That well-poisoner!
Eleven pages all month, and two of them for that well-poisoner?"

He screamed, "Who asked you to count my pages?"

The fact is, I never meant for Franz to be permanent. From
the beginning, I was always expecting my next big love to come
along. I started sending Franz away when we'd been lovers a
week, and I kept sending him away for the next ten years. When I
was in Vienna, I sent him to Breitenstein to write. When I was in
Breitenstein, I sent him to Italy. He'd go to the Hotel Imperial in
Santa Margherita Ligure and sit on the balcony with his box of
cigars and his dish of sucking-candies and actually get quite a lot
done. His first novel was called *Verdi*. It sold very well. Since it
was published the year Schacht ended the inflation, we got a fair
bit of money from it. I bought a palazzo in Venice with a walled
clematis garden, and now Franz had someplace to write all the

time. I'd send Manon there, too, to keep him company. Whenever he finished a play or a book, we'd go traveling for a while. That's what *Verdi* did for us, it gave us enough money so we never had to sit at home together. But I still went around all these vacation spots in the rottenest mood. I suspected all the cooking and I didn't think people were respectful, and I spent all my time complaining, like fat old ladies were supposed to do. It was since Martin that everything started seeming shabby and tainted somehow, and there was Martin's father, sitting across from me, chewing with his mouth open. And I began to wonder if it wasn't all his fault.

In December of 1926 we went to the Prague première of Berg's *Wozzeck*. Alban Berg was a pupil of Schönberg, whom I'd promised Mahler to look after. So when he wrote his opera I made Leiser give him money to print the score. I seldom bothered to remember a promise to a person, but a promise to music, now, that was sacred. Once *Wozzeck* was published, the more advanced people saw its worth, and it had a very nice première in Berlin. But the Prague production was a misadventure. Prague was now the capital of the new Czech Republic. If you spoke German, they thought, *Like a Jew. Wozzeck* mixed everything together, the suite, the rhapsody, passacaglia, rondo, plain speech, and Sprechgesang. When the Bürgermeister of Prague had a stroke at the dress rehearsal, everyone said he died from this degenerate music. On opening night, Alban showed up drunk. He scrambled up the step as our train rolled out of Pilsen station, still clutching his glass of Pilsen beer. I had to dress for the opera in our compartment, with the curtains closed and Franz and Alban standing guard in the corridor. We got there just as the curtain was going up. The set was another insult to the new Republic. There weren't any glorious courtyards or pure forests, but just a bare stage, some army cots, and a few dirty soldiers. And then the soldiers began to snore.

So there was a riot. The Bergs had made Franz and me sit in

front of them, to see this opera Alban had dedicated to me, in their box, which he'd filled in my honor with flowers, and because of these flowers everyone knew our box was the composer's box, and they roared, "*Hanba!* Jew! Jew!" The Bergs weren't Jewish – in fact, Helene was one of Franz Josef's illegitimate daughters – but they didn't stick around to explain this. Prudence! The velvet door flapped behind us, and Werfel and Manon and I were alone.

"What does *hanba* mean?" I said.

"*Shame*," Franz said, pouring sweat. "For God's sake, let's go before they kill us."

The performers opened and shut their lips, but couldn't be heard. It was a bit like one of those nightmares in which you can't make a sound. I turned my glass upon the faces in the orchestra seats below. Each seemed distorted by some ill-expressed ruling passion. One of them was reduced to a great mouth, another to an Adam's apple like a bludgeon, another a set of ears waggling in rage, another a great belly pushing blindly along. *Hanba!* Jew! Manon frowned at the noise. She was ten years old. She sat on the floor, tracing the straps and lozenges in the carpet with a leaden elephant. It had come from the mold without a trunk and was her favorite. I put my hand on her head to keep her down where she couldn't be seen. She held her elephant against the carpet as if she was afraid of losing her place. She looked so pure, and Franz looked so wet and unseemly, that I thought, No wonder they shout at him. He doesn't belong here.

"There's always a riot at Berg concerts," I said. "We'll wait for the police. *Mutzi's* not frightened. Try to show a bit of breeding."

At home I got out two schnapps glasses.

"They wanted to kill me!" Franz gasped, his eyes popping from his face.

"Nonsense," I said. "They thought you were Berg."

"They shouted *Jew, Jew!*" he said.

"Because they thought Berg was Jewish," I said, and gave him his glass. "Why don't you think before you make such a fuss?"

The one good thing is, we kept traveling. In Naples I bought a tuning fork, made a sketch of a keyboard, and taught Werfel the musical interval system. In Palestine, the Zionists gave us tea in rusty iron bowls. We sailed up the Nile to Luxor and Karnak and bought attar of roses in the bazaars. We went to a carpet factory in Damascus. Between the looms, bony, crippled children were gathering up spools or stirring the dirt with a broom. Afterward the owner took us to a coffeehouse. Werfel was fascinated by the water pipes, and he bought himself a mouthpiece and smoked. "Who were those children?" he asked, puffing.

"Turkey," said the carpet weaver. "Poor." He showed us an empty palm. "Orphan."

Franz stopped puffing. "All of them?"

"Armenian," the carpet weaver explained.

Back then, no one had heard about the massacres, so the carpet weaver explained, Pasha's Young Turks were Moslems. The Armenians weren't. When the war broke out, Pasha had told the army to make Turkey one people.

Werfel had malaria, as he often did on our travels. A few days later he took to bed. I kept scooping embers from the iron stove to light his new water pipe. All he could talk about was Armenian orphans, and at last I asked our friend Count Clauzel to send us the French embassy's dossier on the subject. Franz scattered the pages over the bed and read steadily, patting his big lips together. He said, "Alma, do you realize the Armenians were the first nation to accept Christianity as their official religion?"

"They seem very dirty," I said.

"In 1915 there were two million Armenians there. In '17, one million. They marched them until they died. They drowned them in their own wells."

"Dreadful."

"Out in the country, they'd beat any beardless man with rakes. You had to have whiskers, at least a fistful," he said, and gripped the air by his bare chin. I'd never seen such a sweaty face. It seemed fashioned of gray glass beads.

"You look awful," I said, and wiped him down.

"I have a taste in my mouth," he admitted.

"You'll worsen your condition with all these massacres." I went to the bureau, put two piasters in a twist of writing paper, and leant out of the window. Outside was the market and the smell of donkeys, roasting pistachios, and urine. I didn't like Syria. I didn't like the dark skin and the yammering voices. Everything was old and chipped, and I objected, in this desert country, to the lack of flower boxes. "You!" I shouted in German. The sweets peddler below held up four fingers. I smiled and held up a forefinger. He made a casting-away motion, looking disdainful. There was a shiny, scooped-out place next to his nose.

"Your big fanny blocks all the light," Franz said behind me. "Alma, pay the poor fellow his price."

I held up two fingers and flung down the twist of paper, and the peddler flung up a bag full of fig balls rolled in poppy seeds. I gave a few to Franz and took a few for myself, and we sat side by side, chewing.

"They're good," he said. "Well, I'm going to write it."

"Oh, for God's sake."

"It will be a statement—"

"You've soaked your shirt through. Sit up a minute, you'll get a chill." I pulled his shirt from his fat little chest and wiped him down with a kerchief. Then I buttoned him into another, saying, "Isn't that better? Another statement. Why must these awful things fascinate you? Illness, poverty, bugs. You should hear yourself talking about those poxy children. You practically lick your chops. Gorge your imagination on any sort of swill – what are you making of your gifts? Here, do you want your pipe?"

I watched him puff away with his sticky lips. I couldn't believe he was going to do a whole book of this rotten stuff. I thought, Like a little dog that eats its vomit. I had a picture of my life, of two sweaty old people in a hotel, and the whole world foreign and smelly.

"Poor Alma," Franz said. "You always fall among low companions. Well, I'll still have to write it. A civilized government ordering the extermination of its own citizens! Of an entire people!"

"As a historical subject," I admitted, "it would be unique."

I WAS STILL DOING a lot of entertaining in those days, and after the enthronement of Cardinal Innitzer, I brought everybody home and gave them lunch. That's where I met a young priest named Johannes Hollnsteiner. He was the cardinal's protégé, a slender, owl-headed gentleman with pale eyes, thick spectacles, and very smart clothes. He'd been making quite a name for himself as a theologian. Everyone said he'd be cardinal after Innitzer. "What's the Mass, after all?" he asked me. "A choir recital? A nice little party one throws for one's soul? No, the Mass is nothing less than Christ striding the earth, *perpetually*." It was very impressive, how he could talk like that while he was eating and still seem mannerly. "Really, I always liked Martin Luther," he said. "He made the most ingenious mischief. But what a chip on his shoulder! After all, the sale of indulgences – he needed a better grasp of the old German concept of *Wergeld*. This man Hitler's a sort of a minor Luther. There are, of course, disparities."

I'd seen Hitler once, in a hotel lobby in Breslau, and was eager to say so.

"What did you think?" Hollnsteiner asked.

I said, "Well. His voice..."

He smiled. "Like the honk of a goose, don't you think? I'm afraid he's not a very prepossessing man. By now, every nightclub comic along the Ku'damm can do the Hitler-voice to perfection."

"I just saw a bit of him, peeping out from behind a young SA man. He had sort of clutching eyes, like a youth at his first dance."

He laughed. "Yes, there's something a bit adolescent about idealism. He spends his days in a bare little rooming-house room. A washstand, a writing desk, a folding screen. During the day it's his office, and at night he sleeps there on an iron bed, like old Franz Josef. Such things don't concern him. After all, the man's used to prison! He won't touch meat. He lives entirely for doctrine."

"I'm not sure he's entirely sound," I said. "My... dear companion is a Jew."

"An illustrious people," Hollnsteiner said. "Though perhaps a bit prone to pride of intellect. I'm afraid we Jesuits know something about that!"

I always loved these luncheons of mine. I loved the clack of my best china and the sheen of good fabric. I loved the grave talk of intelligent men, taking their ease at my table, and I was very impressed with this young fellow. In my diary I called him *the essence of a priest. If I consider the tough, incomprehensible workings of a Hollnsteiner, for whom it is all the same whether he sleeps or eats, then I have to recognize the difference between the well-bred and the mongrels. He is 38 years old and has never met Woman.*

At this point in my life I was a pretty dangerous character. I was in the mood for drastic measures of some kind. On the one hand, I kept examining my life, to see what I'd been up to for the last fifty years or so and if there was anything at all good ahead. On the other hand, I was a middle-aged woman with bleached hair and a sour mouth, who betrayed her men, ignored her children, wasted her talent, and drank like a fish, so when I examined my life, I didn't want to get too specific. What I really wanted to think of was something higher. Well, I knew how you got hold of something higher. You looked around for a man who'd already got it.

I started inviting Hollnsteiner over a lot. He was a professor of canon law at the University of Vienna, an editor at the *Reichspost*, and a judge in the Court of the Vienna Diocese. I used to say, "I could listen to that man by the hour!" The truth is, when we met, I was always talking my head off. I told him how I dreamt I was leading my son home, and that he had golden hair, but streams of muddy water were flowing from our house. I told him how my feet were always cold. I told him how the Bolshevists had spoilt everything fine and uplifting and I read to him from my diary: *Kafka, cubism, communism – it's all the same mange of the heart!* I told him how Jewish melodies all began with a dissonance, because they hadn't found their Messiah yet. I told him how I'd put Franz on a milk diet but he was still very fat. Then after I'd been complaining about Franz awhile, I'd get angry, as if somebody else were criticizing him, and start singing his praises until Hollnsteiner said, "What a great love! It transcends all barriers."

Everybody always told me I was beautiful – even then, if you can believe it – but Johannes was the first man who made me feel like I had political ideas. He explained how people of good will like me were already working to free themselves from old errors. He made it sound like the Church and the Nazis were really advocating the same thing: purity. I thought, *Purity.* You know, that sounds pretty good.

The funny thing was, it was Franz who first got me thinking about the Church again. I wasn't even a Catholic anymore. Back in 1900, I'd gone along with Gretl when she became a Protestant to marry Legler. She was scared to go alone. The pastor prayed with his back to us. I thought the whole thing was terribly funny. The only religion we had growing up was a few prayers our Catholic maids taught us. I told Johannes all this, and it just made him more enthusiastic about what he called my problem. I was awfully fond of him. You should have seen him polishing his spectacles. Like a scientist adjusting his microscope, and when he was done, how they gleamed! His nails were perfect, his hair was sleek, and his shoulders were narrow. I could have flung him from hand to hand like a medicine ball. His voice was supple, and he had a way of making things seem decent and logical. He'd drop a lump of sugar in his tea, crush it with the tip of the spoon, and say, "Ah, perhaps you're too hard on your friend. He sounds like a fine man, very tenderhearted. And perhaps you haven't made allowances for his, how shall one say it? His spiritual disadvantages."

I was confessed by Father Müller and received back into the Church. Each afternoon I went to Mass at the Stephansdom. My heels would clack as I walked in, and the echoes would rise up and sound very stately, and I thought God must be listening with approval. Father Müller would nod to me as I slipped into my pew – always a little late – and I'd look round until I found the back of Hollnsteiner's well-barbered head. And then I'd forget God and spend the rest of the Mass thinking about Johannes. He was very busy just then. He was writing newspaper articles about Elisabeth of Thuringia and Germanism and Mahatma Gandhi, and trying to finish his second book, A Survey of the Jurisprudence of the Rota Romana Regarding the Annulment of Marriages. I thought they were expecting too much of the poor man. One day when we were all kneeling waiting for the Host, I decided Johannes needed someplace quiet to work. Scholars used to have patrons, I told myself. Why shouldn't I be Johannes's patron?

It didn't take long to find him a smart little flat, with diamond-shaped panels in the doors and wallpaper striped diagonally in taupe and ecru. Once I got him settled there, I used to show up with a basket of food, because I thought he was too skinny. I'd bring cold sturgeon, bread and goose liver, pear preserves, chocolate truffles, mandarines, beef tea, and a bottle of champagne. I'd pile it all on the table and he'd be almost stammering. "This is –" he'd say, "this is most..." But I'd already be looking around for something else to fix up. "I don't like these little rugs," I said one afternoon. "What's the idea of all these little rugs?"

He said, "They're quite the thing now. Herr Wärndorfer's got a few in his study and they look quite smart."

"That's what I mean, it's Jewish taste. You'll slip on one and break your neck." I was at his desk, counting his pages. "All this Latin!" I said, approvingly.

"It's not a difficult language. The logic's so clear it almost teaches itself. A musical woman like yourself could pick it up in no time."

I read, "*But to speak of the soul's 'purpose' is to mistake the matter entirely. The soul has no earthly purpose; it is God's instrument.* Really excellent. People need these ideas. When there's so much confusion and nonsense about. You should write a book about it."

"About...?"

His manners were so good that I wanted to ruffle his hair up and then smooth it back again. I wanted to take charge of him. "You should write a book. We'll plan it out together. I'll *help* you," I said, and I drew him into my arms.

Aflame and appalled, he covered my mouth with his, as if he was afraid of what I might suggest next.

So I returned to the Church, but I returned in my own way.

ONE AFTERNOON a bit before my fiftieth birthday, Manon came in from the garden with her fist against her breast. Her fingers were shiny and black as raspberry jam.

Franz was in the parlor, listing the emotions he intended his next book to arouse. He leapt to his feet and screamed.

"What a noise you make, Franz," I said. "Mutzi, what have you done?"

She'd gotten kicked by a deer.

"It's nothing," she said. "It was my fault. I only need a bit of sticking plaster. Please tell Onkel Werfel it's nothing."

"I don't know what's nothing until I see," I said.

Obediently she unfastened two buttons behind her neck and lowered her dress to her waist. She cupped a red hand for the blood. Her muscles were clean as folded linen, her collarbones were fine and straight. Breeding! We were shocked by her breasts. The tips were stiff, as if pain excited her. "It was my fault," she said. "I frightened her. I knelt down and she didn't know what I was doing. I thought I could teach her to shake hands, like a dog. Why would she want to learn a stupid thing like that? So I got a hoof in the chest, and now she thinks I'll hate her."

"Shame!" I shouted at Franz. "What are you looking at?"

"Oh, she's growing up," he said, full of sorrow, trotting from the room.

"I only need a sticking plaster," Manon said, "and then let me go back out? so she sees me, and knows it's all right."

"Sit here in the light," I said. "Press my handkerchief against it. It's clean. Mutzi, you're becoming a young lady and you mustn't run about nude."

"Yes, I expect you're right."

"Well, thank heaven it's down where no one ought to see. What a scare you've given us."

"I'm sorry."

"You think you make a lovely picture with your cattle. But they're filthy beasts and put their hooves in anything. And what if you get blood poisoning so your teeth lock shut and your toes turn black?"

"I expect you're right," she said.

It was two o'clock. I'd drunk maybe a third of my daily bottle of Bénédictine. I was full of indolence and couldn't understand why the world was such an awful place where daughters got hurt and you never had any peace. And what if there was a scar? Didn't anyone think of these things but me? "My heart," I said, patting it. "My heart won't stop."

Franz shuffled back into the room with a hand up before his eyes, holding out a steaming pot. "I had them boil some water."

"Oh, Onkel," Manon said, laughing, "are you making soup?"

I rang for Manon's nanny, Sister Ida, and the first-aid box, and she came and led Mutzi away. "What were you leering at?" I said to Franz. "Shame. She's not your daughter."

"And if she were my daughter it would be all right to leer? I was surprised, that's all. Pup, there they were," he said, and set the pot down on the end table.

"Not there, you fool!" I shouted, and snatched it up before it could ruin the varnish. I didn't know what to do with it, so I bent down, with some difficulty – I was getting quite stout – and set it on the rug. When I stood up, I was puffing and red-faced, and all at once I was in a rage. "You and your hot water," I shouted. "You just wanted an excuse to come creeping back. You're a dirty man and I'm not surprised your pulse is spotty and your seed is degenerate."

"What," he gasped, "what was that about my seed?"

"And I'll tell you this: I'm not going to marry you. We're not suited."

"Fine!" he yelled. "You're right! You're a millstone around my neck! You've never had the least bit of faith in me, the least bit of respect! All you do is belittle! You can go straight to hell! I'm leaving, I'm leaving this minute!" Then he said, "What do you mean, not suited?"

"We're not spiritually suited," I said.

"You called me your miraculous miracle," he said.

"You don't really want to marry me. You won't do what's necessary."

"What do you mean?"

I got up and went to my desk. I fetched paper and pen.

"Here," I said.

"What? What are you doing?"

"It's time for a decision. We've talked long enough." I held out the pen and paper and said, "Choose."

Until that moment, I'd never seriously thought about turning Franz into a Christian. It had just been one of those notions you kick around. But suddenly it seemed like the answer to everything. All at once I decided that Franz had been muddling along for ten years, living like a pig, admiring the wrong people and thinking the wrong things, dragging me down just when I was trying to go higher, and that he needed to do what I'd done, what Mahler had done – Mahler, who created noble things like the Eighth and who'd never dream of writing squalid books about Armenians with dirty feet. I told him, "You're not a bad man, Franz. You've just got a head full of all this café garbage. You come of an illustrious tradition, but you suffer from pride of intellect. You imagine all these degraded types only want a bit of kindness before they'll be proper little glovemaker's sons. You enjoy troweling around in the muck because the heights, the true heights, frighten you. But the man I marry won't be afraid to join me on the heights. The man I marry will understand that his soul is God's instrument. He won't pollute himself with tobacco and self-abuse and all sorts of sordid theories, and he'll be a fit father for Mutzi. Now, you've been nattering on about your *magna mater* the Church since the day I met you. What I want to know is, has it all been just talk?"

I was a bit out of breath, but pleased. I felt I'd been speaking very well.

"You want me to convert!" Franz cried. "To abandon my people!"

I said, "Well, Franz, you'd better abandon something."

"You want me to sign an *oath*? Under *duress*? I won't!" he shouted. "Not... like this. Not now."

"Then do something to show good faith. Write that you've renounced alien laws. Write that you've resigned from the Jewish community, or I'll tell you right now, the wedding's off for good."

I saw a word between his stained teeth: *No*. And then it turned, and crept back down his throat.

"I shall not question your decision," I said, as Mahler had once said to me, and then I went off to see about my daughter.

Ida had bandaged Manon and tucked her up in her bed. "Nasty," Ida told me. "But it's all right. I cleaned it with a bit of vermouth. That's the best thing."

"I didn't mean to cause such trouble," Manon said.

I sat on the side of her bed and smoothed back her hair. "What a fright we've all had. I shouldn't worry about having a scar."

"Do you think there'll be a scar, then?" she asked.

"Exactly," I said comfortingly, because I hadn't heard her. "And what if there was? It's not such a bad thing for a woman to have a few imperfections for a man to discover. It makes him feel he knows secrets. Besides, if a woman's too perfect, that denies a man the pleasure of forgiveness."

"All right, Mummy."

"Who even knows if they'll be wearing décolleté dresses in a few years? Fashion is a funny thing. Such lovely dark hair," I said, stroking it slowly. "Does that feel nice?"

"Mmm," said Manon.

"Just like your father's," I told her. "Soon it'll be time to start putting it up."

FRANZ FINISHED his Armenian novel three years after we were wed. He called it *The Forty Days of Musa Dagh*. It was about the massacres, and about five thousand Armenians who gathered in the mountains of Musa Dagh and fought the Turkish army for forty days. Actually, they fought for twenty-four days, but Franz liked forty better. It sounded more biblical. The rest of the world must not have agreed with me that Franz's subject was squalid and unsuitable, because the book was an enormous success, and eventually got published in eighteen languages, and made Franz the hero of the Armenian people, because no one had ever told their story before. We went to Paris and mobs of Armenians tore our suitcases from the porters' hands at the Gare du Nord. They dragged us to a fête on the Left Bank, where they roasted truffles in the embers of the fireplace and drew water glasses of brandy from big casks. After a while Franz disappeared and I had to go looking for him. I found him in the lavatory, running cold water over his neck. All this was very nice, and I forgot all about how I'd objected to the book, and was pleased with myself for making Franz work. And, of course, I was pleased with all the money. I right away started looking for a bigger house, because by now my salon was the foremost in all Vienna and I felt it needed a better home than the Elisabethstrasse flat where Kammerer's lizards used to climb the breakfront.

I was very particular about what I should do with Franz's money, but at last I bought a villa in the Hohe Warte next door to the villa I'd lived in with Mami and Moll. Hoffman had built this one, too, and it was one of the biggest houses in Vienna. It had three floors and twenty-eight rooms trimmed in marble, and the same good view of the vineyard hills of Kobenzl and Kahlenberg that I'd used in my late girlhood to help me think fine thoughts. In the halls I hung paintings by Oskar and Papi. I put Mahler's manuscripts in glass cases, like a museum. There was a nude statue in the garden, but I had the gardener grow ivy over the danger spot, and for Franz I made a big studio in the attic, with a spinet on which he could pick out *Rigoletto* with one finger and a soundproof iron door, so he could write undisturbed.

Then I threw a party that lasted from eight in the evening until two the next afternoon. It was probably the biggest I ever had. The *Neues Wiener Journal* needed a full column for the guest list: the Chancellor, Elias Canetti, Berg, Schönberg, Conrad Veidt, our friend Felix Salten who wrote *Bambi*, Georg Reimers of the Burgtheater and Generalmusikdirektor Bruno Walter and a dozen Burgtheater stars, including one who was Countess Thun in her private life and another one who was waiting to become Princess Starhemberg. Franz went giggling out into the garden with a litter of little pink-nosed baronesses and stripped the ivy from the statue's groin. Hollnsteiner was in his usual place by my elbow. I twisted the cap from a bottle of Bénédictine and said to everyone, "Have you met my daughter Manon? From Gropius, a tall handsome fellow. Aryan to his fingertips – the only man who matched me racially. No one can hold a candle to her. You don't mind my saying that, do you, Gucki?"

Poor Anna was used to this sort of thing. All she said was, "Well, it's getting a bit late for me. Good night, all."

"For me, too," said Manon. "I'll just go say good night to my friends."

"Yes?" said a red-faced *chargé*. I'd known him for years. He always used to be chasing after me. Now he watched Manon very carefully as she walked onto the back lawn. Manon was fourteen years old and still slender, but she was no longer equally slender everywhere. "Her friends?" he said.

"The swans," Anna said. "Good night."

"I wouldn't mind seeing these swans," said the *chargé*.

I took hold of his wrist and drew him across the room. He said, "Ow."

I said, "Now, here's something that should interest you. A fresco by Kokoschka himself. We're great friends. That's me you see up in the sky. Hm. Perhaps in the next room."

"In your Breitenstein house," Hollnsteiner murmured.

"And here's the original score of Bruckner's Third. I have locked it in this box. Bruckner always had his hair cut by Wagner's barber. One sees genius in every stroke of his magnificent hand."

"Might we see it?"

"No. Here is Mahler's desk. Here is Mahler's Tenth. The cover sheet!"

Von Schuschnigg leaned close and said, "He's written something on it. Yes. *Why hast Thou forsaken me?*"

"Oh, he was excitable."

"Hung on the wall like a trophy," sighed Zemlinsky, who'd come with his wife.

Gerhart Hauptmann bowed and said, "In another life we must be lovers. I make my reservation now."

Frau Hauptmann said, "I'm sure Alma will be booked up in the next life, too."

"Where's what's-his-name?" I said. "The *chargé.*"

"I think I saw him go out on the lawn," someone said.

"Purity," I said between my teeth, "was a great theme of Gustav's. Surprisingly, he proved himself *the* great interpreter of *Tristan.*"

"Surprisingly?" Franz yelped. "Why surprisingly?"

"One never ceased to be surprised," Hollnsteiner said, "at the richness of Herr Mahler's gifts."

"Now, Franz, not every word everyone speaks is aimed at your heart. Even you won't claim Mahler was German? I merely meant that, for a man of another race, Mahler had a fine understanding of the German spirit. Very pertinent to our current struggles. To forge a national will one requires an active, resolute sort, a Siegfried."

"Siegfried! Tristan! Gristle-heads, butchers, braggarts, louts!"

"Franz," I explained, "is kind."

"Slaughter the dragon for his gold! Slaughter the old man who raised you! The place is going to hell!"

"Oh, now. I dined with Chancellor Brüning –"

"*We* dined," Franz shouted. "Ex-chancellor."

"– and he explained it all very neatly. German unemployment is actually nonexistent. For instance, there is a standing army of eight hundred thousand who are fed for three years."

"My God."

"Franz is angry with the Germans because they won't sell his books anymore. Well, Franz, I suffer from this too. But you mistake the thinking behind it. My friend Margharita Sarfatti, Mussolini's close companion, is very clear on the subject. Anti-Semitism is actually an alien policy."

"Always this obsession with what is and is not alien!"

"Now, Franz," Hollnsteiner said. "Surely you won't deny that each of the world's peoples has its own – well, I won't say 'soul.' But what's wrong with a nation trying to strengthen its own essential character? Don't you do exactly that when you write one of your novels? Try to clarify what's central?"

"There," I said. "No one's calling Jews inferior."

"Merely extraneous? I am a Jew," he shouted, all purple. "And I am your husband."

"I love your higher nature," I said.

"I have one nature," he roared, "and it is Jewish and I shall never forsake it."

"But you did," I said. "I have the paper in my files somewhere."

He rushed out in a rage, he rushed back, he roared, he cajoled, he cited statistics, he quoted the Kabbalah and the *Deutsches Volksblatt*, but to everything I said *It's an alien policy* and *I love your higher nature* until Hollnsteiner was afraid for Franz's heart. Two hundred guests watched the sun come up in our back garden, but Franz ran off, in his creased evening clothes, smoking furiously, and met with Anna at a café.

By now Anna had left her third husband – Franz's publisher's son. She'd set down her paints and begun to sculpt great mythic forms. She was thirty years old and declared it was wrong for a Socialist to wear cosmetics. The truth was, she knew she didn't need any. She yawned in Franz's face with her hard lovely mouth and said, "You haven't been to bed yet, have you? Poor Tubby. What's Mami been doing to you now?"

"I'm being asked to bear too much!" he hissed.

"Ah," she said. "That little creep."

"The thing is, I like him," Franz said sadly. "I have a great, great deal of love for genuine and serious priests."

"Serious? *Genuine?* Sweetheart, not another cigarette, you look ill."

"But I've got to sit and hear how incomprehensibly tough he is and how he doesn't care if he eats or sleeps! Oh, he doesn't mind eating, I can tell you! She stuffs him with champagne and caviar, and buys it with *my* money, because it's *all* my money these days, now that they've quit doing Mahler, but do you know what she calls it? What she spends on the house, that house she bought in *her own name*, she calls *our money*, and what she spends on herself she calls *household money*, and the few pitiful kreuzer I beg for myself, do you know what she calls that? *Franz's spending money.*"

"Your face is the most frightening color. Franz, what are you saying?"

"Oh, I should show a little generosity. After all, it's her last fling. It's heartbreaking to watch her with those creaking gallants – do you know what it is these days to worship the divine Alma? An ancient Viennese ritual! One links one's name with Mahler, Kokoschka, Klimt. But it's Mutzi they stare after, and can you imagine their fat faces if Alma asked them to come upstairs and worship in comfort? And she *knows*. So why shouldn't she have a last bit of fun with a man who doesn't know what a healthy young woman's like? Heaven knows I've no right to prate about fidelity."

"Oh, not with a priest! Even Mami, Franz, she couldn't!"

"But I owe her so much, Annerl. If I hadn't met Alma, I'd have written a few good poems and gone happily to the dogs."

"Well, what are you going to do?"

"But if she calls me her *man-child* one more time, *even one more time...*"

"What are you going to do?"

He placed both elbows on the table to call himself to order.

"I'm going to leave her!" he said.

Quite often he made this decision.

THE BIG STOCK-MARKET CRASH was awful for Germany, but it was excellent for Hitler, because he understood it perfectly and was always happy to explain. He went around saying, Who whispered in the ears of the November criminals, the authors of this criminal peace? Whose stealthy fingers ran the printing presses spitting out worthless marks? The Jews, he told everyone, were a ferment of decomposition. They'd managed to preserve their race and character by millennia of inbreeding but lacked the organizational ability to make their own nation. So they schemed to press other nations in the vise of unearned interest. By 1932, six million Germans were out of work, and in the Reichstag elections, the Nazis got six million votes. This number they'd soon make famous. And Hindenburg dismissed von Schleicher and made Hitler Reichskanzler in his place.

In his diary Franz wrote, HOW TO GET RID OF HITLER: *Have papal bull sent to German bishops. On boycott days, Jewish restaurants should establish Christian-only free lunches.* In Insterburg he tried to lecture on Art and Conscience and the police let the students chase him from the hall.

I found Johannes a great comfort while all this was going on. "Unpardonable," he said. "But why give the louts an excuse?"

I said, "I'm always telling Franz he ought to think."

Hitler burnt the Reichstag and said the Communists did it, and that now he had to have emergency powers over everything. The students in all the university towns burnt the works of Kafka, Freud, Einstein, and Franz. The SS bands played beside the bonfires.

"Now, the very worst thing Franz could do," said Johannes, "is make a fuss. This isn't the time to plead for special exceptions."

Hindenburg died. *Musa Dagh* was banned, so he tried, poor Franz, to join Goebbels's Reich Association of German Writers. He wrote that he was German in his heart.

"Franz is being very sensible," Johannes said.

Our own chancellor, Dolfuss, was a tiny fellow. We called him Millimetternich. When he closed the Parliament, there was a general strike and Prince Starhemberg fired his cannons upon the strikers. "You've got to stand up to worker provocation," I said. "What are these so-called housing projects? Fortresses. The walls are full of ammunition."

"You've thought this through," Johannes said.

"I had it directly from Starhemberg's lips."

Von Schuschnigg, the Minister of Justice, invited me to his house to be safe from riots, but I was comfortable. I packed a trunk, called for champagne, and drank it standing.

"The nerves of a soldier!" Johannes cried.

The Austrian Nazis killed Millimetternich, so Schuschnigg was chancellor.

"A distinct improvement," Johannes said. "A civilized man. I think Franz would agree."

But I still wasn't easy in my mind. One day I saw a crowd on the Schulerstrasse. I could tell by the noises and the way they held themselves that someone in the middle was getting a beating. In fact it was just two drunken students having a brawl. But the first thing I thought was, *Oh, God. They've got Franz.*

The worse things got, the more I needed Johannes around to explain things. I packed Franz and Manon off to Venice again and went to see him every afternoon. It was a funny affair we were having. I was proud to have bagged a priest, a big one – oh, yes, I was proud of it – but it wasn't what you'd call a white-hot romance. I'd just had my time of life. The act didn't really inter-est me anymore. The little we did left him exhausted, and he'd drop right off to sleep. I never slept much, so I'd go to the side table and have a schnapps. By my feet was one of those annoying little rugs, which I'd slide back and forth with my toes, and I'd watch him sleep, jerking his legs around like he was fleeing.

I used to pass the time playing Patience and humming. I'd think of Franz and Manon in Italy, in that nice house I'd gotten them, taking it easy in the sunshine. I'd tell myself that I'd bring them home just as soon as everybody calmed down. I dreamt up a special medal for distinguished Jews with which Franz could travel safely through the Reich. It would be a bronze swastika entwined with a six-pointed star, surrounded by laurel leaves. I was pleased with this idea, and wondered who I could suggest it to. I unlatched my journal and wrote: *I'd like to see the Emperor come back. Let's have splendor and pomp to look up to again, and a knuckling under, a silent knuckling under of the servile masses. Their howling is a hellish music to any refined ear. Tolstoy thought he heard angels in it, but it was his own voice he was hearing, just as in great silences or empty spaces the sound of your own blood pulsing rushes in from outside. What do you earthbound morons know of the vast happinesses I derive from my imagination, from the intoxications of love, of music, of wine – and my strong religious feelings underneath?* Then I'd pour another schnapps and scuff my feet on the rug to warm them up.

One evening the telephone rang. "I'm sorry?" Johannes said, blinking. Without his glasses, his eyes looked bruised. "I'm sorry? Alma," he said, with his gleaming hand over the mouthpiece, "I believe this woman wants you."

It was Sister Ida, from Venice. There was an awful din over there, everybody wailing. *"Camphor!"* she sobbed. *"Camphor!"*

Then Franz got on the line and said, "You'd better come."

Manon was sick. I flew in on the morning plane with Anna, von Zsolnay, and a Viennese specialist named Friedmann. Manon's face was all wet and yellow. Her lips seemed thinner and I could see her teeth. There was something desperate about her teeth. She looked like a little animal that survives by biting things. I was stupid with panic, and all I could think was, *She looks so awful. She looks so awful. Maybe if I combed her hair, she'd look better.* "What a crowd," she drawled, with the sweat trickling down her neck. "Is it really so boring in Vienna?"

Friedmann took her foot in his hand. "Press against my palm," he said. "Press, now!"

"I'm pressing. I think."

"And now the other."

"Perhaps this one's a bit better?" she said.

"Poliomyelitis," Friedmann whispered in my ear, like a beau. "I'm sorry."

I NEVER CARED properly for any of my children, but I liked thinking about them, especially Manon, and for years I'd carried round a little reverie of her, as tiny and clear as a picture in a locket. It had come to me one night as I was dropping off to sleep. I'd seen Manon flying over endless rows of youths in uniform. Their cheeks shone like lead as they looked up. She held a sword before them, to drive them back or maybe to urge them forward, and she kicked slowly along the way a swimmer does, her legs bare, or maybe she was naked, but there was nothing unseemly about it, because she was beautiful and graceful as, I thought, Truth. That's the way I always liked to think of her, beautiful and pure and above everybody. And now her legs were hopeless dead stalks and she moved her arms like a crab.

They'd declared a quarantine for polio victims, so when we got Manon home, we had to shut her up in her room. Franz and I would try to chat with her through the closed door. He said she always sounded very calm and witty in there, but I couldn't hear her and my replies never made any sense. From then on, I didn't picture her as flying around. I pictured her as that shut door. Wherever I went, I always knew just where that door was: just down the hall from me, or just up the stairs or, when I went to town, just a few kilometers west, at the end of the Number 37 line.

I'd sit at my piano and reckon it up. When I was sixty, Manon would be twenty-three. When I was ninety, she'd be fifty-three. And she'd still need someone to dress her and undress her and wash her, and give her an enema when she couldn't move her bowels, and wipe her when she succeeded. There'd never be an end to it, and every year she'd get uglier – that's the only part I could really imagine. And when I thought of her locked up in her room, losing her looks and being so calm and witty about it, I knew the world was a worse place than I'd ever dreamt.

At last she was well enough to come out. She toured the house in her new wheelchair.

"It feels delightfully lazy to roll about like this," she said. "However, you've all grown quite tall."

We tried to take her mind off things. She had an American friend, with whom she'd correspond in French, a publisher's daughter who could have been her twin. I brought this child to visit so she'd have company, but it didn't work out. Manon was too weak for so much French. Franz taught Mutzi the leading role in his translation of La Forza del Destino. We rented costumes and I played the piano. Carl Zuckmayer the playwright declared, "Once she's well, I'll marry her, paralyzed or not." He gave her a little snake, and she kept it on her counterpane and called it Carl. Horch gave her acting lessons, and the actor Krauss was there every day. Manon cast him as Hamlet and directed him from her wheelchair and made him recite the soliloquy over and over until he got it right.

Franz found my old saucepan, all smeared with lead, and on New Year's he insisted we have a lead casting. We let Manon wear a pearl necklace of mine she'd once admired. She folded her hands and looked pleased. "Can you pour, do you think?" Franz asked.

"You needn't baby me," she said. It was true, her lovely arms had grown hard from rolling the chair. She was nineteen years old now and her face was shaped with great decision. We'd put on her leg braces so she could use her crutches. The knobs and bolts were visible beneath the silk. They made her seem armored, like Saint Joan. She said, "Just get me near enough."

"The metal," I warned them, "is hardening."

Franz held her lightly by the shoulders so she could take one hand from the crutches. She wound a cloth round the saucepan's handle and lifted it. A little twist, and a spark of lead curved down into the pot, with a hiss that had stopped before you'd properly heard it. Then she carefully set the pan back on the grate.

"You've hardly poured any," Franz complained.

She said, "How much do you need? Well. It seems seed-shaped, doesn't it? So smooth, with that little nubbin tail. Let's look it up. Here. SEED. *Youth & Secrecy. Buried Beginnings. A Year of Endeavor.* Hm – that's all right. I don't mind that. And now you, Onkel."

Franz poured in a great gush that hid him in steam.

I said, "Franz, must you pour *everything* in?"

"This way," he said, "I'll have lots of future."

He needed two spoons to lift it out – a huge, knotted, dripping lump. "This will take some thinking about," he admitted.

I said, "It's a monstrosity."

"Tut," he said. "And now it's your turn."

"No. I'm too old for this nonsense."

"Come on, Almschi. There's still a bit left."

Shuddering, I cried, "*I'm not going to pour out some last little bit you've left me!*"

ON GOOD FRIDAY 1935, Manon was diagnosed with bowel and stomach paralysis. She got X-ray treatments, but that just worsened her fever. On Easter Sunday she asked for the priest, but on Monday she seemed a bit better, and I sat on her bed and discussed her *Hamlet*. "Where you make your mistake," I said, "is in imagining him as a heroic type. A prince with an itchy conscience is a man beset by feebleness. He mustn't swagger, he mustn't pull noble faces. Now, if you ask Werner to read his lines like a coward! Ah, then I think your play would be considerably more successful."

She considered for a moment. Then she said:

"Let me die."

I couldn't say anything. It was as if she'd emptied all the air from the room.

"I'll never be well again," she said. "Let me die. This, this horrible play – You'll get over it, Mummy, as you always get over everything."

I made a *Mutzi* with my lips.

"I mean," she said contritely, "as everyone always gets over everything."

Mutzi was buried at Grinzing beside Mahler and Putzi. I took to my bed, and Franz went alone. When he came back, his face was swollen and trickling like a pricked wineskin. He'd been trying to drink liquor. "You were unkind to her," he said.

"No, Franz," I said. "We did all that could be done."

"You wanted her to teach Italian."

"I... what?"

"*You wanted her to teach Italian*," he wailed. "You only liked that she was pretty. But oh, no, you didn't want to spend your life nursing a cripple. You've been waiting to play the bereaved widow. Oh, you'll do it well and they'll admire you, but you're cold. You're cold. I've given my life to a cold woman, and you should have been minding your daughter instead of off somewhere fucking priests."

"You're upset," I said pleadingly, "you don't know what you're saying. Watch what you're saying," I gasped. "Be careful!"

"The great *femme fatale*, the great *amoureuse*!" he wailed. "But you don't love anyone, you've never loved anyone – you haven't the knack. You bought him champagne and caviar. With *my* money."

"You horrible man!" I shrieked, and began to weep.

"All you know how to do is put on a good show. Even your tears are big enough to be seen from the fourth balcony."

"*Stop it!*" I screamed.

"A teacher of Italian, a poor dead skinny teacher of Italian."

"*Stop it! Please, please!*"

"We were both unkind, but you were her mother. No, I won't listen. You were unkind," he cried. "You were unkind."

Weeping, he climbed up to his studio in the attic and shut the iron door.

XI

Franz never forgave me.

After this, it was Franz's turn to decide that I was to blame for everything. I'd sent Manon off to Venice to catch the plague, and now my pal Hitler had passed the Nuremburg Laws, and it was all because I didn't know how to love. He slept up in his studio and stopped coming by my room at night. At mealtimes he stared at his plate. If I sat down at the piano, he left the room, and he wouldn't sing for me anymore, except sometimes he went around humming *La Donna è mobile:* Woman is fickle as a feather in the breeze.

Later this made me horribly sad, but at first it just riled me up. The more he scorned me, the more I thought, *I'll show you.*

I didn't know what, but I was going to show him.

Soon after this, Hitler summoned Schuschnigg to Obersalzberg. Franz and I were in Milan at the time, in Verdi's old rooms at the Grand Hotel, which is where we stayed whenever we were in town, and we listened to the whole thing on the radio. It was quite an aria Hitler sang. He told Schuschnigg that all Nazi prisoners had to be released. He said the Hitler salute and the swastika had to be made legal. Otherwise, he wouldn't wait to annex Austria. He'd do it right then. Franz got up and wandered into our parlor to touch Verdi's old pianino. *Plink,* he went, *plink.*

"Your friends," he said.

It's funny how quick I forgot all the nonsense when I heard

the news. About my special little medal, and Johannes's nice talk, and all the rest of it. I remembered the crowd on the Schulerstrasse, that had looked capable of anything. I thought, So much for Vienna. My mind got very cold and clear, as if a man had been loving me, and I began figuring at a great rate. We couldn't just go to the Venice house – Mussolini and Hitler were too buddy-buddy. We had to pack and close up two houses and get hold of our money somehow, but if we went home, they might not let Franz go again. I started getting angry. I felt as if everybody was suddenly telling me where I could live and where I couldn't, when I'd been having them all to my house for tea and cake! And I was angry at Franz, too, because I could tell by the look on his face that he was expecting me to do something low.

"Let's talk about what we're going to do," I said.

"Do?" Franz said. "Maybe I'll see you after the war."

"Don't be absurd. You're my husband."

"We can fix that."

"Don't be absurd. If Vienna isn't your home, it isn't mine."

"No need to trouble yourself," Franz said, plinking away at the pianino. "Your friends will be happy to see you. I'll go to California and write movie scenarios."

"Franz, you couldn't find California on a map."

"I'll find someone who reads maps," he said.

Alma, I thought, this man doesn't like you.

Europe must be finished, if there was a man in it who didn't like me.

I left Franz in Milan and went back to Vienna alone. I started packing our trunks and emptied out our bank account in hundred-schilling notes – larger bills were forbidden. Sister Ida and I spent all day sewing the notes into her girdle, and then she put on the girdle and went to Switzerland. Each night I listened to the Stukas groaning in the sky. Each day I passed the German Tourist Office on the Kärntnerstrasse. They'd put Hitler's picture in the window, and weeping women heaped up flowers beneath it until they blocked the pavement.

I took a last walk round the Ringstrasse. Moll lent me his swastika armband so I wouldn't be bothered. I said to myself: *There's the Hofoper, where my late husband so often... There's the Burgtheater, whose former director so admired me that...* But I couldn't manage a satisfactory last moment. It all seemed unreal, like stage scenery. Only the Nazis seemed live.

On 12 March 1938 the Wehrmacht marched into Vienna and was nearly kissed to death. It was the most gorgeous spring day – people called it *Hitler's weather.* There was a parade, full of torches and immense flags that had been designed by Hitler himself with a ruler and compass. The storm troopers marked the windows of Jewish businesses with a big red J.V. for *Jude Verrecke:* Drop dead, Jew. At last Hitler circled the Ring in a six-wheeled armored Mercedes, black and polished, with the top open. He stood upright in the moving automobile by means of a hidden steel brace. His blue eyes glowed. His face was warm as sun-heated iron. I hated him for banishing my Franz, but at the same time, a part of me hated Franz too, for obliging me to creep away from my home like this when everybody else was celebrating.

I went to see Hollnsteiner and we said our physical goodbyes. The next day Anna and I took the train to Prague. At the station we found a crush of damp shoulders and cheeks. Everyone was black under the arms with fear or joy. When we got on the train, it was so crowded we couldn't even see out the window, and at the border we had to show our baptismal papers. All the Jews were turned back.

Anna went to London to practice her English, and I took Franz to Sanary-sur-Mer on the Côte d'Azur. This was a little fishing village where German and Viennese artists used to summer. Now a number of us came back: Brecht, Koestler, the Mann brothers. We all still thought we were taking a little interlude. The villagers all considered Hitler a fine fellow, but if you spoke German they figured you were an enemy. We'd bribe the gendarmes to let us alone with money, or hot punch on cold days. A shiny-faced captain dug through Franz's pockets once, shouting, "You're a Communist, aren't you? You write for the poor, don't you?"

Franz mumbled, "I write for anybody."

He was taken to La Seyne. I cut out Franzl's picture from *Paris Match*, with the caption *Un des plus grands écrivains contemporains*, and showed it to the interrogating officer.

When I got him home, he said, "I feel heavy."

"You've done nothing but eat your head off since we got here," I said, very worked up. "What did you tell that man? Do you want to murder me?" I put a hand to my breast and glared.

"No, I feel heavy on one side." He lay down.

"What are you doing?" I screamed.

"Oh, Almi," he sobbed, "I'm leaving you!"

I pounded his breastbone with my fist.

"You're hurting!" he cried.

His breath went in and out, as if he was snoring. I wanted to call for the servants, but ah! No servants. I knelt and gathered him into my arms, thinking, *The thing to do in such cases, the thing to do...* I had no idea what to do. I thought maybe he was speaking, so I brought my ear down close to his lips.

"You thought you were so smart," he hummed. "But you made a bad bet when you married me."

THAT WAS Franz's first heart attack. They said it was a mild one, but they didn't have to watch him have it. In Paris, the doctor prescribed injections for his blood pressure, which they said was dangerously high. It didn't surprise me, because by now I'd decided all Jews were gifted little men with diseased hearts. I brought Franz home and tucked him up in bed. I'd rented us an old watchtower to live in, a big ugly stump of gray stucco three stories tall, but at the top was a round room with a dozen windows looking out over the sea, and I put Franz's desk and bed up there because I thought artists and sick people should have something nice to look at. He said the pain was like swallowing a fistful of coins. He said the injections filled his skull with icy water. To ease his headaches he poured my perfume over his head, and then staggered around screaming that he'd gone blind. He complained about the drafts, so I dragged his bed from one side of the room to another. I tore an old gown into strips and stuffed them in round the windowframes. He was afraid to be alone at night, so I slept on a couch by his bed, and now and then I'd get up to see that the rags hadn't fallen out of the windowframes.

For two years we lived in this tiny town, waiting for Hitler to go away. I played Bach in the airless parlor, then stumped down to the market to stand on line for oil, butter, and soap. In Vienna, where I couldn't go anymore, my mother was dying. In Vichy, Franz's father was dying of a stroke. We went to see him and he shouted at us, with his stiff, drooling mouth, because we'd let our American visas lapse. By the time we got home, Hitler had invaded Poland. There was a decree that foreigners couldn't own firearms, so I buried my pistol under a tree.

Franz said, "Don't you know that a tree's roots are in constant motion? In time they'll bring any buried object to the surface. The only safe place is by a wall."

I went out in my nightgown, in the middle of the night, to dig up my pistol and bury it again.

On 23 June 1940, Hitler marched into Paris and inspected the Opera House. He told Speer to build him a better one. The other thing he said was that the Gestapo should round up all citizens of the Greater Reich, which, as far as he was concerned, meant Franz and me, too. Reynaud was on the radio, weeping, begging

Roosevelt to send clouds of airplanes. I packed a dozen trunks in three hours and we began what Franz called our Tour de France.

First we went to Bordeaux, where they said you could get papers. The Bordeaux station was so crowded we couldn't get our luggage off the train, and away went our clothes, *chuff chuff*. A red-mouthed young woman gave us a card to a hotel. When we got there I thought our room was oddly equipped, but we were thrilled to get anything at all, and we feasted on garlic sausage and bread too hard to soften in wine, and Franz was gallant and didn't tell me we were in a whorehouse. It took us less than a week to forget what a nice hot bath was like. In fact, we soon forgot we'd ever done anything but run from the Nazis.

Everybody was in a panic, full of schemes. We got all excited because a man said he'd drive us to Biarritz for eight thousand francs, but every few kilometers the soldiers blocked the road with a wagon, with a church pew, with two donkeys, and reached a lantern through the window of the car and blinded us again. "Not the old lady," they'd say. "We don't want the old lady. Who's the fat little gent in back?"

"My name is Werfel, sirs," Franz would mumble.

"The *writer*," I'd say.

"The Jew," they'd say. "Get out. Stand up. Turn round. What's in the bag, matzohs? Did you come here to peddle your matzohs? We're going to give you to the Gestapo, you know that? Ah ha ha, now he's shaking, but we won't really. They're snotty bastards. Only don't let us catch you here next week."

The orders changed so quickly that the Germans were as confused as we were. But we knew next week, or the week after that, off we'd go to the snotty bastards.

We went from town to town, to Narbonne, Carcassonne, Avignon, Toulouse, Bayonne, Hendaye, Pau. They said the Portuguese consul in Saint-Jean-de-Luz was sympathetic, but when we got there he'd gone mad and thrown all the passports in the sea.

Finally we wound up in Lourdes. There were six long Gestapo cars in front of the Hôtel Vatican. We were like peasants staring at an airplane, it was so long since we'd seen anything clean and new. The innkeeper's wife told us the Gestapo didn't have any jurisdiction here, not yet, and pulled a young couple from their bed to make room for us.

Franz and I had never slept side by side before, but for five weeks we lay on this little bed, with the Nazis down the hall, and stabbed each other with our knees. In the morning we'd go stand in line at the police station, which is where you went to beg for an exit visa. It wasn't far from where the saint used to live, a miller's daughter named Bernadette Soubirous, whom Franz was crazy about. "She was like us," he said. "A prisoner for her beliefs." In 1853 she told people she'd had seventeen visions of the Virgin Mary, but they thought she was lying and locked her up. There was a spring at the grotto at Massabielle where the nice lady had appeared, and millions of sick pilgrims came every year to drink from it, and so Franz went every day, walking with fussy little steps because of his heart, and gargled with the others and prayed, *Get us to America, Miss Soubirous, and I swear I'll sing of you.*

Soon after this we met Varian Fry, whom Eleanor Roosevelt had sent to rescue the intellectuals. He was a stockbroker's son in a pinstriped suit and a boutonnière, and he always looked like he had a tummy-ache. "No sense waiting for visas," he said. "Vichy's cracking down. I propose we meet at Saint Charles station Friday dawn. Agreeable? You'll get out at Cerbère and I'll take your things across the border by train. They've still got some respect for an American passport, I'm happy to say. My colleague Mr. Ball will see you over the Pyrenees into Spain. How soon can you have your bags together?"

"We haven't any bags," I snapped.

But the next day they arrived. The refugees had passed the word from town to town that everybody had to find the famous

Franz Werfel's luggage, and up it came on the morning train to make a liar of me.

We celebrated Franz's fiftieth birthday in a big restaurant by the port. It was actually a marvelous meal. I always wondered what they did to get the potatoes like that. I sat there chewing, feeling ready for anything, and let Franz sip a little beer. He kept saying, "Next year, who knows?" He'd been writing a poem about Hitler called *The Greatest Man of All Time*, and when we got back to our room he burnt it in an ashtray in case we got caught.

Friday morning, he moaned, "It's the thirteenth. Bad luck – let's go another day. Oh, it'll all be on your head if something happens."

His breath was shallow and stale. I stroked his neck and slapped his legs. I warmed his feet in my lap.

"Ah," he said, "that's so nice. Let's just stay here today, you and me."

I put on sandals and a comfortable old dress and tucked our money and my jewelry into it here and there. With a shape like mine, there was lots of room for tucking. I packed my rucksack with the manuscript of Bruckner's Third and packed Franz's with his medicines and some extra socks and the clipping from *Paris Match*. I turned round and Franz was still under the covers. "I'll murder you," I said.

He flung them back. He was all dressed underneath, even shoes. "Ha-ha!" he said.

I thrust my fingers into his collar and took his pulse. "Hm. You're all right," I said. "You'll do."

"My legs are much warmer now," he said, "and feel how dry my palms are."

I said, "Get up before I murder you" and he climbed to his feet, grinning. He was all nerves. I thought, Am I going to have a problem with him?

I expected to feel scared myself, because we'd been hearing

all sort of things about the prison camps, but as it happened I was just grouchy about the inconvenience. And like Leiser said, I didn't like feeling grateful. I liked being the hostess. Today Fry was the hostess. But I always enjoyed the dawn. You don't sleep well when you drink as much as I did, and a lot of mornings I'd be up early and sort of appreciate the world. Things were clean and blue, and the leaves were mysterious, moving around in their own shadows, and the people hadn't come out yet to muck things up, and the birds weren't worried about anything.

Mr. Ball was at the station, a young man with big shoulders and very long blond eyelashes. He was dressed like a hiker, very sporty. He greeted us in perfect French, but he looked so American that I couldn't see the point of the exercise. Fry was way down at the end of the platform, with our luggage and his tummy-ache face, pretending he didn't know us.

We stood there staring down the tracks, where they curved round a little brick shed with no windows and vanished. The rails were almost invisible in the dark. Then, after a long time, they began to shine, just at the corner of the shed. They shone for a long time, the streaks of light getting longer and longer, closer and closer, and then, off in the distance, a single furious eye appeared above them. It seemed to hang there motionless.

I said, "What, have they stopped the train now?"

But then it began to move again and grow.

"No," Franz said. "Here it comes."

I said, "I can't hear you. Why are you whispering? Do you think we'll be *invisible* if you whisper? There's nothing the matter with a man and a woman taking a train."

The train grew faster and faster and finally came up in a rush. It seemed very loud in the blue dawn. Its lights were fierce and yellow. Fry got onto a car up near the front. Our own car wasn't even crowded. It was clean, warm, everything cared for – as if we were taking a pleasure trip in peacetime. "It seems so ordinary,"

Franz said. "It makes you feel nothing so bad could be happening after all."

"Hush."

He whispered, "I thought we needn't whisper."

"You needn't," I said clearly, "but don't talk like a fool."

"Keep it down, you two," Ball said, in that breezy sort of country French he'd worked up. "I'm going to try and get a little shut-eye." His German was also excellent. He was really very proud of his languages. He took any opportunity to speak them.

In Cerbère the three of us got out, dangling our rucksacks from one hand like purses. We thought we'd look more casual that way. Everything was just opening up for the day as we went through town, but we didn't see anybody much except at the fishmonger's, where some men were unloading a truck and we heard barrels rolling along a brick floor. There was an alley along the side of a long stone building with the windows set very high. We turned down this alley and came to the beginning of the path to the mountain. It passed by the back of a café. I could smell them making the coffee, and suddenly I felt the way Franz did, that I just wanted to sit down quietly and drink coffee and not be bothered.

We were crossing a meadow now, and it started sloping up.

Ball said, "I hope you'll forgive my rudeness on the train. I was trying –"

"Yes, yes," I said.

"I simply meant that it's not such a good idea to be heard speaking German. Now, there," he said, gesturing like a tour guide, "is Mount Rumpissa."

"We can see the mountain," I muttered.

"Seven hundred meters. I'm hoping we can reach the peak in about two hours."

"You understand, don't you, that my husband is a sick man?"

Franz said, "I'm fine, Alma. I'll be fine."

Ball said, "One more thing. Since the area may be patrolled by the *gardes mobiles*…"

"All right," I said, "we'll be quiet."

"Wait," Franz said.

He knelt and tied his shoes again. He stood and went step-step-step in place to decide if he was comfortable.

"These are very good shoes," he said. "I'm ready."

It wasn't mountain climbing like Burckhard used to do, with ropes and so on. It was a path that tourists would come and hike. But they were young tourists, not fat little heart patients, and I started wondering if this was such a good idea for Franz. We went stumbling along through the brush, smashing our ankles on stones we couldn't see. When the path was clear, we slid around on slate like glass. If you fell, you had nothing to grab onto but nettles. There were clouds of them everywhere, and soon our hands were fiery and speckled with blood. By now the sun was blinding. The air sang with bugs, a great harsh rising note. It was getting hot. Below us there was a hook of dark shining water, growing broader as we climbed, and a black-green forest settled slowly down like a sheet spread out over a bed. It seemed as if we were climbing away from the world. I started getting the notion my whole life wasn't quite real. My salon seemed a sort of fiction. The Hofoper was red and gold like a child's tale. Oskar, Mahler, youth – gossip. I'd made it all up, or heard it somewhere, like an old song. "What are you thinking?" Franz whispered. "Don't be sad."

He looked ready to weep himself.

I said, "Look at that young swine. This is an adventure for him."

"Alma," Franz said, "he's being lovely to us."

Mostly, I looked at my feet. They were lumpy old-lady feet, and I watched them trudging along. At the base of the mountain there was a loose blackish soil, good for walking. Higher up came an orange gleaming sort that was slippery in the shade but dusty and hard in the full sun. I found that leaning too much on things was a mistake. It just threw you off balance and made you more tired. The idea was to move calmly and make no fuss, but Franz wouldn't let us keep a steady pace. First he'd creep along to save his strength, then get the idea he could climb straight up cliffs and be done at once with his labors. He leaned his belly against a rock as high as his chest and lifted one knee, as Putzi had once done to show I should take her up on my lap. He tripped over a root and was up at once, singing, "Nothing! Nothing!"

"Come here," I said. "Show me your knee. It's fine. Take a breath. You're all disorganized." I stuck my fingers in his collar again. "Boom boom boom. Relax, for heaven's sake. Save your strength. Don't be a little ninny."

"I told you," he said, panting. "I'm fine."

His infant's face was shiny and as gray as spit. "Gently!" I said. "We've a long way yet."

"Ssssh," he sobbed, "the *gardes!*"

The second time he fell, he cried out like a stricken calf. Ball and I lifted him to his feet.

The third time he slapped our hands away.

"Leave me!" he shrieked.

He lay on his side in a stew of weeds. His legs were twisted to the side. He didn't adjust them. He had abandoned them. "Save yourself, Alma. I'm dying anyway. Oh, God, I told you about traveling today."

I bent and turned Franz over with my hands. By now it was a familiar gesture. His eyes were shut and fat, as if I had smashed them with my fist. "Franz," I said.

Ball observed us, like a headwaiter. A mannerly young man.

"Franz," I said. "Please."

"Just keep walking," Franz whispered.

"No."

"You don't owe me anything more. You've already been punished for everything. Oh, God, we've all been punished enough."

"You're talking nonsense."

"Just let me go. Alma, let me go."

"I'll do no such thing. What do you think I'd do in America all alone?"

"You'll make your music."

"No."

"You'll rest."

"No."

"You'll find another man."

"No," I said. "I won't."

As I said it, I realized it was true.

Franz was attuned, like a dog or a child. He saw my astonishment. He sat up.

"No?" he said.

"No," I said.

"Must I forever be taking care of you?" he said.

"Yes," I said.

"Well," he said. "If I must."

And he arose. "Take my arm," he said grandly, and we walked to the top of the mountain. Far below us was Spain, and a tiny white guardhouse on a field of white stone.

Hollnsteiner had been Schuschnigg's friend, and so they sent him to Dachau. When the Russians entered Vienna, Carl Moll and his daughter and his Nazi son-in-law took poison together. I've already told you what the Nazis did with incurables. One afternoon, soldiers came to my sister's asylum. They brought her to the dining room, where her fellow inmates were already standing in rows, nude and weeping, and took her shift from her. She started weeping too, because she was cold. A medical officer walked around with a list. By each name he put a blue slash or a red cross. The red crosses were taken to the cellar in lots of six, like so many Tsar's daughters, and shot. They cut Gretl's brains in slices and put them in a jar full of alcohol, and on the label they wrote *Advanced Paretic Caries, 54-y.o. Fem. Jew. Forebrain* in waterproof ink.

From Lisbon we sailed on the Greek steamship *Nea Hellas*. It was very crowded and dirty, and I was annoyed because the ticket to New York cost what you might have spent to cross on the *Queen Elizabeth*. It was a dull trip. The sea is always dull. Only the coasts are interesting.

THE FIRST THING we learnt about America is how gigantic the place is. I'd only really seen New York, so I didn't know. Maybe a Russian could understand those enormous empty spaces, but to a couple of Europeans it's like you got a knock on the head. New York was so cold we decided to go to Hollywood, so Franz could get a job in the movies like everyone else. The trip took three full days by express train. When you begin, there's a few nice hills and rivers, but soon the whole place is flat, just thousands of kilometers of dirt combed into rows, with now and then a white metal shed where Americans come to buy petrol or hair dye. At the end of the third day we reached the oil fields outside Los Angeles. The pumps looked like huge iron crickets, bobbing back and forth. Above them we saw searchlights in the sky. There weren't any bombers, of course. To an American, searchlights are festive. The Franks were expecting us, but we kept wandering down these curving little streets lined with jungle vegetation and preposterous bungalows, bungalows with Moorish arches, bungalows with roofs like pagodas, and by the time we found the Franks' little house we were ready to collapse. Outside was a crowd of hot-colored automobiles. The Franks were having a get-together. Liesl Frank's mother, Fritzi Massary, was there, who'd been the queen of German light opera, and Bruno Walter, and Brecht, Feuchtwanger, Reinhardt, Schönberg, and the Manns, everyone burnt as dark as Mahler. The émigrés used to gather in the evening to listen to the war news together. There was a nine-hour difference, so the important news came after midnight, and to pass the time they played Charades. When we stepped through the door, Bruno Frank, a big mighty man with a Caesar's head, was crawling round the rug on his elbows and knees, wiggling his nose. "You'll excuse me," he said. "I'm a mouse." And that was our welcome to America.

The next day we had the Franks drive us around. It was a few days before Christmas, but the air was warm and drowsy. Franz clutched the open window with both hands, crying, "Look, look at that! Is that a bathing costume or a dress? Alma, please. I need a woman to explain that hat. What's that, a mosque?"

"No," Liesl said, "a car wash."

"I've seen those," Franz bragged. "They have one in Berlin. There, is that one of your movie palaces?"

"No, it's Fräulein Semple McPherson's church," Bruno said. "They say Herr Hitler models his microphone technique on hers."

"They're like children's drawings of buildings," I said.

"Yes!" Franz said. "My God, what's that one supposed to be, a big sausage?"

"A big tamale. They sell tamales there."

"How excellent! Form, function, Walter would be pleased. What's a tamale?"

"A sort of Mexican crêpe. Filled, I believe, with rice."

"They can eat anything here!" Franz said in admiration. "No – stop, stop!" The car turned into a parking lot, and Franz toddled out into an enormous grocer's shop. I rushed after him, calling, "Franz. Please. The sun."

"You can walk along beside me with a parasol," he said slyly, "as if I were an African king. I'll soon be dark as one, anyway. I'll dress in feathers and have shiny little black concubines and drink from the skulls of my enemies." The food was shut up in immense glass-fronted boxes, like bookcases. They were brightly lit, and cooled by pipes covered with frost. You couldn't smell the food, only electricity, ice, and rubber gaskets. When we returned to the car, Franz was holding a huge glittering grapefruit in both hands. "Isn't it fine?" he said. "They wanted to put it in a paper sack."

"They put everything in paper sacks here," said Liesl. "They're squeamish. Yes, it's pretty, but you'll find it has no taste."

"That makes it all the better as an object of contemplation."

"Well," I said, "we're a long way from home."

"They've got swans in Echo Park," Bruno said. "It makes you homesick for the Heustadelwasser. But then they've got swan-shaped boats, too, which rather spoils it."

"Now that mosque over there," Franz said, "I know that's a movie palace. Because it says Flash Gordon in front. Well? Shall we?"

"No," I said.

"We might as well," Bruno said, "and get it over with."

Franz was still holding his grapefruit as we took our seats. Inside it was refrigerated, and I put my jacket around him. Above the screen was a frieze of hammered metal, a miniature village lit from behind with colored lights. It had a miniature windmill, whose vanes turned. On the screen were silver rocket ships. They moved slowly in circles, buzzing and dropping sparks. They landed in the mountains and then everybody was climbing down a cliff of ice, each holding a roman candle. A beam of light shot through the dust above our heads, twisting and leaping, and over and over again formed a stupid handsome face, huge and empty of thought. "What are they doing in the snow?" I said.

"Looking for polarite," said Franz. "It's the only cure for the Purple Death."

"Those metal men are walking bombs," Flash Gordon said, "operated by remote control."

"What did he say?" I said. "What are those iron fellows, knights? This is awful. They'll be killed."

Shhhh, they said behind us.

I turned around and explained, "We don't speak your language. Why, Franz, it's like *Siegfried* without wits! Franz, your teeth are chattering."

"They keep these places like icehouses," Bruno said. "Liesl likes it."

"Your teeth are chattering," I said. "That's enough of that."

On the sidewalk, Franz moved his head wonderingly, as if kissing the warm air. "I'll be back," he said. "I'll get a car, and bring a coat, and I'll be back, and watch the movies like a real American."

Hollywood was a sort of Vienna for savages. There was the same obsession with perfect young women and historical façades and dramatical productions and putsches among the divas. There were a lot of Viennese there, too, and we were all mad for news. Liesl carried a portable radio from room to room. It seemed horrible that the war was in English, and I enraged my friends by saying over and over, "What? What did they say?" The girls here looked like prostitutes and the young men like bricklayers. It was hard to take them seriously. We imagined these handsome peasants faced with German rigor, once Hitler had gotten done conquering Europe, and we decided we were doomed.

Gustl still had a big pile of dollars sitting in the Lazards' bank, and I bought a second-hand Oldsmobile and May Robson's little house in the Hollywood Hills. It came complete with a butler. We called him Der Schöne August. He'd left a touring German operetta troupe to stay where it was warm and he could look at the boys. It was a very nice little house, but I never got used to it. Our parlor opened right onto the street. In the middle was my grand piano. You went down to the bedrooms on a twisting iron stair, and I bruised my legs black on it. I called it the Chicken Ladder. I'd named my Breitenstein house the Haus Mahler and my Venice place the Casa Mahler, but this little place I didn't bother to name anything, because I wasn't sure I wanted to stay. The California sun gave me a headache, and I detested the stink of acacia and oleander and eucalyptus – like liniment – and I didn't touch the fruit that fell from our rented trees. It rolled down into the Hollywood Bowl, which was just behind us. Whenever they did *Music Under the Stars*, we heard every stupid note.

But Franz loved Los Angeles. He loved the colored lights in the shrubbery. He loved the cheerful voices with the flat, clanking vowels, and the suntans and the nylons and all these huge, enormous girls, and he wrote to his parents, *The Riviera is just trash compared with this.* He went around with his face turned up to the sun, like a seal balancing a ball on its nose. I'd hoped he'd like California, but I didn't think he needed to like it quite so much. When I saw him enjoying himself like this, I felt that motherly ache, like I never did for my own children, that you feel for a child who needs you for everything, but who's plotting, one of these days, to betray you – to need you for nothing.

From being ill so long he'd gotten quite shrunken, so we went to the London Shop on Rodeo Drive to buy him new clothes. American shirts are cut short in the tail. On a man of Franz's physique they come untucked behind. I'd say, "Come here and let me fix you. You look like a bundle of laundry."

"You're pretty," he said shyly, as I thrust in his shirttails. "Harlow's got nothing on you. You've got," he said, mischievously and in English, "*personality.*"

Americans all adored this meaningless word.

He was mocking me a little. He was so relieved not to worship me anymore that he often got very affectionate.

I'd had a lot of worship all my life, but affection, this was a novelty.

Four days after we were in our new house, he began *The Song of Bernadette*, just as he'd promised Miss Soubirous in the grotto at Lourdes. He worked on it the way he worked on everything, like a man having a seizure. He scribbled in black-covered schoolboy's composition books ten hours a day, sometimes in his room, sometimes in a bungalow he'd rented at the Biltmore in Santa Barbara. I wasn't sending him away anymore, but he still had the habit of going off somewhere to write. He hired a secretary named Albrecht, who'd previously taken dictation from Thomas Mann, and Albrecht typed as Franz read the notebooks aloud, or made lists of theological questions for our friend Father Mönius. Just after Pearl Harbor in 1941, *The Song of Bernadette* came out in Swedish, French, Spanish, Portuguese, Hungarian, and English. It was Franz's biggest success – in fact, it was one of the most popular books anybody ever wrote. For months it was Number One on the American best-seller lists – the army alone bought fifty thousand copies to improve its soldiers. A factory in Alabama made a Bernadette-shaped soap. On the radio you heard nothing but a doggerel called *The Song of Bernadette*. It was an awful little tune, and I'd get up and turn off the radio, and then I'd go turn it back on again, just to be sure they were really playing it.

On Franz's fifty-third birthday we were both in a fine mood. We went out for a nice meal, and I let him smoke one of the strong Havanas he liked so much. He patted his chest.

"Are you going to sing?" I said.

"I've eaten too much," he said.

"What?"

He kicked out sideways, then leant over and took hold of my leg. "Help me fall."

"What?"

He brought us both to the floor. I sat with his head in my lap as we waited for the ambulance. "Put his *feet* up," said the waitress. "Not his head, his *feet*."

I told her to drop dead, but since she didn't speak German, she just stood there.

A FEW WEEKS EARLIER Franz had scribbled across the back of a Biltmore menu, *Illness invites us to hell or to heaven. It either* *delivers a being soulless into the hands of matter or else immolates his ego, making it ever more transparent until the moment of death.*

Franz knew what was coming. Me, I had no idea.

By December he had three more heart attacks and his lungs were boiling with embolisms. We kept an oxygen tank by his bed so he could get a little air. He'd lie there holding the mask over his face for hours, peering round the edge as if he were ashamed to be so greedy. Franz had always been a big complainer, but now he was too frightened to say a word. Since I was too deaf to hear him wheeze, I had to watch for little signs that he needed the oxygen. If he was poking his lips out like a boy getting ready to kiss an old aunt, it was time. I'd watch his fingers, too, to see if they were curled up softly or a little stiff and anxious, and I'd part his hair and examine the color of his scalp, which I'd decided was significant. He got digitalis for his heart and morphine for his fevers, and quartz-lamp treatments and herbal tea. His back was raw as a baby's bottom, and I rubbed it with ointment. Each morning I rolled his bed onto the tiles of our patio so he could sun himself. Every now and then he'd scratch a bit in his notebook. *What would Israel be without the Church?* Or just: *Back in the soup.*

A few days before Christmas they had the première of the movie of *Bernadette*. We gave Der Schöne August our tickets, and Franz and I sat home by the radio. "It's America's first great Catholic movie," he said.

The radio said, "*There are still ten free tickets at the box office for the first ten young women named Bernadette. Looks like we've got quite a crowd of Bernadettes tonight, here in front of the Cathay Circle Theater. Have your driver's licenses ready, girls....*"

I understood *young* and *girls* and I told Franz, "You only wanted to go so you could look at all those prostitutes."

"Oh, bye-bye, girls," he whispered in English, and waved at the radio. "*Au revoir.* You know, I've thought of doing a book about Joseph Smith. He founded the Mormons?"

"Franz," I said, "don't you become the village crucifix carver!"

He rolled in his fingers a cigar he was not permitted to light. His eyes were shut. The radio said, "*...and now, on the arm of director Henry King, here comes Bernadette herself, the lovely Jennifer Jones, winner of a nationwide talent search to find the perfect Little Saint of Lourdes....*"

"The arse of an angel," Franz said slowly. "And not a thought in her head."

"Yes? And how many thoughts have you in yours?"

He put the cigar to his lips and pretended to blow a smoke ring. "See?" he said, and pointed. "My halo."

The night before Palm Sunday 1943, Franz had a dream that came all night in episodes. "Like a novel serialized in a newspaper," he told me. "I want to write it. A sort of travel story." He called it *Star of the Unborn.* The book is set in the year 101,943. The globe's been scraped bare by old wars. All that's left is gray grasses and a few Jungle People poking the dirt with hooked sticks. Way below the ground live the Astromentals, who eat pastel-colored essences and fight the Jungle People with trans-shadow-disintegrators. The hero is named F.W. He died in California in 1943, but they summon him spiritualistically to the future, where he meets Io-Squirt, who turns out to be his son, Martin. Martin's been brought back from the dead too, and he loves his father, and forgives him, and together they travel to the middle of the earth, where the Astromentals go when they tire of their long lives. There they're buried in retrogenic humus and planted as embryos in a great field of daisies. All their sorrows and fears are taken from them, all their sickness and weariness and pain, and at last they leave the world, Franz wrote, to become a *light, bright, airy joy.*

Each day he was strong enough, he dictated from notebooks to Albrecht until I called them to lunch. When he went to Santa Barbara, he took a personal physician, Spinak, a little Austrian who looked like Schubert and was called Schwammerl, Little Mushroom. For luck I gave Franz some flowers, which he pressed in one of his notebooks. One day in midsummer he telephoned me and said, "It's done. That was the last page. Do you hear it? I'm shaking the notebook by the phone. Actually, I might take a little rest and then write a twenty-seventh chapter. In it, I will conceal an epilogue that is *also* an apology."

"You sound happy," I said.

"I'm miserable. I miss you so much. It's a scandal, the way I've deserted you, how have you managed? Send August tomorrow. I'm coming home."

"Franzl, not if it's hot like today. A long drive, such heat, it can't be good for you."

"Did you hear that? I was shaking the notebook again. Doesn't it sound like a masterpiece? Send August."

The next day was viciously hot. Late in the afternoon August called out from the curb, and together we helped Franz from the Oldsmobile to his bed. He was gagging and wheezing, and the flesh of his face was like wet sand. Spinak was off on holiday, but a Dr. Wolff came at once to administer morphine, and I sat by Franz's bed all night and watched him roll like gray waves through the blankets. He kept waking to cry, "My feet are numb!"

I rubbed his heart and warmed his feet and hands with hot towels.

"It's your head that's numb," I said. "Didn't I warn you?"

"That feels so good," he sighed. "I wanted to go swimming today. The water looked so pretty. When you go deep down, your ears sing. An endless mezzo-soprano note. As if water were an endless Alma."

"Do you want me to sing to you?"

"No. I want to sit here and dream you're singing to me."

"That's no compliment."

"Oh yes. Dream first, sing later. That's the best way. What will you sing, when you sing to me?"

"I'll sing about a great field where all our sorrows become flowers."

"That doesn't sound so bad."

"You wouldn't rather just dream?"

"I'm dreaming now."

"All right," I said. "Then I'll sing to you."

Mahler used to say, *If only you were old, if only you were sick,* THEN *I could show you how I love you!*

ON THE LAST DAY of July was Franz's father's fourth *yahrzeit.* This is the anniversary of a Jew's death. The rabbis sell you a special fat candle in a water glass, which burns all day, but Franz didn't want one. He just lay in bed and hummed Verdi's *Rex tremendae.*

On 6 August the Americans dropped a uranium bomb on Hiroshima in order to end the war. And three days later, another one on Nagasaki in order to end it again. The bombs had pet names: Fat Man, Little Boy.

In the yard was some sort of bird. It made a sawing or scraping noise and wouldn't leave us.

On 24 August, Franzl dreamt he was in uniform again. He walked through an old Austrian gateway and up some crumbling stairs. Above his head was a shelf full of dirt and bric-à-brac. Someone said, *Take the dog down.* He was afraid to put his little hands in the schmutz. But then the dog became a tiny white horse and galloped away.

When he woke he asked me, "Alma, have you read Broch's book? A white horse is the omen of Virgil's death."

"You're not Virgil," I said uneasily.

Bruno Walter lived next door, and the next evening we went out to dinner with him and his daughter Lotte. Franz had just been to the Schwammerl and we were all in a fine mood. The Schwammerl had said he guessed a journey by water wasn't so bad. We decided to go to Prague and Venice and London to see Franz's sister Hanna. Franz demonstrated how a Londoner gives one change from a purchase, how he looks around for a spoon to eat his melon, how he eats at last with his fingers, how he asks a prostitute her price. We were all merry. It was Franzl's favorite restaurant, Romanoff's.

The next morning was Sunday, 26 August 1945. I let Franzl sleep late, because of all the excitement of the dinner and the Schwammerl's guess. But when noon came and no Franz, I began playing Smetana's *The Bartered Bride.*

Franzl came out from his rooms doing a gigue. Off he danced onto our little patio without his slippers, hum de hum.

"You're a simpleton," I called. "Sit and be sensible before I knock you down."

"Yes, yes," he said, humming.

I pressed him back into a chaise. "Franz, your soles are black. Where have you been running? I'll fetch a cloth. Sit."

"Oh, yes."

I wet a dishtowel at the kitchen sink and knelt before him. Meekly, or maybe in triumph, he put out one little foot and then the other and I wiped away the dirt. "There," I said, "now you're fit to be seen. Sit there until you feel a bit better."

"I feel better now."

"Sit."

"You could cure me," he said slyly, "you could do it so easily."

"When you're stronger."

He sat up. "I'll go to a whorehouse!" he said.

"August has taken the car."

"I feel like a bit of work. A cigarette would clear my head."

"Your head will never be clear."

248

"Well, I still feel like a bit of work. Perhaps in a bit I'll get up and dress."

We had luncheon and Franzl had his nap, and then he dressed and went into his room. I sniffed outside the door but couldn't smell anything. Good. He wasn't smoking. I sat down and played *The Bartered Bride* and thought of his little black feet. I'd drawn the curtains to spare my skin. Outside the light came pouring down. I was a little sleepy myself. I thought, How the piano lid shines. It'll outlast me. A piano outlives a woman, a melody outlives a piano. After the pianos all rot, it can be hummed. A little before six o'clock I knocked on Franz's door to see if he wanted tea. I knocked, then called, then went in. He lay beneath his swivel chair, almost smiling, his hands limp and unclenched, and when I saw him I began to scream.

August appeared at once, but I was already on my knees again, jamming the oxygen mask down over Franz's face – I almost broke his nose – thumping on his heart with my fist and groaning like a poisoned dog. "Madame!" he cried.

"*He's only fainted!*" I shrieked at him. I thrust my hands beneath Franz's body and lurched up on my feet. I was ready to run with him from the house.

"*Madame!*"

Poor August, in a minute he was going to have two corpses. He tried to take Franz from me, and the three of us fell across the bed.

"I'll get the Schwammerl," he said, "please, Madame!"

"Gone!" I screamed in his face, "Oh God, all, all gone!"

Smetana's music still frisked about my head. But now August was gone.

"Gone," I said more quietly, to Franz.

The face was no longer Franzl's. It was becoming a monument of worn stone, growing larger as it went away from me. He needed nothing now, not love nor scolding nor fame. *"Gone,"* I said. Gone. His feet were clean. He didn't even need death.

WE HAD the memorial service at Pierce Brothers' Mortuary. They laid Franz out just as F.W. had been laid out in *Star of the Unborn.* He wore a dinner jacket and silk shirt, with his powerful glasses in his breast pocket and, at the foot of the coffin, an extra shirt and several extra handkerchiefs. He also wore the Bundesverdienstkreuz that Schuschnigg gave him for Services to Literature. Franz had been eager to be buried with such a decoration. Father Mönius, who had corrected the Catholicism in *Bernadette,* refolded his sleeves smoothly on his lap and waited to speak. The Schönbergs had come, the Igor Stravinskys had come, the Otto Premingers, the Otto Klemperers and all the Manns, in fact everyone had arrived except for the widow. While the mourners waited, Lotte Lehmann sang Schubert lieder and Bruno Walter played the mortuary piano. It was fifteen minutes. It was twenty. Lehmann sat down and Walter played the same little lied twice more. At last Albrecht drove to my house and found me rewriting Mönius's eulogy.

"This is terrible," I said. "Up *in the heaven of the Astromentals, Franz Werfel is shaking hands with Karl Kraus.* With that dreadful little man?" I drew a black line through the thought. A glass of Bénédictine sat at my elbow, smeared round the edge with lipstick.

Albrecht squinted at my housedress. "Alma," he said gently. "Everyone is in the chapel forty-five minutes now."

"Yes," I said. "Ah, well. I've made it a little better. You may give this to Mönius."

He said, "But Alma. Aren't you coming?"

"Oh, no," I said. "I never go."

XII

I LIVED NINETEEN MORE YEARS. By then I'd had a lot of practice, and it didn't take long.

The day after the funeral, Mönius and I drove out to the cemetery and secretly blest Franz's grave. The Church calls this *baptism by desire*. I sold the house at a good price and bought a building on East Seventy-third Street in New York City. I rented the bottom two stories and moved into the top floor, two rooms that looked out on the tops of trees. I began, for the first time, to live alone. I called my bedroom The Power of Music. I put my Bleuthner piano in it, the cradle Makart made for me, and a steel safe containing Bruckner's Third. My parlor I called The Power of Words and filled it up with Burckhard's volumes of Nietzsche, Oskar's fans, and Gustav's *My God my God* in a new gold frame. Anna won a Prix de Rome and married Albrecht. I went to Vienna. The Hofoper had been bombed, and the great staircase led up to an empty sky. I came home and every day put on makeup, jewelry, and a black dress, and sat down to write to the municipality, insisting that I had to raise my rents. I corrected my diaries. I burnt my letters. I began to go a little mad. I asked visitors, "Why does everyone say I'm sleeping with Bruno Walter?" Der Schöne August sent me poems on Mother's Day, and on Fridays I ate bouillabaisse at the Chambourg, and at night I bit my tongue, so that it hurt.

On my eightieth birthday Oskar sent his last letter. *My dear Alma, you're still the same wild brat.*

I called Anna up and asked, "Who won the war?" I told her, "I met Crown Prince Rudolf on a mountaintop. He wants me to have his child."

She came from California to look after me.

"Ah, Gucki," I said. She was now sixty years old. It seemed to comfort her to hold my hand. "See my little ruby?" I put out my tongue again, with the sore that wouldn't heal.

"Mami, won't you let me get Rossner?"

"I won't see that quack. He thinks I've got diabetes. A Jew's disease! I want you to put me in Mutzi's plot, not Gustav's. He was rude to me."

"Yes, you've said."

"Said what?"

"Your plot in Grinzing."

"Don't be so quick to finish me off," I said.

Eventually I decided I was back in Plankenberg. Good, I thought. Now I'm here in my own home, and I've gotten rid of all the interfering people, and I can really start sorting things out. At this point, I was actually pretty happy. Anna kept the window blinds closed so the light wouldn't give me a headache. I'd trace the cord of the blinds with my eyes, from the top to the little satin tassel at the bottom, and sometimes the way it twisted round itself proved certain things to me, and I'd smile with satisfaction. Sometimes I felt something astonishing gathering in my body. Then the light got so rich and golden that it gathered in little clumps. There'd be little golden clumps pouring in through the window, little clumps in the shadows of my blankets, and I'd grip Anna's hand and say, "Hold on."

One afternoon I looked at the little clumps and said, "He's putting flowers in my bed."

"Shall I stop him?" Anna asked.

"No, little miss," I said. "It doesn't concern you. But I'll tell you this. When I'm well again, there won't be any of this moping about. When I'm well, I'm going to make an absolutely fresh sincere start. You know the only one who ever understood?"

"Tell me."

"If he came though that door," I said, and pointed straight ahead at the ceiling, "I'd go with him *this minute.*"

"Who, Mami?"

I smiled slyly.

The flowers on my bed were starting to pile up. They began to make a rustling noise, like birds rearranging their wings for sleep. I didn't want to mention it – it would have seemed indelicate – but they began to block my view of Anna, and soon there was nothing but a weight of flowers driving the breath from my body. The truth was, it seemed silly to breathe. The flowers were rich and rustling, and if you listened to the rustling, you began to hear great chords.

"I always knew –" I said, but by now I only imagined I was speaking. "I always knew I was lucky. I was born on a Sunday."

Then the flowers piled up over my mouth.

"Mami?" she said, and I let go of her hand.

She wept. She saw I'd begun to know everything.

Note

To put it mildly, this is not a work of scholarship. Although all major events in this novel adhere closely to the historical record, I've invented minor incidents and fiddled some matters of chronology and detail for the sake of narrative coherence. When conflicting accounts of an event exist, I've used the one I liked best. When quoting from published writings, I've exercised the letters-column editor's prerogative of reworking texts for concision and style. I've also occasionally collaged together bits from related letters or diary entries, or filched sentences for use in my characters' dialogue; they sometimes say what their originals wrote.

Since she's been retelling her story for many years, I hope Alma may be forgiven for reusing favorite phrases. The following lines from this novel are quotes or close paraphrases from translations of her published writings: Marriage brought a narrowness into my father's life. We all ran around with our hair loose, like holy women. For a joke once, I took everyone's rings and put them on my fingers. He was a pagan and hated Christianity. When you've had a drop or two, nothing's better than a cycle ride. The daft faces, the dreadful pivoting motions of the male. Until my hair fell over my shoulders like a cloak. Gustav Mahler was a fidgety little man with a fine head. Mahler, I felt, had dragged them around since his youth like leg-irons. Mahler tried to prevent seasickness by lying stiff on his bunk like a stone cardinal upon his tomb. He explained that he'd made Sonnenthal and would now make

Mahler. He bought smart waistcoats and beautiful shoes. He walked sloppily, as if he was shoving himself forward. Each morning the women sat down on their doorsteps and combed their hair to the side, like a picture by Blaas. This I'd already heard from the lips of another egocentric par excellence, Gustav Mahler. I had the gardener grow ivy over the danger spot. We lay on this little bed and stabbed each other with our knees. The sea is always dull. Only the coasts are interesting.

I owe a great debt to (and have taken great liberties with) the work of Angelica Bäumer, Antony Beaumont, Herta Blaukopf, Kurt Blaukopf, Friedrich Buchmayr, Françoise Giroud, Elaine S. Hochman, J. P. Hodin, Edith Hoffman, Reginald Isaacs, Peter Stephan Jungk, Susanne Keegan, Baron Henry-Louis de La Grange, Karen Monson, Christian M. Nebehay, Susanna Partsch, Egon Schiele, Heinz Spielmann, Alfred Weidinger, Frank Whitford, and Stefan Zweig, among others. I've also drawn on Oskar Kokoschka's magnificent if somewhat inventive autobiographical writings. In particular, O.K.'s military training and the Silent Woman's début incorporate several of his own images and turns of phrase. The late Felix Galimir, founder of the Galimir Quartet, was kind enough to share his memories of Alma and Alban Berg. Antony Beaumont provided me with sections of Alma's diaries currently unavailable in English.

Charles Ardai, Cindy Bosley, Sarah Burnes, Garrett Deckel, Michael Elmore, Benjamin Grzimek, Bruce Holbert, Marka Knight, Elizabeth McCracken, Fritz Mc Donald, Kathleen W. Jones, Noah Millman, Ted Reichmann, John Whalen, Dr. Manfred Wolf, Michael Wolf, and my parents, Constance and Irving Phillips, were all generous with their intelligence, expertise, and time. Jack Macrae, Katy Hope, and Maggie Richards at Holt provided wise counsel and tireless advocacy; Raquel Jaramillo and Fritz Metsch provided endless patience and skill. John Weber and Chuck Kim at Welcome Rain made this revised edition possible. And my agent, Henry Dunow, as always, was a constant friend to the work.

DECEMBER 2002

About the Author

Max Phillips is the author of the acclaimed novel Snakebite Sonnet. His fiction and poetry have appeared in The Atlantic Monthly, The Village Voice, and The Threepenny Review. He lives in New York City.